Fabien Delage

JURASSIC PARK: DEAD ISLANDS

PROLOGUE

The air was heavy with rain. Beads of liquid crawled up the glass of the trembling airplane window. It was a dark, bone-chilling night. The plane's titanium fuselage vibrated in the damp wind. Kenneth Turner was anxiously tapping his fingers against the armrest. He couldn't sleep, and this trip seemed to last forever. He'd tried listening to every radio station available, but in vain. Turner was restless. For hours, he'd tried to lull himself to sleep by listening to Mozart's Piano Concerto No. 9. He'd watched both in-flight movies earlier that night, but they weren't boring enough to let him relax and doze off. Nothing had worked. He just simply couldn't sleep.

Turner scratched his head and tousled his thick brown hair, which fell in loose strands over his high forehead. His fair-skinned triangular face bore elegant features: almond-shaped hazel eyes over a small, defined nose and expressive mouth. At the moment, that face was twisted into a melancholy frown. Turner clenched his teeth; his jaw was tense. His damp shirt clung to his muscular chest. It'd been almost 24 hours since he left his hotel room in Natal with his daughter. Since their layover in north-western Brazil, Turner had had only one thing on his mind: going home. He'd had such a fun, relaxing vacation with his daughter in South America. They were both going through hard times but they'd grown even closer on this trip.

His wife had passed away 4 years ago and the anniversary of her death was approaching. The day before, Turner had celebrated his 38th birthday with his daughter. He'd always tried his best to be a great father to her. Aileen was only 10 but she was a strong kid, and she'd shown surprising resilience in the face of hardship. Turner hoped this trip would make her happy. Brazil was the perfect location for his daring little traveler with an eye for natural wonders. Turner wanted to make sure he'd always have a special place in Aileen's heart. They'd already enjoyed some great times together and had many fond memories. They'd both lost someone very dear to them but they'd held on and stood strong. They had to carry on loving; sorrow wouldn't bring them down anymore.

So Turner had made it his mission to entertain and surprise his daughter while he still had time. Once back in Brisbane, he'd have to go straight back to the office. Cases would pile up on his desk and he'd be up to his neck in paperwork. The Good times were almost over. Turner glanced out the window. It was so dark outside; he could hardly see the wing. Only the flashing navigation lights outlined its shape in the darkness. For a while, he gazed into the night. Then he turned to his left. Aileen was quietly sleeping, curled up under her blanket. She looked so peaceful with her blond hair framing her round face and falling over her delicate little nose. She was wearing a flowery dress, clutching her lace collar in her sleep. The next two seats beside her were empty. Turner had told her to make herself comfortable and lie down but she wouldn't do it. *Kids can sleep anywhere*, he thought. Turner felt trapped in his seat and his legs were getting numb.   Each time he tried and stretched his legs, his ankles would hit the front seat. This night flight was a nightmare. It'd already been 10 minutes since he asked the flight attendant for a whiskey.

It was 4 in the morning. The cabin was dark and quiet. What was taking her so long? It was the only thing that'd help him get some sleep. Had she forgotten about him? It was quite a simple request... Turner was getting more and more irritated.

The service on this flight was so bad, he was beginning to think the crew had fallen asleep too. The lack of sleep made him edgy. He looked over at his daughter again. Her golden hair was shining in the darkness; her skin was dewy and soft. She looked just as lovely and innocent as the day she was born.

His love and tenderness for her knew no bounds. Suddenly, the plane jolted for a second and the cabin lights flickered for a while. Aileen remained fast asleep. Turner fastened his daughter's seatbelt over her blanket. They still had a few hours to go before they reached the Australian coast and it seemed to him this flight was dragging on and on. He put his headphones back on and browsed through the airline's music selection all over again. Once more, he picked the classical music station. Listening to the same symphony for the umpteenth time would probably help him curb his impatience and let him enjoy the rest of the trip. He pushed the armrest button to select the program but it wouldn't work. He angrily pushed the plastic button harder and harder with his index finger. The digital screen turned black. *Of course!* Everything was conspiring against him. When he turned to Aileen, he saw that her screen had switched off too and so had those on the other seats.

Could he really be the only one having a terrible time on this flight? And where on earth was his whiskey? Feeling slightly worried, he pushed the armrest button once more, hoping a flight attendant would finally show up. He pressed his temple against the ice cold window and took a look around. How could everyone be so quiet? Not a whisper, not even a baby crying. Five minutes went by. The waiting was getting unbearable. He wasn't a drinker but he couldn't stand this anymore and he unfastened his seatbelt. He was determined to have a word with the cabin crew to take his mind off this flight. Besides, he was now determined to get this glass of whiskey and there was no way he would go back to his seat empty handed. This flight had cost him a small fortune and as a passenger he was entitled to a certain standard of service. He needed whiskey. He stood up from his seat and slipped quietly past his soundly sleeping daughter.

As he was heading to the cockpit, the airplane jolted violently. The floor shook; Turner was thrown on a seat and his shoulder hit the plastic shell. The cabin and seatbelt warning lights turned back on. A child started crying a few rows ahead of him. *Well, all it takes is a little turbulence for the passengers to react!* Kenneth Turner kept on walking up to the front of the plane. As he was

—

reaching the cabin crew area, there was a loud noise and the plane jolted again. The airplane lurched toward the ground and the Australian crashed to the floor, then slid down the aisle. A terrible clanking sound echoed outside and a flash illuminated the left side of the plane.

Turner stood up; people were screaming in the back rows. He ran to a window on the left side of the airplane and was stunned to observe that one of the engines had caught fire. A flight attendant running down the aisle shouted at him: "Sir, get back to your seat and fasten your seatbelt immediately!" It seemed that whiskey would never come after all. Turner silently complied and scrambled back to his seat. The turbulence had woken Aileen. She rubbed her eyes and looked around, bewildered. Turner could now feel the anxiety of the other passengers. Some of them were screaming with fear. Turner sat beside his daughter and held her close. The fifty-something man sitting at his left had closed his eyes and was pressing his medal to his lips. He had blond hair, a round face and a sharp nose. Sweat dripped from his receding hairline down his pale, pursed lips.

The man crossed his arms over his large stomach and smoothed the four-leaf clover embroidered on his green Guinness polo shirt. He looked up. Fear filled his blue eyes, which grew hazier with each jolt. Turner and Aileen saw a ball of fire and black smoke outside the window. They heard an alarming unidentified thud and the smell of burning kerosene filled the cabin. Turner felt the plane abruptly slow down as it made a sharp U-turn

—

9

toward the ocean. Over all the screaming and crying, he managed to hear a message from the pilot. His trembling voice crackled over the speakers: "Due to engine failure, we have to perform an emergency maneuver. Preparing to ditch. Brace yourselves! "

To ditch? Turner thought that to survive such a procedure, the plane should be coming in at low speed, nose pointed up, as if it was landing on earth. But the plane was nose-diving. Could the pilot pull the level? Did he have the experience? Fear gripped the physician, and he did his very best to hide it from his daughter. He could feel her shivering against his shoulder, hiding her face under her dress. He rested his chin on her angelic little head and whispered sweet words in her ear. The plane leveled off for a few seconds and then abruptly tilted to the right again. Oxygen masks dropped down from the panels above and the lights started blinking. An alarm went off in the back of the plane. One of the left engines was on fire. The flames licked at the fuselage and set the emergency exit ablaze. A young woman was praying a few rows down. The plane nosedived again; Turner caught a glimpse of the ocean some thousand feet down. The flames glinted off the raging sea. Could they land safely on those waves? At their current speed, the water surface would be as hard as concrete. Ditching was impossible. The airplane would be crushed. Turner lost hope. He and his daughter were going to die in the most terrible way. He choked back his tears and remembered his wife. Soon they would be reunited. He whispered all his love into Aileen's ear, but he didn't know if she could hear him.

The sheet metal roared and the burning lead edge of the wing was ripped away into the night. The ocean rushed up toward them and the pressure drop threatened to burst Turner's eardrums. He played over and over in his head the images of the worst air crashes in the past ten years; in every single documentary he'd watched, ditching had failed. Dozens of people had died and sunk into the ocean depths. The year before, in 1983, a child had been the sole survivor of a plane from Yemen that crashed into the ocean. Rescuers discovered the shivering little boy near the tail area - is blankets had protected him from the flames. They said it was a miracle. Turner looked down at his daughter once more. Aileen had her whole life ahead of her, and Turner couldn't stand the idea that it was over. She had to live.

He quickly unfastened his seatbelt and then hers. He slung her arms around his neck and made his way to the emergency exit at the plane's tail, gripping seats to stay upright and collecting blankets and pillows as he went. When he reached his destination, he sat his daughter in an empty seat in the final row. She looked at her father with fear and confusion. Without meeting her gaze, he strapped several pillows to her with the seatbelt. The fuselage moaned, about to collapse under its own weight; they were falling too hard. The other passengers breathed heavily into oxygen masks. The second engine exploded and ripped off a wing. With a thunderous screech, the plane tore itself apart; rows of passengers disappeared into the gaping night sky.

The wind rushed into the cabin, sucking out luggage and bodies. Its engulfing howl drowned out the noise of screams as another piece of steel tore away from the plane. A dozen more passengers plummeted into fire and darkness. Turner faced his fate. The time had come to atone for his sins. He prepared himself for excruciating pain. He wrapped the blankets around his daughter and then covered her with his own body. Turner was trying to grab the neighboring seat belt and buckle himself up to his daughter's seat when his time ran out. The plane tilted to the left and he felt his stomach turn with it. He looked out the window to see the ocean rushing toward him.

There was a deafening crash. The cockpit exploded and the fuselage shattered as they slammed into the waves. The plane dove into the roaring sea. What was left of it skipped over the choppy black surface and burst into flames. Turner saw fire coming up the aisle, devouring the seats and the carpet as it went. The elevator tabs and fin collapsed as the tail fell off. The tailplane and rudders disintegrated. He could feel the flames on his back; his blanket was on fire. He held on tightly to Aileen's seat. The girl had wrapped her arms around his waist, screaming.

The tail of the plane crashed into the ocean. Turner was immediately sucked down into an icy whirlpool. His damp clothes felt heavy and he could barely move. The impact flung him backward and he let go of the seat. Turner was underwater.

Debris tore his shirt; he hit a piece of the fuselage and ripped his trousers before he finally reached the surface and caught his breath. He felt rain drops on his head and looked around him. Kerosene burned on top of the waves, sending tendrils of flames into the sky to set the darkness on fire. Turner scanned the wreckage for Aileen.

Nothing. He had to save his daughter. He took a deep breath and dove back under the water. Electric arcs from short-circuits flashed in the ocean depths. Turner could make out pieces of the plane slowly sinking in the blue-ish light. The salty water hurt his eyes and blurred his vision. His heart was racing. The crashing of waves and sheet metal had now been replaced by a deafening silence. Turner located the tail. It was sinking, leaving a streak of bubbles in its wake. He kicked his legs harder and dove deeper to reach his daughter. Aileen was still strapped to her seat. Her blanket flapped underwater, caught beneath her seatbelt. Turner made it to what was left of the last row of seats and reached out for his daughter. His fingers brushed against hers. The girl was holding her breath.

Desperation filled her gaze. Her father tugged at her seatbelt and somehow managed to unlatch it. Burnt pillows floated up to the surface, where flames illuminated the ocean depths and showed Turner the way up... He pulled his daughter to him and desperately kicked away from the sinking piece of aircraft. His heart pounded and he exhaled the air from his lungs to reach the surface more quickly. It was only about 30 feet away now. He lost a shoe kicking. His body felt heavy and carrying Aileen didn't help. A cloud of bubbles suddenly blinded them. Father and daughter felt themselves lifted up as the water grew clearer, the light brighter. Turner and Aileen surfaced. They breathed in and coughed out salty water. They had just barely caught their breath when they were swept away by the current and waves.

Turner held his daughter closer and they drifted for a couple dozen feet between the flames. The water was freezing and their muscles grew colder and more rigid with each movement. They had miraculously survived the crash, but would they survive hypothermia? They were both in shock. All hell had broken loose on earth. Well, on the ocean. Debris floated all around them, sheet metal rippled underwater. Were they the only survivors? Turner flipped his daughter to her back and dragged her through the water by the arm.

Raindrops and foam splashed in his face. He swam and drifted in the wind toward a piece of fuselage. He grabbed an iron bar hanging from the shattered debris and climbed onto the platform with great difficulty. His ripped clothes were heavy with water. He helped Aileen up onto the fuselage. She was shivering, her tears were mixing with sea water and nearly freezing as they rolled down her cheeks. Her dress stiffened with frost. The piece of fuselage they stood on was slowly sinking as it drifted away from the flames, carried on the waves.

Black smoke faded into the night. Aileen snuggled up to her dad. He wrapped his arms around her in an attempt to keep her warm and then gave her a kiss on her soaking blonde head. He stroked her hair with his shivering fingers. Aileen was silent. Turner noticed her gaze: she knew they were in big trouble. She surely had suspected that her father didn't know how to cope with such terrible conditions. *Every hero has his limits*, she was probably beginning to realize. Turner and his daughter were in a hellish nightmare. Was it even real?

Aileen moaned, gripping the sheet of metal. The storm was subsiding, but the sea was still rough. Lying on his side, Turner couldn't even think, his limbs hurt too much from the fear and the cold. The plane had crashed at sea. When would the rescue squad get there? Was there going to be a rescue squad? How could they find them in the middle of the Pacific Ocean? Could they survive on their own out at sea? The piece of fuselage wasn't going to last much longer, their weight was dragging it down quickly. Turner was sick with worry; he pinched his lips and blew away the water from his face. He had absolutely no idea where they were. Somewhere near the Equator? Was the current taking them ashore or dragging them far out to sea? How could anyone see them?

A shout interrupted Turner's thoughts. Someone was calling; there was another survivor among the debris! He could hear a man's voice over the lapping of the waves. "Help! Please! Over here!" The man clung to an emergency door as best he could. The poor survivor was shoulders-deep in the water and moaning in the dark. Turner's makeshift raft floated in his direction. He caught a glimpse of the man's face in the light of the flames. It was the guy with the Guinness polo from the plane! Turner beckoned for him to join them. The man swam toward the piece of fuselage and climbed onto the iron. The sheet bent and the platform tilted under his weight. The survivor lay down on his back, panting and dripping wet.

He turned to Turner and whispered: "I thought the waves were going to take me. Thank you so much for putting off my doom. At least I'll die in good company." Turner answered in a low, broken and tired voice: "This debris is gonna sink; we have to stick together and tread water if we want to remain above water." The Irishman looked at little Aileen. She was covered in frost and quietly shivering. "Thank God she made it. Can she swim?

- She learned two years ago. Still a bit afraid of the deep end though...
- And the deep end has never been so deep. How deep do you think the wreck is by now? 200, 300 feet? 600?
- It doesn't matter; we have to remain at the surface no matter what.
- All those people... cattered...
- Well, let's try and stay alive. We need to focus and keep warm.
- Keep warm? In this icy water? We'll freeze! Everything was torn to pieces, nobody knows where we are.
- Keep calm, buddy. You'll scare my daughter.
- Sorry, I didn't mean to worry her... more. She survived... that's a good sign. God doesn't let angels die.

- Sometimes he does, Turner sighed.
- Your daughter will live even if you have to eat me first!" He held out his hand to Turner. "I'm Cole... Cole Prescott." The Australian shook his hand.
- "I'm Kenneth Turner. And this is Aileen.
- Nice to meet you Aileen. "

Both men watched a piece of scrap iron rocking on the waves. An engine propeller was floating into the night away from the inferno, as were the three survivors. Their fuselage was sinking. Turner and his daughter were soon surrounded by water again. The platform tilted downward and was engulfed by the sea. Prescott, Turner and Aileen slid into the water to grab the sheet of metal and use it as a raft.

Aileen kicked her legs in the foam and her sandals hit the debris. Turner pulled her closer and leaned on the platform. Their clothes were not going to dry any time soon and he was worried his daughter might suffer from dehydration. For a while, they drifted in the sea. Aileen closed her eyes; she rested her head on her father's shoulder. Using the little strength he had left, Turner clung to the debris and to his daughter. Cole Prescott remained silent for a long time; he was trying to hold on too. The piece of fuselage eventually disappeared under their feet; their raft was swallowed by the ocean. Turner began to tread water to keep his body vertical. He kept his head high above the surface and encouraged his daughter to breathe normally. Prescott joined them, and the three sloshed together in the waves.

The rain had stopped, the clouds had cleared and the sea shimmered in the moon's silver light.

Minutes turned to hours. Turner struggled to stay awake. He'd been trying so hard to fall asleep on the plane and now he was desperately fighting sleep back. He scanned the horizon, looking for a boat, a light. Screaming for help was useless; no one could hear them in the middle of the Pacific Ocean. Suddenly, he noticed a glimmer in the darkness. It looked like a flame.

Another piece of debris had drifted away and the waterproof kerosene was still burning. Turner's vision was blurred and his body was exhausted. He was struggling to find his balance with the weight of his daughter around his neck and was having a tough time treading water. He squinted to see the debris floating in their direction. It was a piece of fuselage, at least 10 to 15 feet long! The curved sheet metal was upside down. It seemed to be sinking too like every other debris, but it was larger and flatter and was going down slower. It was their chance to conserve energy at least for a few hours. The structure itself wasn't burning; only a metal rod sticking out of one wall. A piece of fabric was wrapped around the tip, burning and flickering in the darkness. And... could it be?

Two people were sitting on the fuselage! A man and a woman! There were two more survivors floating on the water, drifting away like Turner's trio! Sparks illuminated the man's face. His eyes were dull, his angular jaw dirty with ashes. He was beardless; he had probably shaven right before boarding. He was tall and thin with a torn t-shirt

Dear Mummy,

Well done! You are amazing - I I love you so much!

love mummy! ♥ !! 🐵 😊 ♡

and jeans blackened by the fire. His pale eyes gazed down at the surface, but he seemed to see only his own despair. Salty water ran down his long nose; his tense, thin lips whispered noiselessly. He was younger than Turner, probably by a dozen years, and deeply in shock. The girl sitting behind him was even younger still, in her early twenties. She was looking at Turner and trying to discern whether his trio was still alive, or just more of the lifeless bodies floating for miles around. Both survivors seemed locked in a new world of death and salt.

The girl's short, wet brown hair covered her ears and reflected the moonlight. She, too, looked pale, thin, and exhausted from the accident. She bore no visible wounds. She had wrapped her arms around herself to keep warm. Upon seeing the survivors, Prescott came to his senses first and called out to her: "Help! Over here! We are alive! There's a little girl here who needs help!" The two survivors quickly made room and invited Aileen onto their piece of fuselage. Turner guided her to the debris and guided her safely up onto the sheet metal. The young woman wrapped the little girl in her arms. "You're going to be fine now, you're safe with us. Have you ever seen pirate movies? This is our raft. You can be our captain if you want and I can be the second mate, what do you think?" The little girl remained silent as she sat down on the makeshift raft. "I'm Katherine," the woman offered, "but you can call me Kat if you want. And you see this man over there? He's not much of a talker, but I believe his name is George." The man nodded to Aileen and helped Turner up onto the platform.

As soon as he rolled onto the fuselage, Turner felt his strength leave his body. He tried to stay awake but the cold pierced his bones. The four survivors distributed their weight evenly on the piece of fuselage so it wouldn't capsize. Cole Prescott swam freestyle toward them. He fought against his heavy, damp clothes as they tugged at him under the water. The Irishman struggled to stay at the surface. Suddenly, the water heaved and tossed the middle-aged man. Something was moving under the water right next to him. Something big. Prescott panicked; he increased his pace and worked his arms harder. Something unyielding brushed against his foot and water suddenly splashed in his face. A corpse came up from the depths and landed on Prescott, who let out a shriek of terror and surprise. Turner put his hand over Aileen's eyes and held her closer. A metal rod impaled the male corpse. His skin was bloated and blueish and his eyes were bulging from their sockets. The ocean was throwing up crash victims. Prescott was terrified; he pushed the corpse away with disgust and leaned on the fuselage.

The surface was once again disturbed by more splashing. The man heard the water lapping, but the tone had changed. The water was no longer lapping against steel, but some other material. Something softer. He heaved his torso onto the fuselage moments too late. The water split in two, and something large, slippery and muscular sank its jaws into the meat of Prescott's calf. Prescott let out a howling, animal wail and struggled to free his leg from the shark's razor teeth. The animal must have been at least 10 feet long.

Within the span of a few short, terrifying seconds, it whipped back down into the deep, dragging the poor man with it. They disappeared underwater. Only Katherine and Aileen's screams broke the silence. Turner and George barely had the time to see the monster's pointed snout and black, lifeless eyes. Kenneth had spotted its white ventral side. Its back was blue. It was a fierce predator, probably a Mako shark with a deadly bite. The plane crash had offered these creatures an all-you-can-eat corpse buffet. Soon, the dark waters would be swarming with more sharks, if it wasn't already. The surface rippled once more and water sprayed the debris. Prescott suddenly resurfaced and grabbed the platform! He was alive. Turner and George dragged him up on the fuselage. The man moaned and muttered unarticulated curses of pain.

His leg was drenched in blood. The shark had torn shreds of skin from it when it dragged him down. Though the shark had released its meal, Prescott was losing a lot of blood. How could they stop the bleeding in these conditions? The vital fluid dripped from the wound onto the steel and mingled with the water. This wound was going to attract more sharks. The survivors were at risk of another attack; they had to keep Prescott out of the water and stop the bleeding. Turner ripped bits of fabric hanging around the Irishman's calf and tied them above the knee to stop the wound from bleeding. A tourniquet was the only solution.

Turner tied it as tight as he could. Prescott was passing out.

Suddenly, Aileen screamed in terror. A Mako shark sprang out of the water, eyes dull as death itself. Its jaw closed on the debris and its sharp teeth tore through the metal. The fuselage tilted forward. The shark's strong body fell on the steel sheet; its pectoral fins slapped against the water as it tried to reach the party. The shark kept snapping at them, its rough skin shining under the moonlight. George suddenly slid toward the water, right into the mouth of the beast! He cut his hand open trying to grab the side of the fuselage and tried to kick away the shark. Water was splashing on his pants; he broke one of the shark's teeth that fell into the sea. One of his adrenalized kicks made contact with the Mako's nose with his shoes and the shark eventually gave up and slipped back into the ocean. The beast glided a dozen feet away underwater, where it lashed out at a dead passenger dragged her underwater.

Turner pulled George back onto the fuselage. The young man was having a hard time catching his breath. Katherine and Aileen were stunned; they sat voiceless on the other side of the steel debris. The raft had almost capsized and was now taking on water. Cole Prescott had passed out. Turner lifted Prescott's leg and rested it on his own so it wouldn't be in contact with water. He didn't want to draw attention to them; their lives depended on keeping the sharks at bay. His head was spinning; he felt sick and had trouble keeping his eyes open. Turner was exhausted. He reached out to his daughter and stroked her leg. The clouds had cleared and the sky was getting brighter in the East. The day was about to dawn. How long would they survive?

Hours went by and thirst became more and more of a problem. They couldn't drink sea water. There was nothing but the ocean as far as the eye could see. It was quiet and infinite. The sound of the lapping waves was lulling Kenneth Turner and his daughter to sleep. All were quiet. They knew the end was close. A whole day went by without anyone uttering a single word. Turner was running a fever, he couldn't move his jaw, and his mind felt sluggish. Was he going to collapse like the Irish guy? He couldn't let his daughter down. Aileen was counting on him. His duty as a father was to protect her, to save her from this ocean of desolation. The fuselage was sinking slowly. Soon it would be fully submerged.

The sun had been beating down all day and was now about to disappear into the horizon. All bodies and all pieces of the plane were now gone, they were alone and defenseless in the water as night was creeping on. Prescott was an easy prey. He wasn't moving anymore and it was hard keeping him awake. The situation was critical. Turner was hopeless. Suddenly, the water opened in front of him; huge tuna were now wriggling at the surface. The sea shivered with flapping fins. The big fish swarmed around the debris, looking for food. Their erratic swimming disrupted the water's surface and rocked the platform. In the water, Turner's feet felt the vibration caused by the large school of easy prey. He feared it might attract more sharks. As if on cue, a fin sped right by the raft. This one looked bigger than a Mako's, and darker. Could it belong to a great white? The Tuna flapped around in the foamy water. Something made a scraping sound underneath the survivors. Were they under attack? Had their time come?

Turner remembered vividly a comic he'd read as a kid. It was an adventure magazine for men publishing scuba diving testimonials from people who'd braved the sea and fought sharks with their bare hands. Kenneth keenly remembered the advice that had so riveted his pre-adolescent imagination: to survive a shark attack, go for the eyes! Time to see if that really worked. The father was ready to fight back and protect his daughter, even if he had to die in the process. The debris jolted again. Something was knocking against the metal. It wasn't a shark. It was a rock. The piece of fuselage had crashed into a reef! Bank reef, a large coral growth developing over submerged highs. Was it a miracle or just a fever-induced mirage? Turner's mind was becoming more and more confused. His vision blurred and his body dripped sweat. His mouth was dry and he was white as a sheet. He began seeing double and his tongue went numb. In the falling darkness of late sunset, he saw a light about 50 yards away and then a large gray shadow. Dizzy, he spun his stiff neck to look around him once more. His daughter and the other three survivors had fallen asleep.

Turner thought he heard voices. He saw black spots and then silhouettes. He felt water rise up to his waist and felt a net brushing against his hand. The salt water stung his eyes, and he ran out of breath. He passed out.

BIG FISHES

The lightning struck outside the room and a mighty clap of thunder roared right over his head. Turner awoke with a start. The first thing he saw was condensation on the window. He was lying on a lifted folding metal cot. The small window was composed of tilted glass slats to let the air in and keep the rain out. It was dark outside but through the misty window, Kenneth Turner caught a glimpse of palm leaves beating against the wall in the rain. He tried to get up but his aching limbs kept him bedridden. He gulped and immediately felt a burning pain in his throat. The dense air was hard to breathe.

He was running a severe fever from spending so much time in the ocean. He was a doctor; it was crystal clear to him. His aching tonsils and dizziness indicated that he was sick, probably a nasty tropical cold. Dehydration and hypothermia had weakened his whole body. The rain was tapping on the bedroom walls and still the heat was unbearable; the humidity was so high he could feel it on the sheets. Or was that his sweat? Turner straightened up on the bed. At his feet, white hospital sheets, a light khaki woolen cover and what looked like military linens. He looked around. He saw concrete walls painted a shade of glossy gray. The room was impeccably organized. On the left stood a small desk and a metal table, at the back, a small green faux-marble tiled-floor area with a basic shower hose and a white plastic curtain. Built-in toilets were concealed on the side. Where on earth was he? Had he ended up in an Asian hospital? The color of the room reminded him of a military hospital. Had he drifted so far west? Why wasn't his daughter with him? Was Aileen in another room similar to his? How was she?

Suddenly, Turner started shaking. What if the fever turned out to be stronger than him? If he had such a hard time fighting the thermal shock, what about his daughter? He tried to calm down, but he feared for his daughter's health. He knew what he and his daughter needed: antibiotics. And he wasn't talking about some Asian generic drug that would never work on him. He remembered what had happened in Indonesia. He had to get better quickly so he could see his daughter immediately; only he could take care of her. There was no way he would watch her survive a plane crash and shark attacks only to die in a tropical hospital because of a misdiagnosis. No one could take his daughter away from him.

He was about to get out of bed when the neon tube over his head started flickering. The sound of the rain on the walls got louder; the drops were hitting the shivering sheet metal roof. Turner could hear the water pouring down the window. Outside, the palm trees moved to and fro and the branches brushed against the walls, dancing in the rain and singing a strange jungle melody. The rattling softened. Nature's symphony was interrupted by the sound of a door bolt being drawn and a door opening." Good, you're awake! I'm glad to see you're still alive. It'll be easier to rehydrate you now that you've come round."

Standing in front of him was a beautiful young woman, handing him a plastic water bottle. She had long, wavy red hair and a thin face. Turner was surprised and disoriented. For a second, he let his eyes wander from her bright eyes to her perfect mouth and then remained silent as he grabbed the bottle and drank from it.

"Your nervous system went through a lot these past few days; you need a lot of rest."

Turner paused. "How's my daughter?" he asked with irritation in his voice.

- She's fine. She's just next door. She's great actually, she even asked for a coloring book last night.

- Last night? - How long have I been out?

- Two days. I guess you needed a lot of sleep after what you've been through.

- How do you know what I've been through?

 - The other crash survivors told me. They're here too with your daughter.

- I want to see my family. Let me see my daughter."

He stood and realized he wasn't wearing pants. Someone had undressed him while he was asleep. He didn't remember putting on this white t-shirt and underwear.

"What have you done with my clothes? Please ask the nurse to bring my pants. My passport is in my pocket.

- I know. But there are no nurses here.

- What are you talking about? There are no nurses in this hospital?

28

- Well, it's not really a hospital... More like a medical center... a small medical center.
- Well then, where is the doctor who took care of my daughter?
- Your daughter doesn't need a doctor, you're the only one here running a fever. But you're in luck; we have everything we need to treat you here.
- I'm a doctor; I know how to take care of myself.
- So am I. I'm a doctor too.
- Are you?" He stared at her from head to toe. She was wearing a beige tank top and combats. Her hair was clinging to her face because of the rain and humidity. He noticed she had several mosquito bites on her arms.
- "I took care of your daughter and of the others, they are fine. I've also taken the liberty to change your clothes. They were quite dirty... You'll see Aileen soon.
- I need to see her now.
- Lie down and rest now, I'll tell her to come and see you.
- Where are we?
- On an island in the North Pacific. Your plane got lost and you drifted toward volcanic reefs. That's where some fishermen found you.
- I knew it! We *are* on an Asian military base!
- Far from it! What makes you think you're in Asia?
- I don't know. The Pacific... and the jade-colored bathroom I guess."

She gave a faint smile.

- "I'll check on Aileen. In the meantime, take the white pills on your bedside table.
- What are they?
- Good old antibiotics to fight the infection and lower your fever."

Turner smiled back. This woman was definitely his type.

"I'm Kenneth, thank you for everything you've...

- My name's Julia."

The young woman picked up some sheets and stepped out of the room. Through the doorway, Turner saw someone waiting in the corridor.

The man entered the room silently as Julia walked away. He closed the door behind him, then walked up to Kenneth and sat at the foot of his bed. Julia was in her thirties, but this man looked a lot older, fifty something maybe. He was wearing similar attire: combats, beige t-shirt and black leather boots. Kenneth thought he was less charming than Julia... This fat and sweaty man looked like a Chinese mobster about to offer him a shady deal. The man took off his glasses and smoothed his mustache, squinting. His eyes almost disappeared in his cheeks. He started in a hearty voice: "We're very happy to see you awake and well, Mr. Turner. You must be in terrible shock right now. You survived an air crash, fought sharks with your daughter and you're still here to tell your story. I've always enjoyed a good hero story and I can't wait to hear yours. My name's Raymond Chua, I'm in charge of most operations here. I picked up the call from the crew that rescued you. They usually fish for red tuna in the area, but they never made such a catch! You're lucky it was fish delivery day or you'd still be on that reef with your daughter. Do you like fish Mr. Turner?

- How do you know my name?
- It was on your passport.
- So you should know that people are looking for us. What did the authorities say when you told them you'd found us?
- Relieved. The authorities were relieved. Everyone's so happy you made it, it's a miracle. The rest of the crew wasn't as lucky.
- When are they going to pick us up? I have great insurance. Have you called them? I need to see my daughter and make a phone call. Could you find me a phone?
- Sure, you'll be able to make any phone call as soon as we get clearance. I'm sure the appropriate measures were taken.
- What do you mean by 'clearance'?
- Well, Mr. Turner, I'm sure you'll understand that our communications with the continent are very limited. The government is aware of your situation and is doing its very best to get you and your daughter home very soon.
- I'm not going to wait on them. I just need to call my insurance and they'll take care of our repatriation.
- You're on a tropical island and external communications are down. We're not allowed to use our satellite phones at the moment. A helicopter will come and pick you up and bring you back to the continent.

- When?
- Very soon."

Turner didn't like his sweet-talk, but refrained from showing his feelings. He sensed that Chua was buttering him up, making small talk. Turner didn't feel safer listening to him. Even though he looked nice, he didn't seem reliable.

"May I see my daughter now?

- Of course. Just one thing: for your own safety, you're not currently allowed out of the medical facility. Take a look at the rain. It's very dangerous. You're already sick; you need to get better so you can go home healthy. It's the rainy season; you don't want to catch a cold, do you?" Raymond Chua gave a little smile. "You won't get out of here until you're fully recovered. You've just woken up from a grueling experience." He got up and walked to the door. "Germs aren't welcome on this island. We're very concerned with health risks. Some chicken broth, a few shots and you'll be back on your feet in no time! But who am I to say that, you're the doctor, aren't you?"

Chua nodded to Turner and stepped out of the room. In the corridor, Turner could hear his daughter's merry shouts. Then he heard her laughing and running to his room. "Daddy!" She jumped in his arms. The pain was sharp, but the joy of seeing his daughter safe and sound again made up for it. Both had gone through hell and had now experienced a whole new range of human feelings. Well, at least that's what Turner thought. So many ideas and emotions went through his mind as they crashed, so many questions and theories he never thought himself capable of having. The old saying "seeing your life flash before your eyes" had never rang so true. It should have been such a shock for Aileen; Turner felt immediately relieved when he saw her so lively and loving. On the doorstep, the lovely Julia was watching their embrace with a quiet tenderness. Kenneth Turner and his daughter were alive. They'd been given a second chance!

Katherine Harrison had always had a taste for drama. Drama and writing. Wherever her job as a journalist took her, she'd find inspiration in her surroundings to write articles. These past few years, her quirky human interest stories had made her queen of the unusual scoop. After a few unsuccessful love stories, she had decided to concentrate on her independent journalist work and to sell her articles and pictures to prestigious magazines. At only 25 years of age, she'd managed to make a name for herself in the publishing business even though her family had tried to talk her out of it.

She'd traveled all around the world despite their misgivings. In Malaysia, she'd met a cannibal tribe living in the jungle, hidden away from the modern world. In Japan, she'd followed the tracks of a mysterious creature called Kappa; she'd even photographed a disturbing corpse in a river in

Hokkaido. She'd been paid big bucks for her story about the suicide forest at Mount Fuji. But what Katherine loved above all else was freedom, space; having the choice to travel and to grow wise discovering new cultures. So naturally, after surviving a plane crash at sea, she had only one thing on her mind: writing about what happened. It'd been a huge shock, but she was ready to put everything on paper. What about a novel? Plane crash and survival stories were selling really well, she might even win a few prizes. Her wild imagination took her to places only she could enjoy and she lay there, daydreaming. Besides, that was the only thing she could do locked up in this room, cut off from the outside world.

Since she arrived on the island, Katherine, like the other survivors, hadn't been able to get out. Well, she visited the corridor and the other rooms, but the adventure stopped at the end of the hallway. A steel door was blocking the way. She'd been there for a couple of days already and hadn't been allowed to leave the premises, stuck in a large corridor providing access to seven aseptic rooms. Prescott, the Irish businessman who got in trouble with the Mako shark, was recovering from his leg injury in his own bedroom. It was located next to the security door. Only authorized personnel visiting them were allowed inside. They all had a pass they scanned in front of a laser device. Katherine had never seen such technology. It seemed to be a very advanced security system. Why was she isolated from the other? Were they infectious? She was happy to be back on solid ground, but she hadn't had the chance to enjoy the fresh air yet. She couldn't care less about the pouring rain; she just wanted to get out for a walk around the medical facility.

And this morning she felt more and more trapped as the hours ticked by. Sitting at her desk, she started to feel frustrated. If only she could write. What was the point of having a desk if she didn't have any pen and paper? What was hiding behind that steel door to the outside? What if this room was actually a cell?

For all she knew, she could be on a radioactive site in the middle of the jungle. She could be infected and quarantined. If they refused to give her more information, she would find answers by herself. Her mind was made up. Katherine rode horses as a young girl. She was slim and athletic. She figured she could fit into the air duct above her desk. She would pull herself up and put her shoulders into the metal compartment and then she would investigate the facility and crawl over the security door. She had noticed a small hatch of braided metal in each room. The air duct ran along the corridor and through each of the seven rooms and over the door, on the other side of the wall. If she could go past the wall, she could probably see other rooms; even get out of the building before crawling back to her room. Tonight, after dinner, she might go on a little evening stroll.

A familiar voice interrupted her stream of thoughts. "Good morning Miss Harrison, it's almost lunch time." Raymond Chua was standing in the doorway. *Should have closed the door, she thought...* "We're going to bring your food tray very soon. Marinated yellow fin tuna and pineapple cake, I think you'll enjoy it!"

Katherine snapped back, visibly irritated.

"When will I get out of here? Why has nobody picked us up yet?

- As I told you, there might be a biological hazard on this island. For your health and safety, it's better if you wait for a little while."
- Wait for what? I've seen you walking around this place without a protective suit on. You're not sick, there's no virus. Why aren't the crash survivors allowed out? Do you really think we can tolerate this much longer? "

A paramilitary soldier appeared in the corridor behind Chua and entered Katherine's room without invitation. The man was fully kitted out.

He wore a black vest with many pockets, had a knife on his left leg and a gun on his right hip. Underneath his vest, Katherine caught a glimpse of ammunition; he was wearing them across his body. He was hefty and must have been in his fifties. He was wearing a black baseball cap and sunglasses but she could see his face was stern. He had blunt features, a square jaw, and an impressive military bearing. Chua got closer to Katherine and laid the tray on the table. The soldier spoke in a cold, aggressive voice:

- "Do you feel trapped on this island? Well you better get used to it. You're right, there's no virus. But it doesn't mean you're allowed to leave. You'll stay here until you can be evacuated. Our facilities can't be exposed. No one should know about what we're doing here, whether you like it or not."

Katherine straightened up on her chair and faced the man. She was young, but she was tough and she addressed the soldier confidently:

"I demand a phone call; I want to make sure my family knows I'm fine. What facilities are you talking about? What gives you the right to keep me locked in here?"

Chua shut the door.

"Miss Harrison, let me introduce you to Bradley Conway, he's a general and deserves to be addressed with the highest respect. General Conway and I only put your safety first. You see, we're working on an extremely sophisticated food-processing program here. Mr. Conway mentioned that we cannot communicate about it, so as a journalist I hope you'll be happy with the little information I'm authorized to give you. Our labs present serious hazards for untrained personnel, both on a physical and technical level. We fear our cattle might be at risk of contamination and we don't want our animals to be exposed to any human disease. And we're also concerned about industrial espionage. That's why our men are carrying weapons. You've just landed in the wrong place, at the wrong time."

Bradley Conway interrupted him. "You've said too much already. Chua is right about one thing: you're actually risking your life on this island. It's hostile.

Believe me, you're far better off here and that's where you'll remain until further notice.

- I won't! No way! I want to go home now! I can't see any badge on your uniform. There's no evidence that you're actually a general!
- You're right; I haven't been a general in a while. But my experience in the Marines is very valuable here. Here, you have to obey my orders and I'm the one dealing with local authorities. Everything goes through me. You want to go out, that's your problem. For now, you'll stay here until I'm told what to do with you.
- So I'm officially here against my will? What if I refuse to stay?"

Conway pushed the door handle and before he went out he turned around and said: "We'll take the necessary measures." He stepped into the corridor and disappeared behind the metal door. Chua gave Katherine a neutral look through his small sunglasses. He wiped his sweaty forehead with the back of his right arm. "Enjoy your food, Ms. Harrison." The man walked out, leaving the door open. Katherine watched him heading toward Aileen's apartment. She heard the little girl greet him. She already knew she wouldn't be as polite next time she saw Chua.

The young journalist was infuriated. She looked through the window, through the zig zag glass. The leaves were still swinging in the rain. Even though the sun was up, the light was dim and the visibility was low. The forest was probably misty. Katherine Harrison glanced at the tray lying on the table and then at the vent grid above her desk. A gust of wind made her bedroom wall shiver; a damp warm current came out of the air duct and swept across her skin. Katherine was determined to leave her room tonight.

Cole Prescott was struggling to put on his new pants. The pair the pretty doctor gave him had quickly gotten stained by blood. His right leg was hurting like hell. Julia Barret had cleanly stitched his wounds and cleaned his injury but the healing process was going to take some time. He'd been bitten twice on his thigh and calf. His leg wasn't a pretty sight. He had trouble moving around as no one could find him a pair of crutches. Prescott felt weak. But unlike Turner, he hadn't run a fever or had an infection. And he could consider himself lucky he still had his leg. When he got back on his feet, he'd try his luck in the casino again. He'd survived an emergency sea landing and a shark attack, and he was still there. It must be the legendary luck of the Irish! Once he returned to Dublin, he'd place bets at the greyhound tracks.

Betting and forecasting had insured him a comfortable income which he'd quickly invested in real estate. He owed his property to the greyhound tracks. Prescott eventually managed to put on his pants. It was a pair of khaki synthetic cotton sweatpants. Everyone was more or less wearing the same thing around the facility. And, even though everyone had been really good to him, he couldn't wait to get back on his feet and go home. Wearing his own clothes would feel great too; what happened to the Rolex he was wearing when they crashed? He was still wearing it on his wrist when he'd washed ashore. Could a fisherman have helped himself? It didn't really matter anyway. He was alive, that was all that mattered. He might learn a little bit more about what happened to him when Julia came to change his bandages; he hadn't been there long, but he'd already noticed how kind she was to him. She didn't just care for him; she also gave him information about the repatriation of the survivors. Communication wasn't the strong suit of these paramilitary soldiers.

Regardless of whatever they were doing on this island, Prescott wanted only one thing: to go home to his wife and kids. He wanted to tell them so bad about what happened and to hold them again. No one had told him whether his family knew he was still alive. He already missed his wife and son terribly before the crash. His business trip had lingered on and he hadn't found much time to call. He missed the cool Irish weather too. The suffocating heat of this island was really bothering him, he wasn't used to such temperatures. Night was falling and he was eagerly waiting for dinner. He secretly wished they wouldn't serve tuna again. It seemed to be the fat Chinese administrator's favorite food; Chua wouldn't stop talking about it. Prescott was getting really tired of fish. He couldn't stand the sight of tuna anymore. Even though he loved fish and chips, tonight, he'd give anything for a good steak with some fries and a cold beer. There was nothing like meat to gain strength and quicken the healing of his leg. His bedroom door was open and Prescott was keeping an eye on the security door, eagerly waiting for either Julia or his meal. He was wondering what lay hidden behind that door. So far, everyone had been acting so weird about it. Anyway, Prescott didn't mean to interfere in their activities, whatever they could be; as soon as the helicopter landed, he'd leave this island and all this yellow tuna behind.

He owned apartments in the Boyne Valley in Ireland that he'd turned into very profitable tourist rentals. His wife, whom he had left in charge, was a very bad administrator. She was an artist, a painter. He started worrying about his business. Who was going to collect the rents while he was away? Surely not his son. Even though he was in his thirties, he was just a layabout, watching TV all day. His wife had coddled him and now he couldn't cut the cord or keep a job. Being born in a wealthy family had made him lazy. Prescott had always encouraged his son to be hardworking. He'd always pushed him; in vain.

The main door slid in the hallway. Was it dinner? No, it was just Raymond Chua again. He was heading to the end of the corridor; he probably wanted to check on the survivors while waiting for a psychological support unit.

A man was walking ahead of him; Prescott had never seen him before. He looked like a paramilitary soldier but he didn't carry any gun. At first glance, he looked as old as Prescott's son, between 25 and 30; Hispanic. From Latin America perhaps. He had dark hair and a well-trimmed beard. He was wearing the same black cap as Conway, the other paramilitary soldier, but backwards which made him look cooler and more laid-back. With his gray shorts, black pocket vest, benevolent face and style, he reminded Prescott of a kind of volunteer from an international organization, an environmental activist from Greenpeace or a new generation scientist. The security door slammed shut behind him and the man stepped into the first room of the corridor; it happened to be his.

"Good evening Sir, I'm Segundo, Julia is busy tonight so I'll be changing your bandages.

- Very well! Nice to meet you. My name's Cole. Cole Prescott. What kept Dr. Barret from coming tonight?

- She had business to attend to somewhere else on the island, but don't worry, I'm a trained caregiver. So I'll be your nurse for the night! I'm usually more into vehicles and tractors, but I never miss a chance to practice my nursing skills on people in need.

- I see... I'll have to take off my trousers in front of you, won't I? If you're changing the bandages..."

Segundo answered with a smile: "You will, Mr. Prescott.

- Tell me Segundo, what is Julia doing on this island? What kind of services is she delivering?
- Unfortunately, I can't talk about that. See, we had to sign a non-disclosure agreement.
  The young man changed Prescott's first calf wound dressing. I heard a Mako shark did that to you. It's quite an unusual war wound!
- Yes, it will leave a lovely scar. Prescott sighed.
- Many scars…
- Any war wounds of your own?
- Not one Mister Prescott.
- I also noticed Conway had massive scars on his neck. Do you know what happened to him?
- It dates back to when he was in the Marines. An explosion in Vietnam if I remember well. Burnt his shoulders. Everyone calls him Lizard Neck. Some Marines used to go by that name.
- With a neck like that, it's quite a funny coincidence. He doesn't look very nice.
- I barely know him. All I know is that he's in charge of operations on the island and he comes from New Mexico. He executes the orders of the Costa Rican government. They made a few deals with the company we work for. The company funds their operations and the President is a shareholder in major Central American companies. It makes for a more dynamic economy in the Republic of Costa Rica. The activity on the island is

covered by the government and the company can do anything here. Which means Conway is the boss. You'll be glad to leave this island! *He cleaned up the wound on his thigh before dressing it.*

- So, you're saying we're in Central America?
- Not exactly. You're in South West Central America, off the Pacific North coast.
- And does this island have a name?
- What makes you believe it has?
- And what about you, what are you doing here Segundo?
- I told you, I operate trucks, I handle containers, construction site stuff, you know... I send money to my Mom every month. She's sick.
- I'm sorry to hear that.
- I hope I can go home to San José to visit her in a few weeks.
- You seem like a loving, caring son. You said construction site but what are you building here? I work in the construction equipment rental business. What are you building, a research center?
- Something like that. Yeah something like that."

Aileen was lying on her bed, quietly coloring exotic birds. The book Raymond Chua had given her was the only way she found to escape reality and anxiety. She'd gone through such a terrible time and the images of the plane kept on coming back to her. Her recent ordeal at sea seemed like an old nightmare, a terrible and recurring distant memory. Everything was still so vivid in her mind. The little girl was still in shock and it'd take a long time for her to process what happened. Coloring toucans was a good way to keep going. She was still away from home, the vacation had taken a brand new turn, that's what she told herself to pass the time and keep her mind off things. Spending days in a corridor wasn't much fun for a 10 year-old child. Fortunately, her father was there too.

Kenneth Turner was sitting next to her, watching her, deep in thought, half tired and anxious, half blissful. His fever had subsided. His skin and lips were still dry from the salt water, but the treatment had worked. He was quickly returning to his normal self and had his daughter with him. The rain was still pouring on the sheet metal ceiling, the air was still stuffy and Turner was thinking about the future. He'd survived a plane crash with his daughter and he now had to go back home and take care of her. He felt homesick. So many things were waiting for him back there. How was the practice? Had patients stopped coming in when they heard he'd disappeared? Did everyone know they were both safe and sound and about to come back to Australia? This question had been tormenting him for a while and he'd tried as best as he could to keep a brave face in front of his daughter, who hadn't noticed his anxiety. Aileen used her imagination to escape and had fun with whatever was surrounding her; kids are endless dreamers. Her mother would be proud. Sometimes, Turner would speak to his late wife in his head. He told her about his life without her, about Aileen growing up. From time to time, he enjoyed a conversation with his wife, as if to keep her in his mind forever. In truth, he would never be able to forget her. Thoughts of her instinctively kept on coming back to him. He wasn't mourning, he'd done that a long time ago, but sharing a beloved past, a long gone life, made him happy. His wife would never have imagined this, Aileen drawing on this island after days of suffering. Life was weird sometimes.

Aileen had spent the day talking to the other survivors. Cole Prescott was very nice to her; he had a knack with children. On the other hand, George, the young boy, was quite a mystery. When Turner and Aileen had visited him in his bedroom, he was really quiet. It must have been his way to deal with trauma and feelings. It wasn't easy recovering from an air crash. Since he got on the island, the boy had kept to himself. Just like Turner, he was struggling with so many questions.

"Knock knock!" Raymond Chua came into the room behind him. "I've come to check on the little Turner family." Turner answered warily: "Well, Aileen's fine. She loves the coloring book you gave her. And I feel much better. No more contamination or infection risks, if that's what you're worried about.

- No, no, not at all! I've just come to have a chat.
- Any progress concerning our repatriation to Australia?
- No yet Mr. Turner, not yet.
- My patience is wearing thin; I think you're aware of that?
- Mr. Turner, you're in a very peculiar place. Of all the places in the world, you had to come to this island. We're doing very important work here; you don't have the slightest idea of what's at stake.
- I have a very good idea about you not giving a damn about us. It's all about your militia.
- That's not exactly true, Mr. Turner.
- Stop calling me that.
- Shall I call you Kenneth then?"

Turner made an irritated hand gesture. "Maybe we should take this conversation to my bedroom and leave Aileen to her coloring book, what do you think?

- Of course. *Both men stepped in the next room.* We've taken the liberty to look you and your daughter up, just to make sure you weren't a threat to our facilities.
- You investigated me? In that case, you'd better call a helicopter or a boat to pick us up tomorrow. If you've investigated me, you must know that I'm not the kind of person who compromises if you bring in the

lawyers. If you don't send us home very quickly, I'll be more than happy to sue your paramilitary group, your company and anyone involved in keeping us here.

- Please Mr. Turner, let's not get to that. You may not have noticed, but we've had very bad weather these past few days. The sea is rough and flying conditions are very poor, just a little more patience.

- Since I woke up here, I've been kept in the dark. No one wants to tell me where we are or when we'll be allowed to go home! I don't care what you're doing here, I demand to see a manager, I demand explanations, and above all else, I demand to leave this joke of a medical facility!

- What will you do Kenneth? Are you going to ask the ASIO to investigate us?" Turner froze and looked at Chua in silence. He wasn't expecting this. "How do you know about the ASIO?

- I told you, we took a look at your file. We work with the government; we can access some international information.

- In that case, you should know that the Australian Security Intelligence Organization has nothing against me. I haven't done anything wrong.

- You know, I spent hours reading about what happened to you. It was quite impressive. How can a medical examiner like you get in trouble with the government?

- I don't have a problem with the government; the government has a problem with me. I've always done my best to help all my patients. Those patients had rights, and I don't see why I shouldn't have helped them.
- By patients, you mean clients, right?
- I opened my clinic long after that. I appraised and supervised every accident case I thought was right and honest. Legal medicine's far more complicated than you think, Turner said.
- You accepted so many medical files and took so many cases to court that you cost your clients' insurance policies hundreds of thousands of dollars.
- They're not clients, they're patients Mr. Chua. I had to do them justice and help them get the best financial compensation, despite their insurance.
- But you cost them lots of money. So much, in fact, that you eventually became their enemy. Right?
- That's why they sent the ASIO to my clinic, they looked everywhere, and they came to my house. They were looking for compromising documents, forged invoices, bribes...but they didn't find anything because I was clean. I opened my clinic with the money I made as a medical examiner. What's wrong with that?
- I'm not denying that, Mr. Turner. See, you and I have something in common. We're ambitious and we want to help others.

- And that's exactly what we're doing here. It just so happens that you're a medical examiner and I'm a physician too.
- You are? You too! Is everyone a doctor on this island or what?
- Being here is a gift that requires certain skills. Skills I'm providing my employers with. In return, they give me enough space to work on my own projects, right here, in a lab. It's quite small, but it's more than enough to carry out my experiments.
- What kind of experiments Mr. Chua? What are you working on?
- Something quite profitable." Chua took a flask out of his waistcoat pocket and took a sip of alcohol. He handed the stainless steel flask to Turner who politely declined. "As a doctor myself, I'm trying to develop a drug to treat diabetes, Mr. Turner.
- Wait a minute, are you telling me that all this nonsense is about a pharmaceutical facility working on a cure for diabetes? Everyone's trying to cure diabetes.
- I'm not trying to find a cure; I'm developing a therapeutic treatment that will help diabetes sufferers on a daily basis. Nothing mind-blowing of course, in a nutshell it's just a cocktail of vitamins in addition to medical treatment. You see, I'm trying to help and support patients with a daily treatment, one pill a day. It's absolutely safe and healthy and let me tell you it will be a major

innovation in many domains. Financially speaking, I will hit the jackpot.
- I don't get it.
- Kenneth, think about it: 29 million people suffer from diabetes in the United States alone. It's quite alarming. If only, let's say, one tenth of this population took my pill, which adds up to 2.9 million American suffering from diabetes... A $1 pill every week times 52 weeks every year times 2.9 million, this pill would make me...
- Several hundred million dollars, I get the picture.
- Only 150 million... Per year. And that's only the beginning. I already have the formula and it's quite cheap to produce. I could flood the Asian and European markets too.
- Why are you telling me all this Mr. Chua?
- Because you need to understand one thing. I'm a scientist with an idea, and I mean to make money out of it. Like many other people here, there's nothing I wouldn't do to protect my secrets. You're a doctor, you do understand. Your unfortunate experience with insurance companies and the Australian government all boils down to this: you went too far. You wanted to be the Good Samaritan but in the eyes of the big firms and the economy, you turned into Robin Hood! When hundreds of millions of dollars are at stake, you know people are going to be looking for you. All governments are the same, they don't like you if you're too

nosy or if you're making too much money. Who knows, I might find myself in trouble too with my treatment. The government will look too closely into my business. In this case, it won't be the American administration but the Republic of Costa Rica. They are greatly assisting my collaborators and me. Nothing can stop us. We're ready to defend our interests at all costs, you must understand that. In a way, this is History in the making, but you'll be gone already when it happens.

- Does that mean Aileen and I can leave tomorrow?
- If the weather is nice, you will. You will leave, Mr. Turner.
- Will you charter a helicopter for the five of us?
- Yes.
- Where will it land? Is there a heliport here?
- Unfortunately not, but there's a landing strip further down south of the island. It's no big deal, we'll take you there.
- Aren't you afraid we might see your precious facilities? What are you going to do? Blindfold us?
- If I have to.
- You know, you and I have absolutely nothing in common Mr. Chua. You're just a greedy, self-centered joke of a scientist. You put yourself on a pedestal, thinking you're going to change the world. But there's no goodness in what you're doing. You're just in it for the

money. You're obsessed with your medical pipe dreams and you obey a paramilitary group. There's no magic here. You're just the puppet of pharmaceutical companies.

- Oh, there's magic around here Mr. Turner. Now, you should go and tuck your daughter in. It's getting late. Everyone has to go back to their room before lights out.
- I'll be waiting for the helicopter tomorrow. Aileen and I are ready to go.
- As I said, it'll depend on the weather. Believe me; no one hates rain as much as I do. But what can I say, that's the season!
- Then I will let you go back to your futuristic lab. Good night Mr. Chua.
- What I do in my lab is nothing compared to what I do in theirs. In a few years, you may understand. Here, we make the future. "

It was dark, very dark. Katherine could hear the raindrops tapping on the roof. It was late. Everyone must have been sleeping by now. It was a great time to crawl into an air duct. More daring than ever, Katherine had managed to silently slip inside the duct and to crawl for a few feet. Curiosity had prevailed. She had reached the next room, Aileen's room. She glanced through the vent grid and saw the girl sitting on her desk in the light of the bedside lamp. What was she doing up in the middle of the night? Aileen suddenly looked up and turned around to face the grid. Katherine had been spotted! They both looked at each other. Aileen was about to speak when Katherine put a finger on her lips, inviting silence. She smiled and the girl smiled back at her. The journalist crawled forward a little to get to the end of the air duct. She didn't want to draw attention to her; she didn't want to be turned in. Thinking about meeting Bradley Conway again was giving her the chills. She went past Turner's room and two more empty rooms. The air was damp. Katherine was soaking wet. Alone in this air duct, she had a moment of doubt, but she started crawling again. She looked through the grid above George Alistair's room. The lights were out. The young man must have been asleep. What did she expect anyway? Katherine resumed her progression; only a few more feet. At the end of the hallway, as she was about to go past the security door, the air duct made a right turn. The young woman went past Prescott's room and went right. The air duct went around the corridor and then made a right-angle turn to the left. She was heading straight into another part of the building. She immediately saw light coming from the left. Through the iron hatch, she saw what looked like an armory. Along the walls stood closets full of guns. Katherine spotted a few other rifles and pieces of assault equipment lying on the table. A padded vest was resting on a chair. No one was there. These guys were heavily armed. Perhaps the area wasn't that safe after all. Were they a South-

American militia? Death commandos? Revolutionary armed forces? Perhaps it would be better to go back to her room. It would be silly to get herself killed after having survived a plane crash. But curiosity got the best of her. Katherine overcame her fear and resumed her journey into the air duct. On the left was a far bigger room; a row of vent grids spread out before her all along the air duct; a yellowish light seeped through each of them. As her face got nearer to the first hatch, the young woman saw computers and walkie-talkies. Weapons were lying on fold-up seats. A man was sitting in front of a screen. The journalist tried to be as quiet as possible to reach the second hatch. She was still in the same room, facing a wall, almost above the soldier. She couldn't see his face but she managed to discover two large maps pinned to the wall, this place must have been an operation center. These were maps of the island! The first one was a general map featuring various facilities in the north and south, roads, rivers and mountains. It was a huge island, better not to get lost. The young woman squinted in order to read the map title through the metal grid: "Isla Matanceros, Site C, Maximum Security Prison". It was an experimental penitentiary facility! That explained the weapons. Katherine had surely been rescued on the shore of a high-security island. What kind of prisoners could they keep here? South-American criminals? And what were all these food-processing and cattle plants all about? Was the government trying to turn bandits into gentlemen farmers participating in a top secret food program? And what if this paramilitary group was secretly experimenting on the inmates? The journalist started wondering where on earth she was. The other map featured more islands. The island she was on was the first of the five. It was at the top of an island arc which looked like a tilted "C". The third island was the biggest of them all, but Katherine couldn't read its name. Two others were named after a letter: site C and site B. The three others had Spanish names Katherine couldn't make out. It was the map of an archipelago; there was no trace of an island referred as "Site A". Katherine made one final effort to reach the end of the air duct in silence. It stopped at the back of the room. A grid led outside in the open air. The young, brave explorer pushed the grid without a noise and slid her legs and then the rest of her body through. She dropped outside of the air duct onto crates leaning on the wall. She slipped on the wet wood and almost fell over... The sound of thunder drowned out the creaking noise the hatch made as she closed it; she was outside! She'd managed to bypass the security door and get out into the compound.

The rain was hitting her face and soaking her clothes; her hair was clinging to her forehead. Strangely, she was happy to feel the rain on her face again. There was nothing she valued more than freedom. She walked along the wall and around the building. Through the first window, she saw the control room or the headquarters, she didn't know what to call it yet; She had no idea if the man was still in there. Luckily for her, the night and rain were on her side tonight. She would be hard to spot in the dark. Facing her building was what looked like a plant with two small smoke stacks blowing out steam. Probably one of these "organic food-processing" labs. She turned left to take a look at the medical facility dining hall; it was an impressive cafeteria where a few people were sitting at tables, talking. Behind her: another building, most likely housing quarters. Katherine saw that barrels of fuel were stored in a small cabin behind a fence. An engine roared. A 4x4 vehicle drove past the building. Who could it be at that time of night? Were some men taking part in a nighttime operation? The headlights shone on the foliage and swept through the darkness. Katherine noticed a few massive steel pillars standing behind the buildings and the trees. The Jeep drove quickly by, yet she could see where the camp ended in the headlight beams. Behind the dripping ferns, high fences towered over the village. At the top of each pillar there was a blinking orange beacon. What did that mean? Could it be that the fences were electrified? What kind of inmate could be so dangerous? And where were the inmate barracks? Where were the wardens? Katherine was disconcerted by what she saw. She moved closer, hugging the walls in order to avoid detection. Ahead, in the darkness, she thought she saw a power station and more housing quarters. She went around the building, following the corridor from the outside to her room. Luckily, it was the first room of the medical facility; it would be easy to get into the air duct and crawl back to her bedroom without going all the way back into the night. Now that she thought about it, she could have gotten out that way instead of going all the way up the air duct. She looked up at the vent grid. It was far too high. If Katherine grabbed the duct and hoisted herself up, she would probably rip it off and it would make a deafening crash. It wasn't the best of plans, especially here, in the middle of the night.

The young journalist decided against it and went all the way back around the building before she reached the entrance of the control room again. She climbed onto the crates and into the ventilation system again. By now she was soaking wet. She hoped she wouldn't make too much noise crawling into the aluminum duct. She hadn't completed her mission yet and she couldn't get caught. She went past the armory again, and this time she noticed the security door she'd missed before. Then she made a right and then a left over Prescott's bedroom. The light was on. He was sitting in front of an untouched food tray delivered a few hours ago. Did he choose not to eat or was he getting tired of tuna too? Eventually, he gave in and lifted the fork to his mouth; hunger was stronger. Skipping a meal was hard for someone his age. Every time is a good time to eat yellowfin tuna... The other rooms were dark. Everyone was asleep. Katherine went over Aileen's room before she reached the end of the air duct. She managed to get out and set her right foot onto her desk, still holding on to the hatch. When she let go of it, she cut her finger on the metal sheet, but it was nothing serious. Her mission accomplished, Katherine slipped back into her room unnoticed. She took off her wet clothes and grabbed a towel to dry off. Would she be able to sleep? Her imagination was running wild.

George Alistair was leaning against the corridor wall. He was quiet, as he'd been since he got there. So far, he had ventured a few talks with the other survivors and the facility personnel, but that was it. Like the rest of them, the young man still didn't know where he was exactly and when he'd be able to leave. This part of the trip had been quite unexpected. As usual, he'd been the first to step out of his room in the morning. He was walking to and fro in the corridor to stretch his legs. They wouldn't let him out of the facility, so he had to find some way to exercise in a very confined space. He didn't know what kind of operations they were conducting on this island and he wanted to draw as little attention to himself as possible. Harsh former Marine Bradley Conway and Raymond Chua seemed to know a lot about his mates in the center and he wondered what they knew about him.

George didn't particularly enjoyed being held against his will, yet he hated knowing someone could so easily pry into his life even more. And why? Even if his past might have been of interest, his being here wasn't a threat to Conway and his men. George was in transit and, as usual, he was keeping to himself. He'd had plenty of rest since he'd been rescued by the fishermen. They'd found him scratched and shaking on the shore. But now he was feeling well again and all he had to occupy himself with before he left was watching and learning. Cole Prescott's and Kenneth Turner's doors were open. It was early, yet both men had been chatting for hours already. They'd been talking about their families, their trips, their jobs. They'd been trying to pass the time too, to get to know each other and enjoy themselves. George didn't want to go that far. He preferred to keep things formal and to remain on his own. He knew someone would bring breakfast soon. Katherine's door was open too, but she hadn't shown herself yet. George didn't dare to enter her room and say hello. He would wait. The Turner girl was still sleeping. Her door was shut. A beep rang and the electronic door opened.

Bradley Conway stepped in and stopped in the doorway. Behind him stood Raymond Chua, holding a tray. He entered Prescott's room, asked about his leg and said hello to Turner. He left the tray and went back to get some breakfast for Turner. Conway was stationed in front of the entrance, both watchful and irritated by Chua's constant comings and goings. The fat man entered Katherine's room and dropped off the tray. He went back into the corridor and past George. Then, he stepped into the room next to the security door. It was Prescott's. Chua nodded to George. "Here's your breakfast Mr. Alistair." At the same time, George saw Katherine getting out of her room and walking past Aileen's door toward the end of the corridor. She ignored Conway and tried to get behind him and through the door. Conway stopped her, blocking the way and flexing his muscles. Katherine wouldn't give up so he violently pushed her away and shut the door in his back. He coldly addressed her: "How many times do I have to tell you? You cannot leave this room." Katherine answered, irritated: "Am I being held hostage, Mr. Conway?

- Stay in your room and go have your breakfast.
- Don't you enjoy my conversation? I can think of so many things we could talk about, answered Katherine.
- For the last time, go back to your room and drink your coffee while it's hot.
- Is it a local coffee? A site C delicacy? Are the beans ground here in Matanceros?"

From the end of the corridor, George saw Conway go pale. Katherine had obviously dug up some sensitive information. The man was caught by surprise and glowered at her; his eyes flicked over to George to see how much he had caught. Lizard Neck stood in front of Katherine and spoke to her in a low, throaty growl. "How could you possibly know that? Who gave you that piece of information?

- Even lost in the Pacific, I have my sources. What's going on with you? Are you afraid I might start a mutiny?" Katherine started speaking up so everyone in the facility would hear her. "Are you afraid that I might tell everyone we're all locked up in a high security prison?

 - How did you access this information?"

Katherine glanced at George. "Your attention please! Mr. Bradley Conway here doesn't want me to tell your more about this island we're on! To tell you the truth, there's more than one island!" She shouted louder and louder; so loud Chua stepped out of Prescott's room. It took Turner only a short time to join everyone else. Katherine was losing her temper; Conway didn't know how to get her under control. It was quite a pleasing sight. George had no idea how the journalist had learned so much without leaving the facility, but she surely was resourceful. The paramilitary soldier approached her, his eyes blazing with frustration, and tried to get her back into her room. Chua stood between them and said: "Miss Harrison, this is not the time or place to talk about such details. As you may all know, we're working on classified projects and some subjects should be kept secret. I'm asking you to calm down now.

 - Calm down? Now that I know we are in a prison in the middle of the jungle? What are you hiding here? Are you carrying out forbidden experiments on the inmates? Are you testing a military serum on human subjects?
 - Of course not, you're getting carried away.
 - I saw the map in the operation room; I saw the map of Isla Matanceros. What are you keeping behind those electric fences? Did you

find dead aliens? Are you studying them in your labs?"

Conway replied angrily: "Enough! You're talking nonsense. Go back to your room." Chua backed up the ex-Marine: "Mr. Conway is right Katherine; you'll scare the little one."

The security door opened again and Julia Barret stepped in. George hadn't seen her these past few days. She was in great shape, too. She was wearing khaki pants and an open shirt. A white tank top dirty with sweat and mud clung to her chest. Julia had a backpack and a saddlebag slung over her left shoulder. On her light brown belt, she carried a long machete sheath, also worn out by dirt. The young woman was only passing through; she must have been really busy outside the facility. George hadn't been the only one to notice her badass demeanor. Turner walked up to her, smiling as if her being back was an omen of hope and good news. "Hello Julia, we were worried we might never see you again. Aileen won't stop talking about you.

- Hello Kenneth, I'm glad you're fully recovered. Look at you! This bad fever is just a memory now!"

Conway interrupted their reunion. "Perfect timing. Please try and get Miss Harrison back to her room, she's unbearable." Julia said: "Well, that's understandable. She's been locked up in a small room for a week, just like the others. Maybe it's time for them to get some fresh air, what do you think? "

Chua interrupted her abruptly: "Thank you for your
            suggestion Julia, but these people aren't
            allowed out yet.
-    And who took this official decision by the
     way?
-    You know very well that it's not up to us.
-    Oh really? Who is it up to then? Please
     Raymond, be a dear and go get Aileen her
     breakfast."
Chua cringed; he was a little offended; he slipped
away in silence, glancing at Conway. Julia resumed.
Katherine and Conway were all ears. "Mr. Prescott
needs sunshine; it'll help his leg heal faster. You
can't keep them locked in here; these poor people
have the right to get out before they're allowed to
go home. And when they do, they'll see what's
going on here anyway, and you're very well aware
that they won't leave this island without signing a
non-disclosure agreement. It's not up to
you." Bradley Conway was tapping his feet. From
down the hall, George could see that his patience
was wearing thin and that he wouldn't hear reason.
He looked as if he was about to burst out any
moment. The soldier looked away, silently fuming.
You could tell he didn't like being lectured by a
woman. "Miss Barret, must I remind you that
allowing these people to walk around the
compound might compromise our operations?
They're our responsibility until further notice. We
have to secure and implement the given orders.
-    Do you really think the founders of this
     project would be happy to learn that we're
     keeping air crash survivors locked up in

here? They went through hell and survived, I think they can cope with a worker village, don't you think?

- We have to follow the procedure. No intruder is allowed on the premises." Katherine interrupted Conway: "Intruders?! Do you think we *want* to be here? None of us asked to end up on your beloved Site C! Julia looked at her, smiling. We aren't intruders, we're victims! Nobody cares about your damn top secret paramilitary island arc!" Lizard Neck replied: "You seem to know quite a lot for someone who's never left this corridor. Maybe you're here on purpose; maybe you're a spy.

- A spy? I can't believe it! Do you really want to know how I discovered your overprotected outpost? I used the air duct. I had a pretty nice view of your armory and control room from up there! Your facility isn't as impenetrable as you think! And by the way, what are you monitoring with all your computers? Inmate cells?

- This is none of your business." Then, Turner spoke. "As Julia said, we'll all have to sign a non-disclosure agreement. So you can just tell us what you're doing on this island.

- But there are no legal processes or agreement at the moment." Said Conway. Julia shoot back: "I'm pretty sure Hammond would absolutely condemn that.

- What are you talking about?

- About you, bringing a negative, administrative spirit to his project. Does he know about this? I bet he doesn't, or you wouldn't be here snarling like a guard dog." Chua came back with a tray and headed to Aileen's bedroom, whose door had remained closed. "Julia, listen to me, you know the company will take all the necessary measures according to regulations. We'll make sure to review all agreements with our lawyers. We need to protect ourselves, nothing must leak and we need to come up with legal measures for all this. These cases are always very complicated." He hurried past George, who was watching the scene, and knocked on Aileen's door. "Miss Turner, it's high time to wake up, breakfast is served!" Turner left the group and walked

down the corridor toward his daughter's bedroom. He gently knocked on the door and let himself in. He probably wanted to make sure she wasn't in the bathroom. The last thing a father wanted was for his daughter to be seen on the toilet by one of those mean, fat, sweaty soldiers. George saw Turner looking all around the room; Aileen wasn't in her bed, or in the bathroom. Worry crept into Turner's voice: "Aileen? Sweetie, where are you? Come on, show yourself." Turner tugged the sheets away from the bed and looked over at the desk area. His daughter had finished all her coloring books; one of them was still open. Pastels and felt-tip pens were lying around on the chair but the little girl was nowhere to be found. George looked at Chua stepping into the room too and put the tray on the desk. He scanned the room, squinting, and noticed the vent hatch had been removed and was lying inside the opening. Chua said "Well, it seems that Ms. Harrison's little nocturnal prowl inspired your daughter, Mr. Turner... Aileen is gone." He grabbed his walkie-talkie and lifted it to his mouth. The device crackled when he turned it on. "Chua for North IC compound teams. A little girl escaped from the main building. Find her."

The truck had been driving at average speed on the same dirt road for approximately twenty minutes. The dumpster smelled of cow dung and fish. Hiding behind wooden crates, Aileen listened to the tires rolling on the fresh ground. She tried to look through the thin openings in the metal walls, but all she could see were leaves and branches. In the darkness of the container, the little girl was dazzled by all this greenery. It looked as if the sun was out for once. It was a bumpy ride and Aileen was getting tossed around in the back. She tried as hard as she could to hold on to the crates around her. They were full of fish, huge yellowfin tuna. Where was the truck taking this massive delivery? Earlier this morning, Aileen had decided to explore the air duct; if Katherine was allowed to do it, why wasn't she? She had quickly left the main building and had a brief walk around the compound. She'd seen the steel gates and a few buildings but she'd been particularly drawn to this strange truck. She'd never seen anything like that before. Was it a special military truck? The cabin and the huge storage area were dark green. It looked more like a cage than a container. The framework was made of thick iron bars and metal shutters could be pulled down in order to hide what was inside the cage. It was empty but Aileen had seen Segundo and one of his partners loading it in the morning. She now had a headache from the smell of fish and the ride was giving her motion sickness. Nonetheless, she was happy she had managed to stealthily slip inside the truck before it left. Because she was small and had exceptional secret agent skills, the little girl had remained inconspicuous. Anyway, she wasn't even doing something wrong; she was in good hands. She'd met Segundo before at the medical facility when he came to take care of Prescott's leg. The young man had made a good impression on her. He was very nice and caring; you could see that on his face. He was very active and vigorous, a perfect playmate. Aileen couldn't tell if it was because of the way he talked or the way he wore his cap backward but Segundo seemed trustworthy; like the big brother she never had. Of course, Segundo couldn't see her, he was sitting in the front cabin, driving. The little girl had heard he worked as a driver here on the island and that he drove all types of vehicles, even construction vehicles. Well, even though he was an expert, his driving left a lot to be desired. Or was it because of the condition of the road? The ground had been bumpy for a few minutes now; perhaps Aileen was entering the jungle at last. Good thing she didn't suck her thumb anymore! When she was younger back in Australia, he father took her for rides in his four-wheel drive on remote dirt roads. She remembered how she sucked her thumb in the car, how the car jolted and how her front teeth would dig into her finger; she would bite herself involuntarily. Those were fond memories from a time when her mother was still alive.

Hiding behind the crates full of tuna fish, the girl suddenly felt the urge to suck her thumb. What would her father say if he was here right now? He'd probably be mad at her for getting out without asking for permission. But that was what kids her age did anyway; no one would resent her, would they? She'd just survived an air crash; she had the right to treat herself to a new adventure to clear her head. And anyway she was young; she knew her dad scold her, but he wouldn't be mad for long. She wanted to make the most of this situation. The truck slowed down and stopped. Aileen pressed her ear against the cabin wall and heard Segundo stop the engine. In the front, the two men started speaking in Spanish and slammed the doors shut. Aileen cowered behind a plastic barrel, completely hidden in the back of the container. She could hear Segundo walking in the grass on her right, she also heard birds singing; the place seemed quiet, no one else was there. The driver opened the metal plate at the back of the dumpster. It sank into the damp green ground, turning into an unloading platform. Segundo stepped on it, opened the heavy bar gate and entered the container. He dragged one of the fish crate outside of the vehicle. Aileen, who was watching him between two drums, noticed that all crates had small metal wheels. Segundo unloaded a few and then got out of Aileen's sight. She heard him giving directions to his colleague. The man was stationed in front of the vehicle and Aileen couldn't understand what they were saying anyway. Segundo climbed back into the dumpster and dragged another crate out. What did he need all that fish for? The child decided to go have a quick look at what Segundo was doing; she left her hiding place to hide behind another crate outside. She stepped down the platform without a sound and looked at both men walking in front of the vehicle. They both dragged crates toward a river flowing next to the truck. Segundo's associate had a gun slung over his shoulder. They unloaded the fish on the ground and carried the empty crates to the vehicle. The other soldier grabbed his gun and aimed right, Aileen held her breath. Segundo came back to the truck without looking back, he didn't look afraid at all. What had the other man seen? What was he aiming at? Segundo walked past Aileen to get one last crate. The young man hooked two canisters to his shoulder; he wore a strange tank as a backpack. Both canisters were connected to a long gun with a white rubber hose. What kind of device was that? It looked like a huge water gun. Segundo rolled the crate to the massive fish heap next to the river and knocked it over to spill the fresh tuna on the ground one last time. Aileen heard twigs snapping to her left. She jumped. The other man was still standing in front of the truck, she couldn't see him. The little girl took a look around. The truck had stopped in the middle of a clearing. Aileen looked out over a sea of tree trunks and tall grass. A green hill overlooked the tropical forest in which she was standing. The brook disappeared further down behind trees and creepers.

The clearing was lined with giant ferns, and moss-covered tree trunks were scattered across the wet grass. The place must have been swarming with snakes; perhaps it would be better if Aileen got back into the trailer. The young girl knew the jungle could be full of dangers, she'd read about it in books. She looked at Segundo again; the young man was spraying the fish with a whitish liquid. He was sprinkling the heap with his special gun, emptying the whole canisters on the ground. The liquid was soaking into the ground and flooding the grass on the bank of the brook. As Segundo turned around in her direction, Aileen heard more snapping, like a tree trunk shattering, followed by the rustling of leaves. The girl felt the ground shaking, something was coming from behind the truck; the forest was coming to life. Both men were exchanging in Spanish, Segundo spilled another crate of fish on the ground, right in front of Aileen, as if rushed by his partner. The rustling of leaves was getting louder. The young man took the canisters off his back and put them into the truck. Stepping down on the platform, his gaze was drawn to the remaining crate; he was reaching for it when his eyes met

Aileen's. Her hiding place had failed her; she'd been spotted and had nowhere else to hide. Segundo froze, stunned. He didn't expect to find her here, 30-minute away from the compound. Though startled at first, he comforted her: "What are you doing here? How did you get there? You know you can't be here right? This isn't a place for little girls. I heard a radio call about you. I never thought it'd have something to do with my truck!

- I'm a secret agent on an adventure and I'm here to help you on your mission.
- I believe our secret mission's been revealed. *He told his colleague in Spanish.* "You can't stay here, it's too dangerous. You should never have gotten on this truck. We have to take you back to the village immediately and cancel the rest of our round. You shouldn't be here.
- I didn't want to bother you; I just wanted to see where you were going with all that fish. You're the tuna delivery guys, right? And why do you unload it by the river? And what's that weird goo you spray on it?"

Segundo's colleague yelled something in Spanish. The young man and Aileen turned around to look at the river. At the edge of the forest, a dark shape was crushing the plants to get out of the foliage. Aileen was shocked, she gaped. Segundo grabbed her arm and took her to the vehicle. "Sit in the front, it's safer." The girl couldn't believe what she was seeing. Fifty yards away stood a huge creature. It must have been 25-30 feet. Aileen couldn't tell how much it weighed yet, but it must have been a few tons. The animal crossed a pond before sinking its legs into the fresh humus of the soil. It walked to the river and to the whitish fish heap. It looked like a big lizard, like a huge crocodile. Except it was standing on its hind legs with its forelimbs up, somewhat like a bear. The reptile was swinging its long tail, sending clumps of dirt in the air as it went. Its skin was dark, a shade of greenish brown. Aileen could see darker spots on its back and thighs. Its neck and shoulders were covered in white markings. At the end of its long, wrinkled neck, just like a monitor lizard's, was a formidable head with a long thin snout lined with rows of conical teeth. Its jaws must have been extremely powerful. Aileen noticed a large sharp claw on the first finger of each hand. The beast stepped closer to the tuna fish and started sniffing the ground; it opened its mouth halfway to lick the liquid off the food. The young girl saw a bright pink membrane at the corners of its mouth.

The animal snapped a fish in half between its jaws, buried its snout into the heap and started feeding greedily. Soon, its mouth was covered in white liquid and bloody leftovers. Segundo opened the front right door of the vehicle and ushered Aileen into the car. The little girl had no clue what she was seeing. It was too big. Through the windshield, she couldn't take her eyes off the lizard, hypnotized by this incredible discovery. For the first time in her life, Aileen had met a dragon. Segundo headed to the back of the truck to empty the last crate. Suddenly, there was a rumble next to the car. The jungle opened up in front of a wide-eyed Aileen who didn't want to miss a thing. Another dragon stepped out of the undergrowth, about 5 yards away from Segundo's partner. It let out an ominous nasal roar and snapped its jaws at the soldier. The man took a step back and leaned against the driver's door to dodge the monster's head. His finger was on the trigger of his weapon, ready to shoot. How could he bring down something that big? Everyone knows that dragons are immortal creatures and now Aileen had proof they existed. The animal shook its tail, whipping the grass and trunks around; he walked to the fish, brushing past the truck. The girl could feel the vibrations of its steps on the ground.

The windows were shaking, and she hoped the iron bars over them would keep her safe. The second reptile started feeding next to the first one; that's when two other dragons showed up on the other side of the river. They walked along the river before crossing it; one of them paid no attention to the fish heap and headed straight for the vehicle. Aileen shivered and hid behind the passenger's seat. Segundo's partner stepped in front of the car and aimed at the dragon. It slowed down its pace and started sniffing around; suddenly, it froze. The soldier signaled to Segundo to hurry up. He looked nervous. The young man was loading the crates in the dumpster; he slammed the steel door shut and wiped his hands on his combats. As he was lifting the muddy platform back onto the cage door, the huge lizard approached the vehicle and started bypassing it from the right. The soldier yelled in Spanish at Segundo again. The other three beasts were having a field day next to the brook, but this one had smelled the fish

Segundo had spilled behind the truck in a hurry. As he was lifting the container on the right, the young man found himself face to face with the animal. Aileen couldn't see anything; the creature was blocking the whole window. The dragon, surprised by Segundo, froze again, like a statue. The young man backed away, watching the animal the entire time, went around the truck and reached the driver's door. He let his partner know about his intentions but the sound of his voice startled the animal. It jumped at him. The scaly giant pushed on his hind legs, splashing mud all around. Segundo started running to the cabin as the other soldier got back to his seat. The monster whipped the metal shutters of the cage with its strong, muscular tail. The truck shook for a few seconds. The other dragons lifted their heads from their precious loot, which they had quickly devoured. One of them walked to the cabin and banged its snout on the left window. Segundo hadn't reached his seat yet and he had to face another lizard. It scratched the door with its claws and bent its head toward the young man, hissing. Behind the truck, another giant was swallowing the remaining fish and licking its long sharp teeth with its thick pink tongue; Segundo was surrounded. His partner reached over the driver's seat to open the window. He grabbed his gun, cocked it and aimed at the dragons between the bars. Segundo addressed him in Spanish; the crocodile let out a terrible roar. The man shot. A tranquilizer dart hit the animal in the left leg; it immediately backed away, hissing. The monster took a few steps back and leaned its forelimbs on the hood, the cabin tilted forward. It moved away and whipped at the left fender with its tail; the shock was so great, the window shattered. Segundo's friend covered his face and shards fell on the front seats. Aileen screamed when a few pieces fell on her shoes. The reptile turned its back to the truck and met the other lizard on the left. Segundo took this opportunity to open the door and get into the cabin. He looked at Aileen, wide-eyed, and patted his friend on the shoulder, smiling. "That was close!" He caught his breath and started the engine to put the car into reverse. Of course, the dragons had a very different idea. One of them jumped at the trailer and sent it reeling. Aileen heard the sound of its claws on the steel. Jerking the steering wheel, Segundo jammed the petal to the floor; the wheels skidded in the mud and the wet grass. Both beasts pressed their heads against the trailer, snapping their jaws, as Segundo reversed the truck; ahead, other animals were getting closer. The car struggled back and Segundo tried to make a U-turn. A third dragon began slashing at the cabin with its forelimbs. It pushed its hind claws into the bumper and leaned on the front of the car to haul itself upon the hood; it tried to grab the bars protecting the windshield with its hands. Aileen was expecting the beast to breathe fire and burn down the cabin. Segundo steered left and bumped into a lizard who immediately began attacking the left door. The driver saw the metal warp from the inside. These animals had terrible claws; they could tear the cabin down if they tried hard enough. The driver carried out the maneuver until he fell back into the starting tracks and could engage the first gear at last. While the truck paused, a dragon rammed into the dumpster, knocking the truck off-balance one more time. Segundo managed to stay on course and the creature gave way to the vehicle; the young man shifted to second gear and finally drove away from the pack. Segundo's friend burst out laughing and started cracking jokes in Spanish; he was sweating profusely. Aileen had fastened her seatbelt and sat quietly in the back of the cab, utterly bewildered. The knight had just saved the princess from the evil dragon.

WE MAKE THE FUTURE

The wind was blowing on the hull of the boat and the windows were shaking with an eerie rustle. The sea was heavy; the waves were rocking the boat. Rodrigo Quintado was anxious. It was a small motor boat that could only carry up to 20 people. There were only three people on board, but the freight was substantial and heavy. The captain knew the fuel tanks would soon be empty and they'd need to reach land and refuel. Quintado and his men had been at sea for two days and they were longing to arrive. He was holding the helm, thinking. He was struggling against the wind and hoping they were going in the right direction. Rain started falling on the cabin. He feared the ocean would get rougher and put them off course. They'd managed to cross Nicaragua from East to West, from Bluefields to Granada, and they couldn't give up now. Quintado looked left and saw his reflection in the window. His dark brown beard needed a trim and his face looked gaunt. He ran a hand over his triangular jaw and then stroked his tired face and bushy black eyebrows. The air was humid, and his shoulder-length hair was getting frizzy. His clothes were wet, but at least his boots were clean - unlike his friend Ernesto's. They'd been splattered during a gunshot two days ago. Like his captain, Ernesto was thirty five. They were from the same neighborhood: Santo Tomàs, Nicaragua. They'd been to the same schools, hung out with the same people and got themselves in the same mess. Ernesto was a lot more irritable than his friend; his features were coarser, sharper. He had a straight mouth and almost invisible lips. Buzz-cut dark hair covered his small tanned head and large dark eyes lit up his face. They eagerly surveyed every minute detail in the cabin. Ernesto had become Quintado's right hand man ever since he had upgraded his business from drug to weapon trafficking. Rodrigo Quintado had cashed in these past few years and Ernesto had taken the opportunity to line his own pockets. Together they were a power to be reckoned with; they hadn't hesitated to shoot at the police as they crossed the country. Ernesto had had to get rid of two greedy partners in Acoyapa, just before they reached Granada by the lake with the freight. The famous five managed to smuggle the largest ever cocaine and weapon shipment to Pochomil, where they embarked on a boat and headed South. The goal was now to reach Puerto Jiménez in South Costa Rica near the Panamanian frontier. That was the final delivery site. Quintado and Ernesto had nine million USD worth of drugs and weapons in the back of the boat. Everything was neatly packed in a huge metal crate. Since they'd now be splitting the money between three people, they'd make three million dollars each. Quintado had received a confirmation that a briefcase would be waiting for him in Jiménez, one case for him, one for his faithful partner Ernesto and one for Smokey, the henchman he hired back in Villa Sandino. The man proved to be reliable even though he wasn't the sharpest tool in the shed. His round bald head made him look like a halfwit; he was slower than the others and had a hard time remembering orders. But Quintado knew he could count on him. Despite his stoutness, Smokey had proved he was in great shape the day they had to shoot at the North Pacific water police. The crook had a strong sense of work ethics and hierarchy, which made him a good subordinate. Quintado had managed to shake off the sea cops, sailing at full speed for two days. The authorities had a name for this kind of boat: "go-fast".

The boat was whirring through the waves burning fuel, and no one could keep up. Rodrigo Quintado and his men didn't have to worry about the police or customs forces anymore; the problem now was the low fuel tanks. Quintado knew they had to make a stopover to refuel before they could resume their journey to Jiménez at full throttle. Once again, he hoped he was heading in the right direction. Sitting in his corner, Smokey was grasping a plastic hand-hold for stability, eating a chocolate bar. The man was insatiable. That must have been why he was known as "Smokey" in the business - surely it had something to do with his consumption of food. Or was it because of his complexion? Or because of the way he used his gun? Quintado was deep in thought. He should have been able to see the island by now; did he get his navigation plan wrong by a dozen miles? The sea was getting rougher and the boat walls were shaking from the waves crashing into the hull; it was hard to stay on course and pilot with such a racket. Yet Quintado knew this ocean like the back of his hand; he knew there was an unmapped archipelago in the area. He'd stopped on Isla Matanceros several times with his father as a child and then as a teenager. His father was known as Don Tiburon, he was a tough guy, a godfather; he'd worked with the cartel for twenty years. Rodrigo had had many opportunities to learn the business with him. His father meddled in all kinds of armed groups; he was a tyrant, a somewhat unsavory person. Rodrigo Quintado had never really loved him; he didn't feel anything when he went down for trafficking last year, in November 1983. He was probably rotting in jail somewhere in Panama. He might have even been executed already. Quintado hadn't heard any news of him, and he hadn't been back to Matanceros for almost ten years. He remembered it as a haven of peace, a lush paradise, uncharted and mysterious, a heavenly hideaway for smugglers who used it as a business hub. Human presence was very limited. Nature was queen: the singing of the birds, the sound of the wind in the leaves and rivers. In his memory, Matanceros was brimming with rivers and streams, and swamp mist crawled over the vast landscape, creating clouds in the jungle and the mountains. Quintado wondered if the place still bore the remains of its past as a fuel deposit. Rusty pipe-lines snaked through the land. The government of Costa Rica had ruled out drilling for gas in the 70s to concentrate on petrol deposits in South Pacific. His father had built a small cabin on a river bank, it was his secret lair: a wooden and corrugated metal shed built up against the ditch that led to the creek. After all this time, the cabin must have been vandalized by passersby or pirates, but Quintado knew something they didn't. Buried beneath a tree near Don Tiburon's cabin, there was a very large chest: The "emergency chest", only to be used in the event of a setback; the last resort. His father had told him about it and Quintado had seen it with his own eyes when he was a child.

The chest held fuel cans and weapons, everything you need to get a fresh start. It had never been opened before and no one really knew about its location. Quintado and Ernesto just had to sail up the river for a dozen miles, unearth the chest, load the fuel on a dinghy, sail back down to the ocean and resume their journey. Quintado was counting on the chest. It was his only chance to refuel before they reached the frontier and the delivery point. They had to succeed if they wanted to deliver the shipment and pocket three million. Ernesto, Smokey and he couldn't get it wrong. The sea breeze was getting hard to stand; salt stuck to their clothes and damaged their equipment. The three men wore black military combats and dark multi-pocketed sleeveless vests. Underneath their gear, Quintado and Ernesto wore ash gray tank tops; Smokey, for his part, was wearing a solid pink shirt that contrasted violently with the rest of his outfit. Was he just being eccentric or just plain stupid? Quintado couldn't tell. Smokey stared into the distance and wiped his chocolate-covered fingers on his MP5 rifle. He looked like a fat toddler who had been given a tactical weapon.

Ernesto tried to light up a cigarette to calm his nerves. But with the wind blowing and the waves hitting the hull, he was clearly wasting his time. He couldn't get his lighter to work and angrily stuffed the tobacco back into one of his pockets. The go-fast suddenly nosed down to skim down a really tall wave. Above them, the three partners in crime saw the sky clear up and the sun start shining on the waves with a scorching yet invigorating yellow glow. Quintado stopped the engines and let the boat drift on the water. He rotated the boat toward the south-west. The cabin's plastic walls squeaked and the boat splashed down into the water after a short free-fall. Rodrigo Quintado started the engines again, the propeller slapped the water, quivering, and the boat sped forward. It suddenly nosed up as it hit the trough and then stabilized, carried by a lighter warm breeze. That change in temperature could only mean one thing: Quintado was getting closer to the archipelago. The island group was known to have its own capricious microclimate: some days warm and sunny, some days misty with heavy showers. This time, the sun was on his side. The light coming through the clouds shone on a green horizon. Quintado had finally managed to reach the north face of Matanceros. It was the first island of the group. A dozen miles south, there was another island, far larger, that gave the archipelago its shape. The smuggler didn't know the other islands; he'd only set foot on Matanceros with his father and his men. In less than an hour, he would reach the northern coast, with his own crew for the first time. That was the next step to a new life, the last stop before the finish line. Quintado signaled Ernesto to get ready. Inconspicuously getting fuel would only take a few hours. It was also a great opportunity for Quintado and his men to get hold of a few weapons while they were at it. It was a positive break for the team and there was absolutely no reason why it should go wrong.

A dry heat had replaced the heavy humidity. Cole Prescott could feel it. The sun was shining on the village and felt good on his leg. The daylight caressed his skin and healed his wounds. The fifty-something Irishman was wearing a pair of beige shorts and a gray t-shirt, sitting next to the main building entrance and gazing at people getting busy around him, watching his new environment. Prescott was homesick. He missed his family. He tousled his gray-blond hair and laid further back to get his leg in the sun. A warm voice softly woke him up from his bliss. "When I was a kid, my mother used to rub honey on my wounds for quick healing. I guess the sun is fine too." Standing on the main porch, a man greeted him with a smile. His pearly white teeth and slightly flat brown face made him look very friendly. His small nose made room for his cat-like eyes. His hair was well groomed and he was wearing a white shirt and a brown backpack. His light brown, almost orange pants gave him the appearance of a clown. Prescott smiled back, nodding. "Your mother was very wise, Sir."

- My name's Nurdinah. Fahran Nurdinah. My mother was Indian.
- Really? And where are you from Mr. Nurdinah? I myself come from Ireland. The weather is far chillier there...
- I come from Malaysia; I grew up in Penang, in Little India.
- You too are very far away from home, I guess."

The man took a packet of cured meat from his backpack. He tore the wrapping and started munching on his snack. Prescott looked at him, puzzled.

"What do you have here? Is it beef jerky?
- No, it's even better! It's Tu Yokon. Candied pork. It's delicious. I can't live without it. I have it shipped from Malaysia; I basically live off the stuff!
- But why is there a chicken on the package if that's pork?
- In Malaysia, products are marketed to Muslim customers. So you'll find a chicken on every food package. It's safer that way. Easier. Do you want some?"

He handed a packet to Prescott who opened it suspiciously. Thin slices of sweet and savory meat slipped between his teeth. The man widened his eyes. It was absolutely delicious! The sweet and greasy pork was immersed in slightly spicy oil; the texture of the meat was perfect. The Irishman couldn't refrain from expressing his satisfaction.

"This is grand! How come I've never heard of that before? It's delicious! We don't have this kind of thing in Dublin.

- It's a rare pleasure that my wife sends me from Kuala Lumpur. I'm sure you'd love Malaysian cuisine... Even though Tu Yokon tastes more like Chinese food.
- What are you doing here Fahran? Do you work for the people in uniform? Are you protecting the village?
- No, not at all. I only contribute in my own modest way. I'm an architect.
- Did you build this facility?
- Kind of... I designed the plans and supervised the building process.
- What a coincidence! I happen to be in the property business too. I rent flats.
- That's funny indeed. My mission ends there though.
- Why? You have nothing more to build?
- I do, but not on this particular site. There are more fortifications south of the island. You'll probably go there for evacuation. Works are almost over; they don't need me there anymore.
- So you're heading back to the continent, hey?
- No, I still have a lot to do on sites B and A.

Katherine Harrison, who was just passing by, joined the conversation. "And what exactly are you building over there?

- Wonderful things. You'll see. Any news of the girl?

- Not yet... Julia and her dad are looking everywhere for her. I kind of feel like it's my fault... If she hadn't seen me in the air duct, she'd never have escaped.
- Don't worry, they will find her. This compound is extremely secure. No one gets in or out without an authorization. There's no way she could have escaped those walls. "

Prescott and Katherine looked at the concrete battlements surrounding them. Shadows of branches danced on the structure and the sunlight glistened on the electric fences. An armed man was patrolling on top of the walls and girders. He was walking the narrow path above the security perimeter, keeping an eye on the area. Even in full daylight, Kat could see the light from the orange beacons atop the pillars silently glinting off the soldier's helmet. Fahran resumed proudly: "These lights are here to remind us that these gates are electrified. If you get closer to the fence, you'll see the 'Danger 5000 Volts' signs hanging on cables. I designed them. "

Prescott answered calmly: "The girl's smart. She won't get close to the fence. This kind of apparatus is far too intimidating to a 10-year-old kid." Katherine added: "Not just to a kid. This place gives me the creeps too. What the hell are you keeping here that needs a 5000 volt protection? I've had a walk around and haven't seen any cell. It's a regular worker village, not a prison.

- You're right Miss. It's not a prison. We are not keeping anyone in. These fences protect us from what's outside; this is for our own safety.

- It's hard to believe there's something that dangerous outside. What kind of menace requires such precautions?
- Miss Harrison, could you please stop bothering Mr. Nurdinah. He's our engineer and head technical supervisor. He has a lot to attend to and was about to leave." Katherine and Prescott knew Chua's voice as soon as he entered the building.

"Shall I remind you that our operations here require the utmost discretion? I'm counting on you to follow the rules and stay put. A helicopter will pick you up tomorrow south of the site and you'll be asked to sign a highly confidential file. Until then, just keep quiet and scrupulously stick to the confinement protocol." Conway stepped out of the building and stood right next to Fahran. He held a semi-automatic Baikal MP155 rifle. Katherine could tell from the wood. "Our teams will be away for a day or two. Another mission deserves our full attention. You'll leave tomorrow night. Until then, the North outpost will have limited autonomy. Stay out of trouble and find the girl." Conway stepped down the front steps and headed to an armored vehicle parked next to the little gas station. Chua followed on his heels; a dozen armed men appeared behind the fence. The soldiers came from a building located behind the main construction and its medical wing; it probably was their quarters, their barracks. Some of them got into trucks; others loaded huge six-sided cages on construction vehicles. Fahran said goodbye to Prescott and the young journalist and he headed to the exit door of the perimeter. The wild shadows of the surrounding foliage drew bright patterns on his brown backpack as he walked away. Where the hell was he going?

Kenneth Turner and Julia Barret joined Katherine and Prescott on the steps, the sun was beating down on the concrete; Prescott was delighted, he could feel his wound healing in the heat. He asked Turner about his daughter: "Still no news of Aileen?

- No. We searched every shack, every building. She's nowhere to be found. We've been calling her for hours." Julia looked at Katherine and said: "Aileen is probably just hiding somewhere. No one saw her get out. Have you searched this building? Now that you can walk freely out of the medical facility, you can check the other rooms." Katherine answered: "I looked inside and discovered the dining hall. It looks nice. I tried to get near the armory and the communication room, but they slammed the door in my face. It seems you don't really like nosy people around here. Anyway, Aileen's not inside, I'm sorry Kenneth."

The security gate opened some 50 yards away from them. A three Jeep convoy drove through the electric cage to get out of the compound. For a while, the lights above the fence blinked. The huge tempered steel door opened automatically from the outside and vehicles sped up to drive out of the paramilitary enclosure. Two trucks followed the cars and drove slowly through the gate. They were carrying iron containers of various sizes. What kind of shipment would they place into those cages? As the group of vehicles disappeared into the jungle, carrying Chua and Lizard Neck away, their tires threw dust into the air and cloaked the compound gate in an orange mist. On the other side of the gate, another vehicle waited to enter the compound. The fence lights were still blinking. Could it mean the fences were offline and that there was no electricity running through them anymore? The armored truck rolled through the gate into the compound and parked near the wall. The gate sealed shut behind it. The scout on the fence signaled to the driver, the orange pillar beacons turned on and the personnel got back to their duties. The truck cabin looked wrecked; the body work was covered in mud and scratches. The driver stepped out of the car; Prescott, Katherine and Turner recognized Segundo from his earlier visits. His colleague got out as well, followed by Aileen, who ran to them. She jumped into her father's arms; he embraced her tightly, visibly relieved. The child was giddy with excitement. "Daddy, I saw dragons! I saw dragons! I did! You're not going to believe this, they keep real dragons here, and they're not a myth!" Turner was debating between lecturing or forgetting all about her childish behavior for once. He didn't want to upset her; the young medical examiner was far too happy she was back safe and sound. "What on earth got into you? What were you thinking? Do you have any idea how dangerous it is out there? You can't act like a baby now; you could have died on your little field trip. I was worried about you, do you understand?

- Yes Daddy. I'm sorry I left without your permission. I was too curious." Julia and Katherine exchanged an amused look. "I'll let you off this time. But don't do it again. From now on, you're not leaving my sight. We're going home tomorrow. Go back to your coloring books; you're grounded for the day. I'll come and check on you in a few minutes.
- But if we leave, will I ever see the dragons again?" Turner, embarrassed, answered in a tender voice. "What dragons are you talking about?"

George Alistair had walked away from the group; he was having a look around the village. This brand new type of compound had aroused his curiosity. He'd walked by the worker housings, seen the bunker and the power installations. He'd gone back along the main building and past the paramilitary quarters. That was the biggest facility after the main building. George had turned right to walk alongside the central building and had finally stopped to lean against the wall and smoke a cigarette. One of Chua's colleagues had given him one when he'd finally been allowed out of his room. He'd then realized that the facility was only a small ensemble of rooms with a dining hall and a kitchen.

Only 540 square feet seemed dedicated to communications and weapons. This wasn't such a big deal after all; just a basic military base in the jungle. Except he didn't really know where site C was. The directions the facility guys had given him were purposefully vague. Was it in Central America or further south, in Ecuador? George had caught a quick sight of Polaroid pictures stapled to the walls. What they portrayed was quite strange. His shoulder pressed against the gray concrete, George was smoking his cigarette in silence. His attention was focused on the electric fence and the small factory in front of him. Near the main building stood a small white house that stood out from the others. It appeared to have come straight out of a galactic science fiction movie. It was a small square bunker, longer and higher at the corners and covered in warning signs. The concrete walls were full of vent grids and metal plates screwed to the surface with big bolts. Four large pipes coming out of the left hand wall disappeared into the grass, under the loose and brown soil. The building must have been about 10 feet high and George could see two other pipes and a large antenna on the roof. Behind the factory stood a small rectangular building about 15 square feet, housing a vent system and four large plastic cases. Thick pipes connected the building to two large, 13-foot high silos, which were anchored to the ground by a reinforced concrete structure. George inhaled the smoke from his cigarette; he was more and more interested in this building. This factory in the middle of the jungle was quite strange in and of itself, but the white paint that coated the small facility was even more surprising and made it look quirky and futuristic. The word "AGRO" was stenciled in black paint on both silos. An opaque automatic sliding door opened, the young man heard a de-pressurization sound, like gas or vapor escaping.

A thick white smoke started coming out of the building roof. A woman came out of the factory. She was carrying tanks and a spray gun. Two men came out before her; they were transporting white plastic crates on trolleys. They headed to a loading vehicle. The truck was a custom four-wheel drive with a storage dumpster that was almost 10 feet high. The windows were protected by bars and white wire mesh. The dark green shade of the vehicle contrasted sharply with the immaculate white shade of the factory. The sun shone on the facility and the shadow of the antenna cut the truck in half. It was very hot today. The woman put her equipment at the back of the truck and wiped her forehead. She was hot too. She didn't seem to be a paramilitary soldier; she looked more like a scientist. Under her lab coat, George saw that she was wearing a blue shirt and beige shorts that went down to her knees. She must have been twenty years older than him, probably in her fifties. Her short messy blond hair illuminated her tanned face. The scientist had a thin head and a sharp, well-defined nose. Her delicate mouth and bright blue eyes gave her a charming and friendly look. She stepped away from the vehicle while the others were loading the tanks and crates in the dumpster.

She wiped her fingers on her orange neck handkerchief and walked up to George:

"Hi. You shouldn't be smoking around here. It's not good for the environment. "

George, usually quiet and reserved, answered immediately. "Judging by all the smoke coming from your factory, I believe I might not be the worst polluter in the vicinity...

- Well, you're wrong; that smoke is 100% natural. Just plant steam. No smell, no pollution... I don't believe we've met?"

The woman held out her hand to him. George shook it and was reluctant to give her his actual name. The rustling of the wind in the dry palm leaves gave him confidence and serenity. He was far away from everything here. After so many mishaps and hiccups, he was safe for once; nothing could get to him on this island. No one, not even the militia, could trace him. In this particular place, the young man was free; he could relax and be himself. "I'm George, one of the air crash survivors. They let us out this morning. And you are?

- Tia. I work on this site. Tia Porter. I've heard a lot about you. It was a miracle. They kept you in for quite a while...
- Yes, but now we can enjoy the sun at last. It seems the rain is gone for good.
- You never know what to expect here.
- What are you making in this factory?
- I told you, 100% natural stuff. Nutrients, vitamins, whatever you want to call them.
- Is that what's inside those barrels?

- Exactly. They're food supplements. Powders and liquids. It's a perfect blend of herbs and powdered cuttlefish bone.
- Cuttlefish bone?
- Yes, the same one uses for reptiles or birds. It helps them absorb calcium.
- And for what purpose are you using it?
- To feed the cattle. Well fed cattle produce more vitamin D and are a perfect food source for our residents."

Katherine Harrison, who'd walked around the building, joined the conversation: "Which residents? They found little Aileen, she'd been hiding in a truck. She said she saw dragons. Are they what you call your 'residents'?

- Could be. I bet you're the journalist Chua told us about. I hope you're feeling better after that air crash. It must have been a most traumatic experience.
- You have no idea. The Turner girl claims she saw huge lizards outside. She said they attacked the truck. And when you take a look at the vehicle, you're tempted to believe her. What's hiding behind that electric fence?
- Maybe I should show you. "

George looked at Katherine, she'd lost her composure. She answered: "You've kept us in our rooms for days, coming up with all sorts of threats and hazards, and now you're agreeing to tell us more? I must say, I'm a little confused.

- You're a journalist, right?

- Yes, Katherine Harrison. Sorry, I didn't introduce myself.
- I'm Tia Porter. I'm a biochemist. I supervise a lot of things around here. And if you're a journalist, we can do each other a mutual favor.
- I still don't get it.
- Tomorrow, you'll be leaving the island and signing a non-disclosure agreement. But in a few years, when all this is release to the public, you'll be able to claim that you witnessed it first. You'll be able to say "I was there" and make the headlines! Let everyone know what happened behind closed doors in our company. What we're creating here will change the future of the human race and I want you to tell the world about my work and my part in this wonderful adventure. When the time comes, I'm sure you and I will be awarded many prizes for our contributions. Journalism and science deserve recognition, don't you think?
- I guess...so you agree to show George and me your work and in return, I make you Scientist of the Year writing about your achievement here as soon as the legal prohibition is lifted? Sounds like a good deal to me. I really need to understand what's going on here though... What's your purpose on this compound?
- My purpose is to further science and to offer solutions that will actually change the world. I'm a biologist specialized in bio-

genetics." George, who was all ears, couldn't help but comment: "Bio-genetics?

- That's right; most of our work revolves around cloning. Cloning is essential for developing groundbreaking food-processing solutions that could even put an end to world hunger."

Katherine asked: "Put an end to world hunger? That's quite an ambitious plan. Is that was you're doing in your plant? Cloning cattle? And then, what do you do with them? You feed them to Komodo dragons? Aileen was right?

- It's not exactly what we do. In the past, we cloned a few cows and goats, but the process is too expensive. It's easier to breed them the regular way. We are cloning something else. Let me show you, I was just about to leave the compound anyway. What do you say?"

Tia motioned Kat and George to follow her to the truck. They followed on her heels, looking around, as if they were doing something wrong. The scientist laughed: "Relax! Lizard Neck and Chua aren't there, hop on and enjoy the show. You might be able to write about it in a dozen years."

Quintado was tying his bootlaces, still wet from the sea. He had managed to stop on Matanceros; he'd sailed through capricious waters around the island and stabilized the boat on the north coast. His crew was on solid ground for some time. Smokey was tying a second rope around the wooden dock to secure the ship. Ernesto, for his part, was scanning the volcanic rocky coast eaten by the waves. An impressive sharp cliff rose ahead. Behind, green mountains hid the sky. The singing of birds mixed with the sound of the sea and the three men could see the forest stretch out as far as the eye could see. No doubt, Rodrigo Quintado was back. The smuggler tightened the tie of the knife sheath he carried on his calf and told his partners: "We have until sunset to bring fuel back and get the hell out of here. Smokey, you stay here and watch the boat. Lay low, don't get caught. Ernesto and I are going to follow the river up to my father's chest. Then, we'll come back to the boat with the canoe. If someone comes around, smoke him!"

Smokey, puzzled, answered: "Smoke him? But you told me to lay low. Don't you think people will see the smoke and...

- You moron! You pop a cap in his head, you put him down, you shoot him! Got it? What the hell man! I must have been out of my mind when I hired you... If someone gets close to the go-fast, you take him out and throw the body into the sea, make him fish food, alright? You protect the goods with your life. Keep your walkie-talkie close; we need to stay in touch. We'll be right back. Remember, this is just a stopover, we have to leave before nightfall."

Quintado slid his gun strap on his collarbone and pulled his shoulder blades closer to crack his back. He led the way, and Ernesto followed him without a sound. A few yards away, a path led to the north of the island like a sharp lava flow. The two men left the little makeshift harbor, leaving Smokey and the boat behind. The crashing of waves echoed the buzzing of bugs in the forest that grew taller and taller above them. The path was steep; Rodrigo and Ernesto had trouble climbing the slope. Sand gradually gave way to colorful sandy soil. After an exhausting 30-minute climb, the ground became flat again. The two men carried on stepping over irregular steps of soil, holding on to roots and pushing hard on their legs. It had been raining heavily. Water had turned the path into a torrent and the hardened orange mud had reshaped the surface, making the climb even harder.

Quintado tried not to pay attention to the scorching sun; Ernesto was sweating profusely. They only carried a 33.8 Fl Oz water bottle each in their canvas backpack and they tried to save their supplies, the journey was likely to be a weary one before they reached Don Tiburon's cabin. Quintado couldn't hear the sound of the sea anymore. Smokey the moron and the go-fast were already far behind them, and that was good news. The concealed path was lined with sunburn, blackened trees that reminded him of the volcanic flora he explored as a teen. As they went, more and more bright green ferns grew on the banks and up the trees and creepers. The flora of Matanceros sometimes brought to mind the rain forest, an old-growth forest brimming with life. In the north, ferns and moss covered pine trees and their essence mingled with the tropical scents of the Caribbean. Nature was queen on this island; they'd better keep that in mind. As they climbed the path, Ernesto had positioned himself in front of Quintado to cover his friend in case of an attack and was scanning their surroundings. He wasn't afraid of other smugglers, he feared the island itself. Quintado could see that. It was unknown territory to him; he had to rely entirely on his boss and follow orders. The local fauna and flora were legendary: over ten thousand types of plants, thousands of varieties of orchids, fifteen thousand species of butterflies, nearly ten thousand species of birds and over two hundred species of mammals. The island was the pride and joy of Costa Rica and was blessed with the local climate; like the rest of the archipelago, it was probably magic. There were a lot of threats around here: venomous reptiles, bugs, maybe jaguars. Ernesto wanted to play it safe; step after step, he examined the vegetation that was swaying in the now dry, now humid wind. He was taking deep breaths, as if trying to smell the danger; everything was quiet around him.

The two criminals were heading toward the north side of the island. Soon the ground began to slope away, and it was just a matter of time before they reached the river. Behind Ernesto, Quintado brushed his fingers against a big yellow and green flower with large red ears; it was a Heliconia, an impressive bright red flower that Ernesto knew well. He refrained from mentioning that, however, as he didn't want Quintado to know he had any interest in flowers, or anything other than being a cold-blooded killer. Any sign of weakness would not be tolerated. Ernesto held on to a branch to help himself down the slippery dirt path, as they stepped deeper into the wonderful, wild garden.

The wheels of the truck skidded in the mud. The vehicle careened over a large root; it leaned over to the right and drove away on the dirt road, crushing branches as it went. The ringing of the windows and wire mesh echoed like the buzzing of mosquitoes. Katherine was watching the landscape through the window, behind the trees and the mossy hills; she hoped she would catch a glimpse of those much-vaunted dragons hiding in the forest. She couldn't wait to discover all of Tia Porter's secrets. In the cramped back seat of the four-wheel drive, her right leg was pressed up against that of George, the enigmatic young man. It would have been an intriguing situation, but romance was the furthest thing from Katherine's mind. Her interests lay elsewhere. To George's right sat Tia Porter, who was also absorbed with looking at the landscape. In the front, three men were chatting in Spanish; the driver, a broad-shouldered South-American man, was focusing on the road and jerking the wheel from side to side to maintain his speed. An hour had passed since they left the village and headed south; they were now at the center of Matanceros and site C was about to reveal one of its secrets to Katherine and George. The truck emerged into a flat, bare plain. The truck slid to a halt in front of a small facility protected by 6.5 feet high fences. "Follow me!" Tia Porter stepped out of the four wheel drive and walked to the metal mesh door of the preserve. Kat and George were following her slowly, their eyes fixed on the building standing a few yards away from the barbed wire fence.

Tia Porter drew the bolt and entered. This fence wasn't electrified, the metal gate was thinner and the perimeter was far less secure than the North outpost. A tall concrete building rose ahead. It must have been about 4,500 square feet and about 130 feet high. The grayish building appeared to be some sort of bunker with an automatic security door; black and yellow stripes were painted on the six-sided facade. What struck Katherine first was the large crate hanging on the wall. It was perforated with tiny rectangular holes to let air in. While the scientist was opening the door with her pass, Katherine and George stood still. They immediately noticed how quiet it was; the birds had stopped singing, the wind had stopped blowing. Katherine Harrison felt vibrations coming from the ground when the security door opened. There was something living inside this building, something not human; she could sense it. She and George walked through the door and followed Tia Porter into a small lab. On aluminum tables lay utensils, tubes, various devices and computers. Tia Porter said to Kat: "795 million people are suffering from hunger in the world. It got a little better in the early 80s, but that's not enough. The Food and Agriculture Organization of the United Nations confirms that the situation remains critical in Sub-Saharan Africa and South Asia. Today, we can fight this terrible plague with a cheap and nutritious food source. And we can produce it in large quantities too. It's the food of the future." She walked toward a long control panel and pushed a big green button in front of an automatic shutter. It was about 50 feet long; it started rolling up with a slight hum. Through the window, Kat saw white light coming from neon tubes. Tia Porter resumed her fascinating speech: "Mammal cloning will be made public in a dozen years or so. People are not ready for it yet. It raises too many ethical questions. Still, earlier this year we managed to clone a cow, and we're very proud of this achievement. Three cows were born this year. They're perfectly fine. They're growing up in the neighboring fields, in the open air and in secrecy. Yet, this spectacular achievement was just the start, the first step of the company's plan. We've created something much bigger." The automatic shutter had almost reached the ceiling; a cold light was shining on the control panel and the three people standing there.

Katherine walked to the window; the large Plexiglas surface was perforated with small ventilation holes. The young journalist's eyes gradually got used to the light and to the white walls. That was when she saw them. She screamed with horror, took a few steps back and hid behind George. He cringed and flexed his muscles, ready to fight back. Professor Porter gave them an amused look. Terror showed in Katherine's eyes. George was stunned. On the other side of the glass, there were about two dozen giant crickets. The room was swarming with huge bugs; they were crawling about on the floor and up the walls. Their almost spherical heads had huge bulging eyes on each side and long thin antennae. Their trapezium-shaped thoraxes were thick and seemed strong and sturdy. Cerci grew on the end of their abdomens. Each bug was about 28 inches; some might have been up to 40-inches long. George couldn't believe his eyes.

The crickets crawled up and down the walls on their six hairy legs, looking for food. They fed on blocks of white powder and scattered this thick flour everywhere they went. The gigantic vivarium was filled with a thick fog created by the bugs swarming around in the powder. They were all covered in this floury substance, as if painted white, after spending so much time in their pen wallowing in their food. Their thick, sinewy legs looked ready to launch the insects skyward. Three of the insects clambered across the observation deck window, clinging to the ventilation holes. Katherine caught a glimpse of sharp legs bristling with spines through the thick, clear surface. She screamed again and grabbed George's left arm, who was watching the scene, completely astounded. Tia reassured them: "Don't worry, they can't get to you, you're absolutely safe. Their wings aren't functional. We developed the anterior parts to be hard and strong elytra. They act as shields and stridulatory organs; so the wings aren't locomotory organs anymore. We chose to genetically modify and atrophy them so the crickets are easier to control. They can't communicate and are now completely silent. You'll notice that you can't hear them from the outside or from the inside."

Katherine stared at Tia, appalled. She asked quietly: "Is that your plan? Save the world with giant bugs? How did you manage to create such a thing? It's impossible; no one has the technology to clone living organisms...

- I told you Katherine, we make the future of modern society here. My company owns enough labs to create miracles. Cloning life is just the beginning. We've been working on this project since the late 70s, and now we can implement it here, on this island.

- So, site C is a top secret cricket farm protected by the local government?

- Our domesticated crickets are fed a healthy diet of vegetable and grains. We just add our secret herb and powdered cuttlefish bone supplement. And yes, we raise them here. Bugs are considered a delicacy in Northern Thailand and Burma. And there's a very good reason for that: crickets have amazing nutritional value. These bugs are a great source of protein, vitamin B2 and iron. They are 100% natural with no preservatives or artificial color added. You can snack on them or incorporate them in various recipes.

- I do understand that it's a great scientific achievement Dr. Porter, it's fascinating... But do you really believe people are ready to eat crickets? It's gross, I just can't picture it.

- In the long term, our company will establish cricket farms in countries most affected by hunger. Believe me; they won't be as picky as you. These genetically modified crickets are humanitarian aid; they're a gift from science to the free world. Just think about it for a second: we could fix food inequality in under a year. The creation of genetically modified cricket farms could revitalize local farming industries and generate employment. These people need food and money, and our company is implementing bio-genetic solutions and offering prospects to human beings living in deprived areas. That's my purpose in life: I want to create a better world; I want to save the planet...and by the way, crickets and meal worms are actually not that bad in a curry or with barbecue sauce. Plain, they taste slightly nutty; it's like eating a peanut! It's all about presentation.

- You won't change my mind. Eating bugs is gross. It feels so wrong!" Katherine made a face of disgust.

She couldn't keep her eyes off of the bug pen. She was feeling sick.

Tia Porter pushed the button to close the automatic shutter and ushered Kat and George out. They left the building and walked to a truck parked near one of the walls, its cargo container pressed up against the concrete surface. An automatic shutter, as large as it was tall, was opening in the wall. A man was stationed there; he was activating the door from the outside in order to roll it up to the same level as the steel cage. Those men were about to transport giant crickets! Tia made her way through tall grass to meet the small group of workers. The man was managing the employees, screaming orders over the noise made by the door. "Get ready to close it up. Slowly! Don't crush them. Smith, how many can you see inside?" Standing in front of the container, another man started counting the bugs inside. "4, 5, 6. There are six of them Sir."

- Excellent. Closing the confinement unit gate. Do the same with the cage, gentlemen."

Inside the container, Katherine and George could see crickets flitting from wall to wall and making the metal shake. They'd been lured into the cage with food and were now about to be taken to another location. But where?

The boss came to shake Tia's hand. His face was rectangular and thick arched brown eyebrows grew symmetrically above his bright hazel eyes. He had a slightly bulbous nose above a masculine mouth. He was well put together in a rugged, unshaven way. His brown hair was hidden under his red baseball cap. Unlike Segundo, who was younger, this man wore his cap frontwards. The peak of the hat was rounded; the reddish fabric worn out. Time had taken its toll on this trucker hat! Tia's colleague didn't look like a biologist. Yet he was in his mid-forties and clearly was not a paramilitary soldier, either. He was wearing a thick cream-colored shirt with light brown leather patches on each shoulder. He'd tucked his tapered gray combats into his black boots. His shoes were tightly laced around his ankles. He was wearing hard gray plastic shin guards on each leg and a well-stocked utility belt; he was a field man.

"Dr. Porter, how are you doing today?

- Good morning Joe. Everything is fine! Once again, I see that you are on top of your game. The transfers are going great. I wasn't expecting to see you here.

- I was on my way home from the south; I thought I could supervise a cargo transfer at the same time. So I'll leave you to pack and deliver the merchandise. Take the Ground Tracker and escort the truck. The boys will bring it back and you can drive the Jeep to the North outpost. I'll take the other truck and park it north. Segundo will check the remaining vehicles before our next operation on the day after tomorrow. The demons will feel better in their new habitat. I hear they did a great job with the place; Sorna is ready to welcome them. I'll be happy to get rid of them. Those two, they give the creeps... Well, I see you have company! "

Through the tall grass, Katherine and George were staring at the cricket cage. It was rectangular and about 10 feet long; the steel was painted a shiny light gray shade. On the right side of the container, there was a large 6 feet square opening providing air for the bugs. A dozen thin dark gray steel columns were piled up on each side to create perfectly flat air-permeable surfaces. Two long metal rods connected the corners of the square, they were sealed with a little aluminum box. On each side of the aerated wall, there were two 6.5 feet long vertical thin red and white lines indicating hazard. On the left side, six 15-inches long metal rods acted as a ladder that led to the roof where the door could be activated manually. On the far left side, two short horizontal red and white lines indicated the sliding door. There was a red arrow and a white writing reading "Lock". At the top and bottom of the warning, George noticed bolts, like two latches where cables could be attached to lift the container. Those sophisticated cages could be carried construction vehicles or by helicopters. Where the hell had George landed? He couldn't get his head around the fact that there were giant crickets in this cage, just a few inches away from him. The young man had witnessed quite a lot of things in his life but this particular discovery was astounding. Tia spoke again: "We make the future. That's the company motto. This is how we convey them. Katherine, George, let me introduce you to Mr. Joe Jackson. He's a very valuable and brave asset to our team." Joe smiled and shook Kat's and George's hands. "So you're the air crash survivors, eh? Must have been tough... well, welcome to site C... I see Tia's showing you around before you get repatriated. You won't believe your eyes, but not a peep!" The scientist told him: "We'll be very careful, I promise. Miss Harrison's a journalist. She'll write great articles about the island when this project's official. That's a great opportunity! I'll bring back your Ground Tracker safe and sound later this afternoon, you can count on me. George, Katherine, follow me. These gentlemen will load the cage onto the truck and we'll take Joe's Jeep." The man waved warm goodbyes, headed to the fence and left the perimeter. Tia unlocked the metal latch of the iron door to leave the cricket facility. Behind her, three men were loading the container on the truck with a hoist. The scientist stopped in front of the car, took off her lab coat and threw it into the trunk. George looked at the vehicle. This was the Ground Tracker they had referred to; it was a well-equipped khaki green Jeep Wrangler; all fenders had been replaced and reinforced with black iron rods on the driver's and passenger's sides. The large trunk was empty as if it was a pick-up. George had seen many types of military vehicles but this one was really special. The back of the driver's cabin was covered with green camo netting that went down to the trunk floor. In the back, George saw guns and a long foam protection glove. The framework of that accessory was reinforced with strips of hard plastic covering the whole arm; a genuine defense tool crafted to resist attacks. But what was Joe Jackson protecting himself from? George noticed that there were scuff marks around the wrist area that looked a bit like scratches. Tia was rummaging in her pockets in front of the huge black bumper of the Ground Trucker. Joe was about to get into the car when she called out to him: "Joe, you forgot to give me your keys!" The man paused, and reached into his right pants pocket. He took out a bunch of keys that he threw to Tia with a big smile on his face. She lifted her right hand to catch it but missed. The keys hit her chest and fell down to her feet. "Missed!" Katherine and George looked at each other, laughing, while the scientist, visibly embarrassed, was picking up the keys. Katherine, amused, asked in a laid-back tone: "Do I detect some kind of tension between you and this Joe Jackson, Mrs. Porter?

- I don't think so. At least, not on his side. We barely know each other.
- Well, maybe it's time you take a short break from all your research and crickets and get to know each other a little better." Tia blushed and told Katherine to sit in the front.
- "George, you can sit in the back. Mind the equipment." Hold on tight to the bars, we're up for a rough ride. "

The young man went around the front of the car; the bumper was protected by three black metal rods, a brown can was strapped to the hood. Below, there was a small hatch giving access to the engine or to a storage compartment. Two big round lamps were hanging from the center of the lateral rod above the windshield. When he got into the trunk, George saw a logo painted on the back fender.

Despite the dirt, he could make out the following letters: "inGen". The vehicle rumbled to life and Tia drove them down a rutted dirt path. It took only a few seconds for the Ground Tracker and its occupants to disappear among the leaves. Under the lush forest canopy, George felt the humidity again, and heard bugs and tropical birds singing in concert. A curtain of fresh creepers, ferns and yuccas brushed against the passing car.

The sun beat down on Turner's forehead, burning his skull. He should have borrowed a hat. He was used to the Australian weather, but these tropical temperatures were absolutely unbearable. He was sitting on a boulder; it was burning hot. To his right, Julia Barret was sitting cross-legged on the grass, gazing at the landscape. A few yards below, the ground sank and massive boulders dotted a grassy plain ending in a small lake. Opposite Turner and Julia, a waterfall softly ran down a grayish cliff into a pool of clear water. Below, light white mist clung to the trees. Turner was focusing on the clattering of rocks in the water. He turned to the young woman. She was gazing dreamily into the distance. "Thank you for taking me. I'm enjoying the walk.

- My pleasure. I'm glad you're feeling good again. That cold you picked up is just a memory now. You can enjoy being here. After all, you'll be leaving the archipelago soon. Lizard Neck and Chua are on site B. There are only friendly people on the island now, it's the perfect time to take a break.

- You're right. The view is amazing.
- Aileen took a little trip of her own so there was no reason why you couldn't come with me this afternoon. It'll be our little secret!
- I'm very happy we're sharing secrets now.
- We're not allowed to talk about this island Kenneth. Ever." Turner asked sarcastically: "Or what? Conway will kill us? What is he protecting?
- Lizard Neck has an impressive military background. He's a killer. He leads his troops with an iron fist. That's why inGen hired him. They want only the best, even though the guy is insufferable.
- Did this inGen company hire you on this project too?
- Yes. International Genetics Incorporated funds all research here on the archipelago. They own bio and genetic engineering facilities and bio-technology labs. There are many animals on this island and I'm paid to take care of them and supervise transfers between various sites.
- Are you breeding genetically modified animals here before sending them elsewhere?
- That's right. They're born on site C and then transferred to site B. Here, inGen is

developing food-processing solutions. But they have a few magic tricks walking around; come on, follow me, I'll show you why I took this job."

Turner followed Julia on a little dirt path under the palm trees. The Jeep was parked about a hundred yards behind them. Turner could still hear the waterfall. His shoes sank into the loose ocher soil. Huge dried palm leaves blocked the way and lay on the soft colored ground. Julia went past two big trunks covered in moss and out into a large sunny plain. In the middle of the greenery stood two huge silos. They were so high their shadows darkened the surrounding grass for dozens of yards. The tanks were about 50 feet tall and spherical in shape, two large steel balls standing on concrete pillars and disappearing in the iron surrounding the structure. Weeds had already started creeping up the columns and the round surface. All this greenery growing on steel: what a beautiful example of synthesis between nature and modernity, thought Turner. InGen was indeed at the leading edge of technology. A twelve-flight iron staircase gave access to the roof, where a small walkway with a guardrail led to the center of each sphere. Three aluminum pipes went into the tanks. It was quite the industrial sight. Turner was impressed, he watched Julia walk through the plain and between both silos. "Wow, agriculture is a serious business on Matanceros." Making his way through the tall grass behind her, Turner spotted another facility beyond the tanks, it was protected by 10-foot-high electric fences. Orange beacons shone on some of the pillars that looked exactly like the ones in the northern village. Julia took out her magnetic pass and swiped it in the card reader of the entrance door. Two red lights above the door turned green and the automatic latch unlocked horizontally, giving access to the small security pathway between the fences. Turner stepped inside with Julia, puzzled. That's when he realized it wasn't another worker village, but a farm! Ahead, hundreds of cows were peacefully grazing. Animals moved quietly around the secure perimeter, Turner couldn't believe his eyes. The company had established livestock farming and created pastures in the middle of the Caribbean. Cows were resting in the shade of a large brick building, probably a cowshed. Julia walked around the field, petting the animals that mooed as she went by. The young woman was smiling. Turner asked her: "So, you're a doctor and a vet?

- Let's say I have a large scope of skills, it's a requisite to work here. I'd even say it's a requisite for survival. Site C is quite hostile! I'm not considered a real doctor or vet. Here, I'm what they call a "tracker". I'm not locked up in a lab all day. I'm in the field, as close as I can get to inGen's creations.
- Those cows were created by your company...
- Only two of them. With inGen's magic, cloning has secretly become a reality but most of the cattle come from intensive farming. Regular old-fashioned cows! Here, I can pretend I'm a cowgirl and nobody will make fun of me.

- What's the point of all these cattle?
- Raymond Chua's and Tia Porter's research teams are testing muscle stimulants and high-protein hay. The cows are full of energy and they grow more muscle than other bovines... I'm not going to tell you about GMOs, you know what they are.
- Researchers want to know if their products affect animals? It's a very large scale lab.
- In a way. But we are replacing cattle all the time, these cows don't grow old here. Sadly, their sole purpose is to feed our carnivores.
- Carnivores? What do you mean?
- I'm talking about those creatures your daughter saw this morning.
- The dragons? Are you kidding?
- Your daughter wasn't lying when she told you what she saw from that truck. There are monsters out there; thank God Aileen is OK. Some of them are extremely dangerous.
- Pardon me? Are you saying there actually are dragons on this island? My daughter almost got hurt by a mythological creature? For God's sake, explain yourself!
- The creatures that attacked Segundo's vehicle weren't dragons, they were Baryonyx. And I can assure you, they're real.
- Baryo-what? Sorry, you lost me.
- Baryonyx Walkiri. They're theropods. Fully grown, they can be 30 feet tall. They give me nightmares when they stand on their hind legs... But still, I like them!

- Wait a minute, are you protecting some kind of medieval beast? What is site C? The sixth continent?
- The Baryonyx aren't from the medieval era, Kenneth!" laughed Julia. "You still don't get it, do you? The Baryonyx is not a dragon, it's a dinosaur."

Kenneth Turner was stunned, he put his head back, disconcerted and surprised. He frowned, pursed his lips, he was totally puzzled. "A dinosaur? You mean... an actual dinosaur? With massive claws and teeth... long neck... long tail... huge wings... terrible...

- Terrible horns, yes that's right. You're right Kenneth: it's a dinosaur, a very big dinosaur." Turner stared at her in amazement and Julia burst out laughing: "Stop being a baby Kenneth, what we're doing here is very serious.
- Julia... you keep prehistoric predators on a secret island. Do you even hear yourself? Are you mad?" Turner stopped talking and after a while said as if to himself: "That's why there are bars everywhere..."
- The Baryonyx comes from England, Spain or Portugal. Its sharp claw on the first finger can easily cut through metal. He belongs to the Spinosauridae family and mainly feeds on fish. However, our specimens have been showing signs of aggression for a few months now, as if they were developing an interest in human flesh as they grow up. It might be down to their genetic code.

- Their genetic code? How could inGen create dinosaurs from thin air? What's left of them is trapped in bones and stones, it's virtually impossible.
- Not for inGen. The genetic code of a species comes from fossil DNA. All scientists need is dinosaur blood.
- But how did they get it?
- From mosquitoes.
- Mosquitoes?
- Mosquitoes.
- But why mosquitoes Julia?
- Mosquitoes bite dinosaurs, mosquitoes die, mosquitoes become fossils and inGen uses those fossils.
- How is that even possible? It would be a miracle of nature.
- It is. Absolutely. 65 million years ago, conifers were abundant and their resin was packed with natural preservatives that acted as a kind of magical chemical stabilizer. The mosquitoes that got caught in the sap and survived for ages in their solid amber cells. That's how inGen could collect blood samples of the animal the mosquito had bitten.
- And it's as simple as that?
- Well, it requires supercomputers and advanced equipment. And inGen scientists also need to fill in the gaps in genetic codes.
- And how do they do that?
- They select various species of reptiles to mend the DNA of a particular species. Then,

they incubate the result and bring a baby dinosaur to life.

- Unbelievable. But how do you know which species they belong to?
- Genes are compared in the lab and when the animal grows up, it's studied and identified thanks to paleontology. According to where the amber comes from, it's quite easy for scientists to determine the species.
- So inGen is a food-processing, cloning and archeology company! Quite the resume!
- Once the dinosaur is identified, the scientists create a viable clone.
- Are you saying all the monsters out there are actually the same individual?
- Each birth is different. We like to think of them as brothers. The fact that the Baryonyx could potentially become a carnivore instead of a pescavore has to do with genetic manipulation. These animals grow up and live as a pack. They are used to their environment, to their meal times and to dead fish. They don't hunt in the river. Bringing back extinct species meant inGen would have to face some behavioral modifications. We're all learning here, it's a brave new world.
- And their food is packed with vitamins. You feed your clones all the micro-nutrients they need through the cows. That's smart. Now I understand why Chua likes to borrow some equipment for his own work. He can test his vitamins on cattle.

- Yes, on any kind of cattle. This archipelago is a vast field of experimentation.
- Katherine said she saw five islands through the vent grid, but you mentioned only three.
- There are indeed five. Only three of them belong to the company. InGen owns site C, B and A, which is not part of the island arc. It's a totally different island.
- Have you ever been there?
- No, I only work on sites C and B and I have more than enough to do already!
- What happens on the other three islands?
- Not much. They're quite small and I have no information on the subject. One of them is a hideout for a South American elite commando unit, mercenaries who used to work with the Cartel. They were there long before inGen associated with the government of Costa Rica. I understand that they couldn't kick them out of the island and had to collaborate with them. As far as I know, Lizard Neck and Chua sometimes hire them to participate in operations. I've never seen them. They've settled on Isla Muerta and they have their own helicopters.
- Isla Muerta. What an engaging name."

Julia stepped closer to a cow grazing in front of her; she stroked its neck and ran her hand over its ear; it quivered. The young woman climbed on its back; the animal lifted its head, still munching. She gave it a little kick on the flanks to get it going. Julia steered the animal toward a gate in the fence. Outside, men were loading cows into one of their big cattle cage trailers. One of them was holding a gun and keeping guard.

"So Kenneth, what do you say? Ever wanted to be a cowboy for a day?

- Julia, you're riding a transgenic cow that'll soon be dinosaur food... If what you're telling me is true, I'm not really in the mood to play farmer with you! That's bonkers!
- It's the circle of life, Mr. Turner. The circle of life!
- Considering that my daughter had the chance to see one of your specimens, would you be willing to show me one too? Seeing is believing.
- Sorry Kenneth, that's out of my jurisdiction; I'm taking Daisy for a walk and then I'm taking you back to the village. You've seen cows. Consider yourself lucky!"

Julia burst out laughing as her mount started to make its way across the pasture. Turner followed her, gazing at the wild grass swaying in the wind around him. The plain was coming to life and the green ground was shivering under the sun. Julia's wavy red hair was flowing in the soft breeze. Suddenly, Turner right foot sank into something soft and slimy.

A swarm of flies burst irritated patterns around him. He had just stepped in cow dung.

The Ground Tracker tilted forward as it went down a narrow slope. A big root pushed one of Tia Porter's wheels off the narrow track to the right. The Tracker's suspension squealed. George was holding on to the netting hanging at the back so he wouldn't hit his head. It was a bumpy ride and he could hear the tires of the four-wheel drive struggling on the dirt road. Big clumps of dirt flew through the air in their wake. Clouds of orange dust erupted from beneath the vehicle's tires to diffuse among the sturdy trunks of the sequoia trees. It smelled like pine. George loved that smell. It triggered so many memories. As the Jeep was driving down the forest, the young man couldn't help but remember his childhood back in Georgia. He loved those family walks into the pine woods near Waycross; his granddad owned a country house there. At that time, he spent more time grandpa than he did with his father, who was always away for work. He hadn't minded: he was proud of his father working for the FBI. At least, he hadn't minded when he was little. George had sworn he'd never look back after these last few months of living like a fugitive. He was determined to move forward and leave all sentimentality behind. But the smell of sap was so dear to his heart. It rekindled his feelings. For a while, he was filled with joy, and sadness, and worry. George turned his back on his past life. He was a brand new man. He was reborn; what he'd done before didn't matter anymore. Still, he couldn't help but wonder if he had made the right choice. Lately he was still following in his father's steps. He'd breezed through life and made it as a new agent trainee and then as a special agent. He'd worked for the Bureau and had honored his father's legacy fighting organized crime. Before turning thirty, he'd already solved two major cases and was abiding by the rules to please his father. The Deputy Director of the FBI had to be proud; George didn't want to just stand out. He wanted to be perfect. He started working on his third case. That's when everything went downhill.

The vehicle pulled over near a small ledge overhanging a river. The chassis stopped vibrating and George could let go of the netting. He stood up. Tia and Katherine stayed inside the car. The ledge provided a clear view of the river: uprooted trees were scattered along the stream and disappeared in the depths of the water. A nightmare cloud of mosquitoes swarmed around George and clung his clothes. The young man swatted one of the bugs on his forearm, and its blood mingled with his own sweat. Large pale leaves blocked the path leading to the little stream below. A huge mahogany tree grew on the riverside, the large trunk bent forward, the branches dipping into the water and swaying in the current. A hundred yards away, the cricket truck was unloading its shipment. George looked at the large bugs running down the slope and scattering along the river. Tia followed his gaze. "The first thing they do when they're released into the wild is find a watering place; they're thirsty. They only get water jelly in their container. They discover water for the first time, they've never tasted it before it but they're drawn to it. They know it's good for them. It's in their genes.

- That's gross!" said Katherine. The young woman stood on her seat to take a better look, leaning on the windshield bar. The bugs disappeared into the forest in silence. Katherine was attentive. She suddenly heard water lapping, as if someone was splashing around in the river a few yards below. She frowned and looked hard at the stream. There was a lot of hustle and bustle down there! Branches snapped and the young woman heard a loud snuff, as if a large animal was breathing hard through its snout. She jumped and looked down once more. After a while, she saw the creature. Her heart started pounding; she turned to George who had just seen the animal as well. What an unbelievable sight!

There was an enormous beast standing in the river some fifty yards away. It looked like a ten-foot-long monitor lizard with a long thin tail buried in the mud. What kind of lizard could grow this big? A huge spine sail ran along its back from neck to tail and it stood about six feet high! Katherine was dazzled by the reptile's color. The large protrusion was spruce green with light yellow, almost oval, markings. The rest of the body was covered in large dark green scales; the skin grew lighter on the bottom part of the body. The short legs and stomach were a shade of bright green and it had a turtle-like posture. The lizard stood still, as if frozen, in the middle of the stream. George and Katherine could observe its stocky skull and shortened snout that resembled a Komodo dragon's. Yet this beast's jaws were both more flat and round, like a cat's mouth. The monster opened its jaws, revealing sharp long teeth. Could it be some unknown species of crocodile? It was basking in the sun, perfectly still, like most reptiles. Above the thick veins pulsing at the base of the neck, Katherine could see skull bones protruding under bright, thick skin. Two small beady black eyes shone in deep-set eye sockets below thick brown bones. The animal snuffed again. Katherine had lost her composure and was looking at Tia in amazement. "Gosh! What the hell is that? It's...

- Beautiful. It's beautiful. That, Katherine, is a Grandis, a Dimetrodon Grandis. Its spine sail is supported by neural spines growing from each vertebra. This sail regulates body temperature. Whether the animal places it in the sun or in the shade, it can warm up or cool down its body. This 450-pound creature can increase its body temperature from 80°F to 90°F in 80 minutes. It would take thrice as long without the sail. It's absolutely fascinating. We believe the yellow markings are a defense mechanism. They're like warning signals so larger predators believe the spines are toxic. This amazing species prospered during the Permian period, and now it's back!

- The Permian period you said?" Katherine couldn't believe what she was hearing and seeing. "Permian, Triassic, Jurassic... Are you suggesting this thing is a dinosaur?

- Well technically, the Dimetrodon is closer to a mammal than it is to a reptile. This Synapsid lived 280 million years ago, so it's older than dinosaurs, but yes, it's a dinosaur."

One of the creatures moved slowly upstream. The four-legged reptile crawled easily in the water. It reached a tree covered in ferns and stopped, resting its front right leg on a big root. Its whole body was covered in small, sturdy, whitish scales. Its skin was dry. Katherine couldn't help but notice the pale color of the animal.

"Why is it covered in powder too? Why is it so pale?

- We don't spray Dimetrodons with the same fluid because we don't want them to become targets for attack. This substance means prey or food to them. This animal wasn't sprayed; like every reptile, it's about to shed skin."

George and Katherine stared at the dinosaur as it clambered up some roots to rub its snout against a tree trunk. It rubbed its neck and flanks against the bark, and its thick skin began to peel off in white, thin, dry strips. The lizard then snatched up its own shed skin with its rounded snout and swallowed the skin whole. Tia Porter couldn't keep her eyes off of this sight. "They feed on their own skin and clean themselves at the same time. They're used to having dry skin, it's in their genes. These creatures are originally from dry zones, deserts. Paleontologists think their large protrusion could have been used as a fan on very hot days. Here, they don't really need it. It's a very different climate. But as they were born here, they've adapted to their new environment."

The more colorful animal took a few steps downstream, it bent its head toward the ground to lap up water with its thick coarse pink tongue. It stopped drinking, lifted its head up and looked at the bank. Katherine could hear the wind blowing through the dinosaur's back spines, like it would in the branches. Next to the reptile, a cricket was feeling the brown soil with its antennae. Katherine knew it came from the cricket truck, it was quiet and white. The large bug came out of the bushes to drink from the river; its antennae felt the ground until it froze on the rocks. It dipped its mandibles into the water. The attack was as swift as lightning. The Dimetrodon jumped, spinning to the left; it hit the water surface with its nimble legs and sunk its teeth into the cricket. The prey was instantly crushed and snapped in half by the dinosaur's sharp jaws. The large monitor lizard used its tongue to slip the bug into its mouth. One of the hind legs fell down onto the sand. The monster swallowed the cricket in two mouthfuls and was now totally still again, waiting. Its tongue licked its greenish lips clean of any leftovers. Its beady eye was dull; the animal didn't blink. It looked like a statue. The dinosaur's attack was flawless. Katherine still couldn't believe what she'd just seen. What an incredible phenomenon! What a force of nature! She looked at George and Tia; the scientist was smiling at the scene below. A damp wind buffeted the rocky overhang as the light began growing dimmer. The surrounding nature grew quieter, tree trunks gently swaying at their own pace. A thick mist rose from the water and spread over bark and rock. Katherine could hear cicadas singing in the branches. A bumblebee landed on George's shoulder. It crawled down his arm and flew away and up into the tropical breeze. The night was about to fall on dragon territory.

The sun had turned cold and the jungle was getting more and more humid. Rodrigo Quintado wiped the sweat off his palms on his pants. Then, he combed through his beard with his fingers to remove a twig. He was thinking about his dad, Don Tiburon; he was thinking of the contract and what awaited him. He had to be strong, for Ernesto and Smokey. He had to move on; this hard time would soon be over. Ernesto was walking ahead, holding his gun. He slowed his pace. At last, the two smugglers had reached Don Tiburon's lair. A few yards away, on the river bank, Quintado immediately recognized his father's hideout. A wooden shack stood on the bank, the door hanging on its hinges, having been forced open a while ago. The place must have been plundered. Quintado didn't bother having a look inside and walked directly to a tall sequoia tree growing further inland. Under the creepers and the moss, he found a spade and walked to another tree a little further. The spade was still in the same place, still there after all these years. Behind him, Ernesto was examining the area with his gun. Quintado knelt down in front of a tree stump and stood up again. He took a few steps toward a trunk and started digging. Both men were silent. It only took the smuggler a few minutes to hit the metal buried underground. Quintado scraped the soil off the iron chest and resumed digging. Ernesto helped him pull the object from the ground and they both carried it back to the shack. Quintado put it down. He noticed the leaky wooden dinghy bobbing on the river for the first time. He grabbed his gun and started hitting the chest with the butt of his gun. The lid opened. Inside: three jerrycans, a pump-action shotgun and ammunition. Rodrigo smiled and started counting the cartridges. The wind picked up and the mist shrouded the sequoia trees. Ernesto glanced at the boat and at the shack and then told his partner. "There's nothing else here! How are we going to carry the chest by river? The dinghy is ruined! We can't carry the chest all the way to the boat on our own. Do you have a better idea?

- We take the fuel and we get out of here. To hell with the rest. We have to reach the north before nightfall. Let's have a 5 minute break and leave."

Their conversation was interrupted by an engine noise coming from above. The two men went up the slope and left the river behind. There was a road in the forest; a vehicle was approaching. Lying on the floor, Quintado listened to the vehicle getting closer. He crawled toward the road, climbed up the ditch and saw a truck coming in his direction. Quintado didn't hesitate. This was their exit ticket. He jumped onto the path, brandishing his gun. The plan wasn't to open fire on the truck - after all, he wanted to keep a low profile. Quintado had no idea how many men were in the area. He aimed at the vehicle with a threatening look; the vehicle braked and pitched to the right.

The cabin leaned over to one side and finally stood still on the ground. The mesh trailer squeaked as it settled down and the vehicle stopped. Quintado ran to open the door. Standing in front of the windshield, Ernesto was covering him, ready to shoot. Quintado violently dragged the driver out of the truck and punched him right in the face, the man fell down on his knees in the mud, his lip bleeding. He was wearing a cream-colored shirt with brown leather on each shoulder. Blood was dripping from his mouth onto his gray combats. Rodrigo Quintado grabbed his red cap and threw it to the ground. The smuggler didn't lose time and started interrogating the driver right away. "Who are you?

- I'm Joe... Joe Jackson.
- And what are you doing here Joe Jackson?"

Joe didn't know what to say, it was all so sudden. Who were those men and what were they doing on site C? He hesitated. Quintado hit him in the shoulder with the butt of his gun. Joe moaned, his eyes were fixed on the man. Quintado stood in front

of him. "I see you're on your own Joe. Is there anyone else hiding in the back of your truck?
- No, there's no one.
- Where were you heading?
- I was going back to the compound.
- Tell me more about this compound. Where is it?
- About 30 minutes away from here.
- What's over there? Drugs? Weapons?
- No.
- No weapons. You sure about that?"
Again, Joe didn't know what to say, he didn't want to let those armed men know about the North village. He had to get them to leave and save his skin at the same time. He felt cold sweat running down his back then answered.
"Yes, there are weapons. It's an armed compound. I wouldn't go there if I were you, you'll get shot in a heartbeat.
- You're the one who's going to get shot if you don't tell me what I want to know. Are there other vehicles taking that road?
- Yes, an armed militia could get there any minute. It's a prohibited area.
- Spare me your B.S. I've been coming here since I was a kid. If you don't sell drugs or weapons, why are you armed then?
- It's a farming site.
- Farming? Do you hear that Ernesto? Do you think I'm stupid? Stop it or I'll blow your head off!
- Weapons are for cattle protection and our own.

- Very well, so you must have an armory there.
- Yes.
- And fuel?
- Yes.
- And vehicles?
- Yes...but as I said, you'll get shot before you can set foot in there.
- Me? Get shot? No...but you, on the other hand, won't live very long. I'll kill you. Or maybe Ernesto will. The clock is ticking. If you want to live a little longer, you get back in that truck, take us as co-pilots and you might live to see the sun rise. You're going to take us there. There's a radio in your truck, right?
- Yes.
- Give it to me. Even a short-range device will do. Is there a way to reach the little harbor by road?
- No, the only tracks will take you to the South harbor.
- Listen to me Joe...you see, my friend and I have some goods to take back to our boat. It'll only take a couple of hours. So here's what we're going to do: we're going to load our equipment in your trailer with your junk and then you'll take us to your compound. There, we'll take the weapons and fuel we need and we'll head south to the harbor with one of your vehicles.
- That's impossible! You're out of your mind!"

Quintado hit Joe Jackson in the face again and then kneed him in the chest.

"Stand up! Before we go, you'll get down the hill and pick up my box. It's a family heirloom and I want to take it with me. I got my hands dirty enough to find it, now I hope you'll give me a hand to carry it...if I don't cut some of your fingers first. Go on! Hurry up!"

He pushed Joe with his feet and sneered. The tracker rolled down the slope, trying to grab branches. Quintado called out to Ernesto: "Get in the truck and call Smokey on his frequency. Tell him the stopover will last a little longer than expected and that we'll meet him on the southern quay tomorrow at 6 a.m.!

I hope the fool can manage to pilot the go-fast without us. He's not the sharpest tool in the shed. "

The sky was a deep blue shade, almost royal blue; through the window, Prescott was watching the trees and leaves drink up the sunlight. The grass was shining bright with a yellow hue. Through the wall, he could feel the air getting heavy; the sun was slowly slipping away, inviting nature to rest. In the facility, his leg up on a chair, Prescott caught a whiff of shrimp cooking in the kitchen. Behind him, he could hear the cook frying the prawns in oil, the pan sizzling. Tonight, the facility chef was making his signature dish: Caribbean-style shrimp stir-fried rice. The Irishman's mouth was watering. Too bad there were so few people here to enjoy it. Sitting alone with Aileen and Segundo in the big dining hall, Cole Prescott was resting his leg. The pain was crippling at times; at his age, it took time to recover from such a wound. At least it was getting better.

Next to him, little Aileen was making a pastel drawing in her coloring book. Segundo was sitting a few tables away from them. Prescott glanced at Aileen's work, she was drawing huge lizards over toucan outlines. He asked her, dreamily: "What are you drawing?

- Dragons.
- You seem really interested in dragons since you took that little trip. Do you like legends with creatures and knights? I loved those when I was your age.
- No, no. Dragons are real. They live close by. But they don't have wings.
- And a dragon without wings isn't a real dragon, is it? Your imagination's playing tricks on you. Hopefully, we'll be home soon.
- I don't want to go home. I like it here.
- Good Lord, why? It's just steel, concrete and bars. And I'm not even talking about the jungle and this bleeding weather! Nobody wants to live here! It's no place for a little one like you. This village is dangerous. I don't even want to have a look around. I can't wait to go home and you shouldn't be able to either.

- There's nothing waiting for me at home. Daddy's always working, I don't have any friends. I wanted a puppy but Daddy said no.
- All the same...I don't see why you want to linger here.
- I want to stay with the dragons and go on many adventures.
- Believe me, you don't belong here."

Prescott turned around to the cook who was bringing their plates. The man was in his thirties, he was small and looked South-American. He had delicate, almost feminine features and gentle, friendly eyes. They were dark and lined with thin black eyebrows. A green bandanna held his well-groomed, shoulder-length curly hair back, he was clean-shaven and wore a black leather vest under his apron. He set the plates and cutlery on the table. "Enjoy! I hope you'll like it.
- Thank you Sebastián, it smells delicious." Segundo waved thanks at him and sat at Prescott's and Aileen's table.

"You're having an early dinner today." Prescott was wolfing down his food, he swallowed his mouthful before answering:

"Well, there's nothing else to do really!
- You know, Aileen's kind of right about the dragons." He smiled and winked at the girl; her face lit up.

"What do you mean 'kind of right'?
- This island's shrouded in mystery and legend. It's quite natural to see things here." Segundo showed Aileen a tree outside

the window. The trunk was smooth and shiny. It looked like a kind of barkless tree. "Do you know what kind of tree it is Aileen?

- No, but it looks old and young at the same time.
- Exactly. A very long time ago, well before we were born, other people lived here. They were a native tribe called Huetares. About a century ago, they lived right here, right where our village stands. The forest was their home. And among the islanders lived a witch.
- An evil witch?
- No, a good witch. She helped the villagers, she made potions for the hunters, gatherers and fishermen. And, nobody knew why, but time seemed to have no effect on her. Years went by, yet she looked as youthful as ever. The Huetares asked her what the secret of her eternal youth was. The young witch confessed she had a potion that kept her from aging. But the villagers laughed at her. So she decided to create a concoction and give it as a present to the community to prove she was a powerful witch.
- And she poisoned the potion and tricked them!
- No, of course not! She was a good helpful witch, remember? She summoned a gathering, just a few feet away from here, and revealed her potion. When they saw the bubbling vial, the islanders became fearful and thought the witch had come to take

revenge on those who laughed at her. They refused to anoint their body with the potion. Instead, one of them threw the vial to destroy what he thought was a weapon to kill the tribe. The vial shattered on a tree, this tree over there... The brew trickled down the trunk. Granting the tree eternal youth.

- And what happened to the witch?
- I don't know. The legend doesn't say."

Segundo's story was interrupted by Sebastián calling him from the control room. "Segundo! There's a phone call for you from the continent."

The young man stroked his beard, got up and excused himself. He went to the control room. Sebastián went back to the dining room. "It's a satellite call, your uncle wants to talk to you.

- My uncle? But my uncle's..." Segundo looked confused. He started thinking. Was something wrong with his mother back is San José? Was someone calling to give him some bad news? Had his mother's health gotten worse? His uncle was dead. Who could that be? He closed the door behind him, sat in front of the computer and held the receiver to his ear.

"Segundo Leticia speaking.

- Good afternoon Segundo. How are you? I'm sorry to bother you, I know you have a lot to do." The young man didn't recognize the voice over the phone. It was a male voice, kind of husky, a smoker's voice.

"May I know who's speaking?
- Let's say I'm a friend.

- My uncle's dead.
- I know that. Among many other things. For example, I can tell you what's going on at the infamous site C. I'll be quick, I know your time is valuable.
- Who is this?
- You're sitting in front of a computer, right?
- Yes, but...
- May I suggest you check your bank account right now?
- We have very bad connection on the island...
- Do as I say!"

Segundo typed away on the keyboard to access the outpost satellite platform. He took a notebook out of his vest and looked for his banking details to check his balance on the computer. Data was loading slowly. The strange man on the phone started talking again.

"I understand your mother's sick. That damn cancer...listen, I might be able to help. I can contribute to getting her the best treatment and make sure she gets better. All I'm asking in return is a little favor from you. I know there's another high security compound south of site C. That's where InGen stores all research information about carnivore breeding...they have all sorts of samples and embryos there.

- How do you know that?
- I know this facility is home to many wonders, especially blood samples from your 'Demons' as you call them. And those samples are precisely what I'm looking for. "

The computer finally displayed Segundo's balance. The young man gaped at the screen. He had 500,000 American dollars on his account. He remained speechless. Who could have transferred him that much money? How did they find him? Why him? Questions piled up in his head. Who the hell was that man on the phone?

- You now have 500,000 dollars on your bank account. As soon as you can, take a Jeep, drive down south and steal some of these blood samples. I need these creatures' DNA, Mr. Leticia and you're going to help me get it. Bring it to me when you sail back to San José and you'll get 500,000 more. If we get along well, I might be even more generous.
- That's industrial espionage you're talking about. Do you have any idea...
- Your mother's very sick. You don't want her health to deteriorate when you're away from her, do you?
- ...you wouldn't.
- Yes, it is industrial espionage, let's be honest. We're just two responsible individuals having a little conversation. It stays between us. At the moment, you have 500,000 dollars in your bank account. Take a trip to the south of the island, steal a few tubes and you'll be a millionaire! Is it really so bad to break the rules when there's so much money at stake?
- It's classified information. The genetics administration is located at the heart of

their territory, you can't begin to imagine how dangerous it is. I can't...

- You'll think of something. Your mother's counting on you. I'll be in touch." The man hung up. Segundo heard a remote ringtone, then crackling. He put the receiver back on the main satellite unit and looked around. The computers were on, coding data. Thermal signatures moved around on a map on one of the screens. Segundo was alone in the room.

It was silent. He thought about this abrupt proposition, both terrifying and unexpected. What was he to do? Did he have a choice? Had this man really threatened his mother to talk him into this? Chilling thoughts came flowing into his head. Was espionage really worth it? Who was this man working for? Segundo could lose his job, or worse; they could sue him and he could lose everything. InGen's work on site C was groundbreaking. Their genetic experiments went far beyond modern science as he knew it. And there was no doubt inGen would make him pay for this and ruin his career. Then he would lose much more than this classified job. He would lose his friends, his family, his mother. He gazed at the desks. Copies and photographs were scattered on the tables. A walkie-talkie lay on a Polaroid picture. On the photographs, Segundo could see the dark skin and the impressive size of the predator. The scaly monster was standing on its hind legs. Its clenched jaws bore sharp teeth... This devil, as black as night and as red as fire, stared at the lens with a sly green gaze.

MIDNIGHT DEVILS

George was listening to the song of the birds and the chirping of the bugs, the long forest moan. The engine hum coming from the Ground Tracker wasn't loud enough to cover up the noisy and lively island magic. The young man was holding on to the lateral bar of the vehicle and watching a red ant running up and down his shoe. Would it be brave enough to cross the ankle boundary, climb up his sock and explore his calf? If it did, he would have to do something to stop its climb. His seat shook as the vehicle sailed over the gravel. Tia Porter made a right turn to follow the path leading to the North facility. To her left, Katherine was gripping her seat; George could tell she couldn't wait to ask all the questions she'd been thinking of. She finally broke the silence and asked the driver: "Can I ask you a question? I'm not a geneticist and even if science has progressed these past years, how can you exploit fossils in 1984? I'd have thought amber would have lost all its genetic properties after all this time.

- It was the first issue we had to deal with when inGen started funding the amber mines in Puerto Plata. But we found a way to decode even indecipherable DNA. The company developed a computer program so powerful it could rebuild any genetic code from fossilized blood contained in mosquitoes. In just a few months, it was working like a charm. Once we identify the dinosaur species, we grind bones from museums or private collection to produce a raw DNA powder dating back to 65 million years ago. The gaps are filled with reptile DNA.

- But what about cloning? In order to clone individuals, don't you need a live specimen, a surrogate mother to carry the embryo?

- Dinosaurs are not mammals. Even though the Dimetrodon is related to them, they hatch from eggs. The embryos created by inGen are directly implanted in ostrich eggs and put in a digital incubator for three months. Each newborn is studied in a terrarium or in a cage for a few weeks before it can join the grown-ups on the island.

- But these animals are going to grow up in a new environment that is nothing like their native ecosystem, and that will impact their genetic metabolism. How can you be sure they're actual dinosaurs and not some kind of genetically modified freaks?

- You're now raising the issue of epigenetics and individual history. The epigenome is a layer on top of the genome and not a stem cell. And it's not a differentiated cell either. Our current knowledge in this field is incomplete and this field of experimentation will help us evaluate the evolution of species. Anyway, so far inGen's scientists can guarantee that cloned embryos are over

93% dinosaur, which is actually not that
bad!
- And what about diseases? Can their immune
systems adapt to modern germs? Or can
they become disease vectors and
contaminate us with new illnesses?
- It's a risk we're trying to evaluate and
contain. The future holds the answer.
- Very comforting! "

In the back, George was pricking up his ears to try
and listen to their conversation. All this talk of
genetic engineering was beyond him. This place
was one of a kind. Man and dinosaur, face to face.
What kind of modern magic did those men use to
take such a giant leap into the future? He was sitting
in a gasoline-powered Jeep and yet, beyond those
trees, hidden in the mountains, extinct species were
growing in the utmost secrecy. It was bigger than
any case he'd ever come across at the FBI... Since the
1970s, a complex network of programs and
activities had been developed in the United States
to fight terrorism. Over forty departments,
agencies, services and bureaus were now actively
participating in this international struggle. The goal
set by the American administration had faced the
same problem over and over for years: there wasn't
just one common definition of terrorism.

What was it exactly? Was breeding giant
reptiles without the government knowing an act of
terrorism? No one, not even the FBI nor the CIA,
knew about this for sure. Was this top secret
private activity a threat to America? Who actually
knew? One thing was for sure, the former agent

wouldn't say a word to the FBI about it. George Alistair was miles away from it. He'd lost everything and never again would he be loyal to the Bureau; his stupidity had led to failure. It had all happened so fast, barely a year ago. A few months ago, he was still working for the FBI, infiltrating a German American terrorist group. These guys were tough nuts to crack. They claimed to be part of the Red Army Faction, the Rote Armee Fraktion, also known as RAF. It was a left-wing German terrorist organization presenting itself as an urban guerrilla movement. They'd been active in West Germany since 1968 but only settled in the United States in 81. Amid this climate of social and political violence, George had fallen in love with one of the members. Beautiful Frida had captured his soul and the young agent chose to follow a dangerous path, stepping away from all established principles and laws. After disclosing sensitive information to the terrorists, George had to flee North America with her and settle in Europe. But he hadn't seen Frida's betrayal coming. She had manipulated him into betraying the Bureau, his father, his family... This two-faced woman had played him and gassed him up to her comrades and let him down. His cover had been blown, he couldn't work for the FBI anymore. George was alone. He was now considered a traitor, hunted down by his own people, hated by the RAF who had left him for dead in Colorado. His will to live and to go on had put him back on his feet, but still the young man had had difficulties going dark; getting new papers when you're hunted by the FBI is no easy business. Confronting his father was out of the question after the shame he had brought on his family, and he'd never face martial court. There was no way he'd end his life in a federal prison, but he didn't want to live in exile in Europe either. He'd just had the time to change his name to "George Alistair" before he got on that plane to Panama in Atlanta. He had to start all over again with a clean slate somewhere no one would know him. He had resolved to forget his father, to forget Frida and her betrayal...then the plane crash happened. And now, George was here, watching an ant on his shoe in the Ground Tracker. He was at the heart of the most incredible discovery in all human history, hidden in the depths of the wilderness. No one would ever find him here. Tomorrow, however, he'd leave the island and get back to his own adventure. Once in Panama, he knew the dragons from site C would still haunt him. This kind of magical encounter only happens once in a lifetime. George felt a tickle on his leg. The ant was crawling up to his knee; another one was climbing on his shoe.

Julia steered right; the pick-up truck's suspension squealed and creaked as it bounced slowly along a long straight road lined with earpod trees and passion vines. The forest sparkled with colors. The ocher road was covered in large blades of grass and a light mist blanketed the ground; the tropical humidity was taking hold of the path. Kenneth could hear the empty cage clattering in the trunk behind him. His gaze was attracted to Julia's muddy boots and pants, while the young woman was focusing on the road. The radio crackled with occasional signals from com relays. Turner asked her: "I still don't understand why a woman like you ended up in a place like this. As a GP you could've worked everywhere but here.

- I picked my specialty and you picked yours. You could've been a medical examiner in the USA but you chose to stay in Australia.
- Still, I picked a specialty. I chose life over death. I gave up autopsies to help accident victims. It's more satisfying to have living people asking for your help and to assist them in the legal process.
- I've never really had an interest in forensic medicine. Judicial authority is not really my thing.
- I'm not really sure it's mine either. That's why I opened my own practice and I delegated the tasks to concentrate on the core values of medicine. Still, I don't understand why you're wasting your talent working here, in such conditions.
- Believe it or not, medicine is everywhere on this island. Every single day I learn something new, it's the best place in the world to practice science and save lives.
- Has there ever been an accident on the island?

- Not that I know of. On the contrary, inGen is developing a groundbreaking gene therapy that'll soon be approved and patented.
- What will it treat?
- Cancer.
- Cancer? Are you saying that besides bringing monsters from the Cretaceous period back to life and experimenting with food processing, your employers claim they can cure cancer?
- It's the truth. I've seen the results with my own eyes on site B. It's just a question of months before the formula is approved by the FDA.
- And how does it work? Is it another bitter pill Raymond Chua wants us to swallow?
- They call it GATA Pharma. It's a new generation treatment: it genetically modifies immune system cells to fight cancer.
- And geneticists found this magical formula on this site B you're telling me about?
- GATA Pharma was developed by a Californian lab called Kite Hodge before it was bought and exploited by inGen, actually. It specializes in the treatment of human lymphoma. The immunotherapy involves harvesting immune cells from patients, genetically modifying and cultivating them in the lab before injecting them back to the patient in a single dose. The injection destroys cancer cells.

- That's incredible! If it's true, it's a major step in the development of a whole new scientific paradigm for the treatment of serious diseases. Why haven't they made it public yet?
- They've encountered a problem. Gene therapy can have serious, even deadly, side effects. All clinical tests have shown high fever, a drop in blood pressure, lung congestion and neurological problems. It turns out that 39% of treated patients recovered completely. InGen has found a way to increase the success rate to 87% and to remove all side effects.
- Remove all side effects? That's impossible Julia.
- It is impossible, except if you have a new generation immune agent. GATA Pharma's designed for patients who didn't respond to chemotherapy. They have nothing to lose and that's when they get the best results. With a gene found in the lymphatic system of the Spinosauridae, the geneticists can strengthen the patient's own genes in the lab and remove harmful effects. These Baryonyx are surprising...who'd have thought that bringing dinosaurs to life would solve the human race's own problems?
- Knowledge lies in the past. We study history to understand the future. So, Baryonyx can save the human race?

- In theory, they can. But not just them. Every Spinosauridae can, including the baby Spinosaurus on site B and the Suchos here on site C.
- There are "Suchos" on this island? Are they dangerous?
- "Suchomimus" belong to the same family as Baryonyx, but they look very different. And they *are* predators. So yes, they're dangerous. InGen hatched four of them here and they're raised down south. They're only six months old but they're already deadly! They haven't reached their full size, thank God!
- Suchomimus... 'Crocodile mimic'..."
- I knew you would be good at Latin, Kenneth!
- Do they actually look like crocodiles?
- They're far worse. We don't even know whether they really existed or not.
- Why?
- For the simple reason that it hasn't been discovered yet. Tia Porter sent pictures of the specimens to paleontologist Paul Serano who named them Suchomimus. But it's still a secret. We'll have to wait for the species to be excavated before we can formalize the name.
- It could take decades.
- It could never happen. In that case, the Suchomimus would simply become a new genetically modified species created by inGen. A dinosaur that never really existed.

- And they're running around freely, without any electric fence? Are you sure the helicopter evacuation is safe?
- Don't worry, you and Aileen will be perfectly safe. Rangers operate regularly on their territory and know how to deal with them. Contrary to appearances, they're very shy and they track their prey for a long time before attacking. They're great observers, but they're also natural born killers. You should see how they tear cattle apart! Suchos fear the loud noise made by helicopters as they come and go. The animals on this island aren't very comfortable with the sound of new technologies. I guess there were no engines in prehistoric times.
- How can you guarantee they won't attack my daughter as we get on the helicopter?
- inGen rents a satellite to watch all our animals on the island arc. Each checkpoint has a thermal imaging control system. We've noticed dinosaurs are very territorial and shy. Species don't interact with one another and stay in their sector of the island. They have no wish for conquest.
- Well, these creatures aren't like humans at all!
- No, they aren't. Reptilian blood runs through their veins. They drink and hunt on their territory and stay away from the roads. Thermal imagery allows us to locate and care for them.

- How can the company fund all this? Islands, facilities, dinosaurs, even a satellite...who's paying for all this? Even the largest multinational corporation couldn't afford this.
- inGen isn't just a cutting-edge company. It makes big bucks selling pharmaceutical licenses and patented products all over the world. That's more than enough to sustain the economy and invest in solutions for the future.
- The future is now!" answered Turner ironically.
- No, you're late Kenneth. The future was yesterday."

They looked at each other and smiled. The pickup truck drove over a dead tree that shattered under the weight. Fresh bark splinters flew off into the ferns. The mist covered the mud cracks. The dark silhouettes of the earpod trees rose in front of an incredibly beautiful pink sky. Humans could create amazing things, Turner thought to himself, but they'd never be able to recreate such a sight: life blooming beyond the hills at dusk, giving nature a dewy glow and enchanting curves. Never in a lab could anyone craft the feeling that was now blossoming deep down inside of him. The deeper the vehicle drove into the jungle, the more deeply Turner absorbed the miracle of creation in utter bliss.

Night was falling, and Joe Jackson was off schedule. Not without good reason: he'd been kidnapped by two narco-smugglers. He was driving slowly to get back to camp as late as he could. Jackson was steering with his left hand and running his right hand through his hair, he was worried and sweaty. Midges were flying around his head and alighting on his sticky neck. He was putting his red baseball cap back on when he felt the barrel of Rodrigo's gun pressing against his back. He had no idea why those two criminals wanted to raid the North outpost. The tracker took a road leading directly to the village, he had no other way. Soon, he'd reach the compound gates with two intruders hiding in the back of this truck. What could he do to prevent any incidents? Should he pretend they were out of fuel? These men weren't easily fooled and they'd quickly liquidate him. Should he drive the truck off a cliff and run away? The bearded one would probably shoot him before he got the chance to contact the compound. Each scenario was a dead-end and the barrel of the gun was pressing harder and harder against his ribs. "Hurry up Joe, I hate killing people at night. It gets dirty. And I hate traveling at night too. Get us to your compound and make it quick or I'll put a bullet into you.

- You don't get it, the island is dangerous. You can't enter the compound." Static on the radio interrupted him, a voice spoke: "C1 to

> T6, second batch of grilled shrimp on the
> way! Are you off soon? I got the recipe from
> my mother."

Joe recognized he cook Sebastian's voice. He was always in charge of communications when they were under-staffed. He was a good guy, always friendly and lively. What would happen to him if he brought those gangsters home? Quintado forced him to answer: "Act normal and answer you friend!" Joe complied and grabbed the receiver.

"I'm on my way to dinner Sebastian. See you in a bit. Joe Jackson, T6, over."

Crouching behind the front seats of the cabin, Quintado and Ernesto were gazing at branches and creepers sweeping against the truck, monitoring every move. Ahead, the road was getting narrower and finally, it disappeared in the tall grass; the cabin lurched down into a hole and then drove up a sloping clearing. At the edge of the forest, orange and blue blinking lights shone beyond the trees. The truck drove through a green stretch of grass and entered the forest. That was when Quintado saw huge electric fences in the heart of the woods. He saw the first security gate and the wire mesh entrance. Ernesto caught sight of a man standing on top of the fence. The gates were connected by arched concrete columns; a cement wall walk allowed men to patrol and monitor the area from above. The radio crackled and a South-American worker shut down the power on the other side of the gate; warning lights turned off and the truck drove into the village. The gate closed behind them. Joe gulped, with difficulty. He waved at the man and felt the barrel of the gun digging deeper into his flesh. Suddenly, Quintado let go and jumped in front! He gave Joe a violent kick out of the front seat; Ernesto came out through the right door and aimed at the man standing near the door. He opened fire, gunning the man down in the span of a heartbeat. The gunshots echoed in the village. Joe was stunned. He couldn't get his head around what had just happened. The poor worker, who had been alive just moments before, was lying face down on the floor in a pool of his own blood. Quintado started shooting in the direction of the guard stationed on top of the fence. The burst of gunfire pierced through the cement and hit the man in the chest; he flipped over the railing and down tumbled down the column before he finally slammed into the dirt road. Joe heard him scream until a deafening silence announced his death.

Rodrigo Quintado shot at the truck, laughing. A bullet went through the windshield and lodged itself in the seat behind Joe. He ducked down to avoid the bullets. Both smugglers left running toward the first building they could reach and entered the compound, covering their own backs. They loudly broke into the dining room, kicking the door and pointing their rifles at Aileen and Prescott, who froze and stared at the smugglers in shocked disbelief. Segundo took Aileen in his arms. Quintado shouted: "Freeze! In case you haven't noticed, we won't hesitate to take you down. Stay still, do as you're told and you'll be fine. You don't want any more dead, do you?" Segundo felt the quiver of panicked sobs rise from Aileen's chest. The little girl was scared to death. He held her closer. What a spectacular entry! No one in the room knew who those men were. Workers, who had come there to have dinner like every other night, were now in danger. Quintado scanned the dining room while Ernesto held the staff at gunpoint. Segundo knew the man was ready to shoot. He could read concern and surprise on Sebastian's face. Quintado saw the security door leading to the other rooms but his eyes stopped on the door of the armory that had been left open. He quickly counted the guns and yelled at two workers sitting at the table before him: "You two, put the guns and ammo in the bags, my friend and I have a boat to catch; come on hurry up!" The men complied and nervously entered the room. Quintado had his eyes on them, his finger trembling on the trigger. "I need someone who knows the area. I haven't been there in a while!" He pointed at Segundo: "You! You'll drive us to the South harbor. We're leaving now. One objection and I'll shoot you - I have no time to waste! And we'll take the kid with us. Just in case anyone tries to follow us. We'll leave you at the quays safe and sound if you don't cause any trouble." Segundo nodded in silence. Aileen simply buried her head in Segundos arm and sobbed harder. Prescott stared at the wall in grim silence. He also knew that this could go wrong at any moment. The two workers put the bags filled with guns down at Quintado's feet and walked toward the table. Their meals were getting cold. Quintado spoke up: "Who said you could sit down? Put the bags in the trunk of a truck and let's go out all six of us at the same time." The crook stared at Sebastian and Prescott and walked backward to the exit. Ernesto flicked his rifle at Segundo and Aileen, who shakily got to their feet and staggered out of the building. Once the bags were in the trunk, Quintado freed the workers, who took off running toward the compound. Ernesto forced Segundo to sit behind the wheel and got into the cabin with him; Rodrigo Quintado sat in the back of the truck with Aileen. His brutal appearance and his shotgun silenced all protest - she didn't fight back. She simply sat in stunned silence. Quintado shoved the bags into the truck. It was only a humble military 4x4, but he knew it would be enough to successfully complete his night mission. Ernesto and he would reach the harbor in an hour or two. Then they would load the weapons and refuel on the spot. Ernesto's gun jabbed against Segundo's temple, who reluctantly started the engine. He drove to the gates. Ernesto temporarily slid the barrel off of Segundo's skull and pointed it out the passenger. A bullet erupted from the rifle and lodged in the electronic door box. It exploded in a shower of sparks.

Both gates ground to a halt, still wide open. As he accelerated through the gates, Segundo glanced at the tower guard's dead body. He had bled out on the ground. The fence powered down, the turrets went dark and the truck got out of the secure perimeter. Segundo couldn't see Aileen sitting in the back, as the hatch connecting the cabin to the trunk was closed. He prayed they wouldn't hurt Turner's daughter. The man in the back looked particularly fierce. The truck drove into the forest and out into the clearing. The sun was hiding far behind the tree tops; dark mountains looming in the red distance. The strong heat of the setting sun set the sky ablaze with a blood-red hue. The night would be dangerous.

Turner was sweating profusely in the damp jungle. Julia had slowed down yet Turner could still feel the wind and the speed on his neck and cheeks; he was popping his head out of the window to catch the cool air. Headlights shone on the greenery with an intense white light. A night bird flew just past the bumper. Julia was focusing on the road, furrowing her brow. The lights of the village suddenly appeared behind a big trunk. Julia drove to the electric fence, where Turner noticed that the light bulbs indicating a locked gate were off. He heard workers yelling. Sebastian was kneeling next to the body of a man, lying on the ground. The young cook warned Julia:

"The compound's been attacked by smugglers! I don't know who they are but they didn't hesitate to shoot! We've lost two men!" Julia and Turner met eyes and a shocked dread seemed to overtake both of them at once. What had happened here? Turner practically leaped out of the car and ran up to the main building in hopes of finding his daughter. Julia and Sebastian came running right behind him. Julia asked the young man: "What did they want? How many people?

- Two armed men, they threatened Joe and robbed the compound. They took all the guns from the armory and a truck. They're holding Segundo and the girl hostage."

Turner interrupted him? "The girl? My daughter's with them?

- They had guns! They said they'd kill everyone, we couldn't do anything!"

Turner stepped into the dining room, Aileen wasn't there. Cole Prescott was alone in the room. He was silent. On a table, a record-player was playing "Déjà Vu" by Crosby, Still, Nash & Young. Kenneth knew this song. He was suddenly hit by a wave of nostalgia; he and his wife used to sing along to that song. "Our house" was their favorite. Emotion choked him. His wife was gone and Aileen was all he had left. The mere thought of her alone on the island, taken by rogue crooks shattered his composure. Meanwhile, Julia joined Joe in the communication room. He was badly wounded; blood soaked his shirt. The ranger spoke on the radio, he was talking with Lizard Neck on site B. He'd just told the inimical Conway what happened. What measures was he going to take? Turner entered the room with Sebastian.

"Where's my daughter? How are you going to get her back?" Joe turned to Turner, pale and frantic. He gave it some thought and answered: "They want to reach the South harbor. They're going to drive across the island at night. They said they'll let Segundo and your daughter go as soon as they reach their boat.

- And you trusted them?
- Sir, I really wasn't in a position to oppose them...
- My daughter's life is at stake. Is there really nothing you can do?
- Not me personally." He glanced at Julia. "Conway knows. They're coming up with an evacuation plan to a secure area. As long as the situation isn't taken care of here, on site C, the location is considered 'compromised'. All teams must stop all operations and return to the village or the South compound until it's all sorted out.
- And how exactly are they going to sort this out?
- Conway put Isla Muerta on it, they're going to send a team to neutralize the two smugglers.
- And what's going to become of my daughter? What if she takes a stray bullet? Your mercenaries are going to operate at night, will they mistake her for a narco-smuggler in the dark?
- I don't make decisions. I'm just here to take care of the animals, I don't even know these guys! What do you expect me to do?" Julia was holding her head in her hands. Turner could see how worried she looked. She asked Joe: "Kenneth's not entirely wrong. InGen's taking a big risk letting a paramilitary unit on the island. What about

the dinosaurs? These men are going to kill them all... Or get themselves killed. It's madness. I can't believe Chua and Lizard Neck are OK with that." Turner was running out of patience: "I will not let my daughter die because of your stupid... dangerous world. She won't be collateral damage. I'm going to get her!" Sebastian stared at Turner and tried to hold him back as he was heading for the dining room. "Are you out of your mind? If the pirates don't kill you, the dinos will! You have no idea what kind of danger lies there, you've lost it!

- I won't stay here doing nothing waiting to hear about my daughter's death over the radio. Julia, please, let me take your Jeep! The young woman answered solemnly: "I don't think it's a good idea. You'll die if you leave on your own!" Joe Jackson interrupted them: "He'll need someone who knows the island to track them. Without me, he'll never make it to the south. I'm going with him." Julia smiled faintly: "You two? Alone in a Jeep? Surrounded by the largest predators that have ever walked this Earth? I give you one minute without me! Let's get the hypodermic guns and put them in the trunk, we have to find them before the island gets them..." Joe rolled up his sleeves, stared at Turner and walked to the door. He told Sebastian: "Gather everyone here, ask the workers to fix the gate control box urgently.

We need to secure the perimeter even though we're under-staffed.

- Why should I be the one to ask? I'm just a cook, nobody will listen to me, I have no authority.
- We're dealing with a crisis and we'll have to deal with more, consider this a drill. I tried your shrimp stir-fried rice, the mechanics tried your shrimp stir-fried rice and believe me, they have every reason to take you seriously! You're not just a cook, you're The Cook, do you hear me?"
- For real? You really liked my shrimp stir fried rice? If you're still alive at dawn, I'll make you the Chef breakfast special!" Turner and Julia

left the building and headed up to the jeep. Joe got down the stairs of the facility and grabbed two jerrycans.

There was actually one thing George Alistair knew for sure now: Katherine Harrison was the talkative type. Since she'd met the Dimetrodons, Katherine kept on asking Tia Porter questions. She wanted to know absolutely everything and kept on asking for more explanations. For reasons known only to her, the scientist patiently answered the journalist. The two women were obviously bonding. Porter was dangling a future position as an archivist in front of the journalist. This island, home to monsters of the past, was a real chance for the future. It opened up the scope of possibilities. The Ground Tracker was driving north, headlights tearing up the darkness. In the dark, the former FBI agent was listening to the two women talking. Tia was extremely chatty. "The Dominican amber mines are perched up on rocky hills, away from rivers. Miners dig up petrified wood. The Dominican amber comes from Hymenoea trees, whose resin is rock solid. inGen invested 10 million dollars to exploit amber mines from New Jersey to Mano de Dios in Dominican Republic.

- You need to sell a lot of necklaces! I hope your employers are going to open the biggest amber jewelry factory in the world.
- They keep that in mind to get some return on their investment, but their main concerns lie elsewhere Katherine.
- Here, you can observe and refute paleontological theories. That must give you a sense of enormous satisfaction. It's the end of an era.
- And the beginning of a new one my dear. Obviously, we can now establish with absolute certainty that dinosaurs were warm-bloodied animals, just like birds. It puts an end to the cold-blood theory. The Dimetrodon, on the other end, even though it's genetically closer to a mammal, is a cold-blooded dinosaur. It needs warmth and UVB rays to get the energy it needs to hunt and

digest its food. The other species we're bringing to life are warm-bloodied ones. It makes sense actually; can you picture a 30-ft tall Brachiosaurus having to hide from predators to hibernate? It'd have been extremely vulnerable if it'd been cold blooded. These animals need to eat very large amounts of food to produce warmth and defend themselves; their body temperature doesn't depend on the sun but on their ability to find food. It works for carnivores too. Bipeds are warm-blooded in every sense of the world.

- How long do you think it will take for the word 'paleontology' to disappear from the dictionary?
- At this pace, I'd say... 5 to 10 years!" Lights suddenly blinded her. Tia, Katherine and George couldn't see anything. Another vehicle was coming their way. Who could be leaving the North village at this time? thought Tia. She recognized the truck. It was painted with a camo pattern and blended into the surroundings despite its big black tires. Even though the unique suspension and large bumper inspired respect, it was just a maintenance vehicle; there were no bars on the front cabin. Going on a night trip in this type of four-wheel drive was quite daring. Who could that be? Tia stopped the engine, got out of the Ground Tracker and walked to the vehicle. Katherine and George followed her. Behind the driver's window, she saw Segundo and waved incredulously at him. The young man seemed nervous. A man sat next to him. She didn't know his

face. "Good evening, it's a little late to be driving around in this area. I know there's no actual curfew...but it's just common sense! Why are you driving at night? Aren't you looking forward to going home for dinner?" The passenger came out of the vehicle and walked up to Tia Porter. "I don't think I know you Sir. Are you one of the building workers?" The geneticist stopped talking; the man had a machine gun slung over his shoulder and looked menacing. Someone slammed the truck's rear side door. Another man stepped out of the shadow. He stood in the headlights. George was monitoring the situation too. He noticed that he too was armed. This was hardly surprising on this island. The man pointed his gun at them. Apparently, these two weren't part of the team. The bearded one looked like a soldier though. Who was he? A terrorist? An agent infiltrating inGen? The grim character addressed them in a sarcastic tone: "Good evening. It's a little late for a walk in the woods. The moon is shining but it's dark out. You could trip on a root." Tia Porter snapped back: "Don't worry, we have a ride, thank you." Quintado raised his rifle and started shooting at the Ground Tracker; bullets bounced off the hood and pierced the front tires. George heard the compressed air escaping from the wheels and the cartridge cases falling on the ground. The gunshots echoed in the jungle. Quintado grabbed Tia by the collar of her shirt and said: "Correction: you *had* a ride. Now, you'll be walking." George's blood was boiling; without pausing to consider the repercussions, he leapt on the gunman. Quintado dodged a straight right and punched George in the stomach. George staggered. The smuggler hit him on the head with his gun and kicked him in the ribs. His accomplice slammed his boot into George's back. George spun and landed a solid uppercut under Ernesto's chin. The young man felt his fist slam into Ernesto's jaw, and he immediately followed up with a left cross to his face.

Quintado took advantage of the lapse in George's attention and stomped George's extended leg; it bent and crumpled to the floor. Katherine screamed. Ernesto was aiming his rifle at her, a grim, spiteful expression twisting his face. Quintado walked to the back of the vehicle, screaming: "Enough! Get out of the way. We have a schedule to follow. Go home before you get shot...wherever home is. Your Jeep's dead, so you won't be tempted to follow us. I don't know what the hell you're doing here, but you have quite a compound waiting for you up there. It's better if we go our separate ways. We've killed enough people for one day. You don't want this to end in a bloodbath, do you?" Rodrigo Quintado disappeared into the back of the vehicle and his partner went back into the cabin next to Segundo. The poor guy was pale and paralyzed with fright. Ernesto gave him a nudge in the shoulder with his rifle and Segundo started the engine. The young man was scared, he was thinking. Aileen was sitting in the back. She was a hostage too; he had decided that keeping quiet was safer for her sake. These monsters were vicious, and the girl's safety came first. Besides, both of their lives were at stake. The truck maneuvered around the Ground Tracker, crushing leaves on the side of the road. Segundo drove away from Tia Porter and the two air crash survivors.

The scientist looked stunned. If Segundo didn't burn in hell for this, he was going to be in a world of hurt when inGen heard the story. The forest quickly closed down on them, and the truck bounced along in the green darkness. Segundo put his cap forward on his head, then nervously put it backward again. He wiped his sweaty hands on his vest and grabbed the wheel. He swerved the four-wheel drive down a southbound road. The young man felt awful. Ernesto looked at him through slitted eyes. He asked Segundo a question, and Segundo suddenly became aware that he was hearing the gunman's voice for the first time: "The guy who punched me...who was he? It's the first time someone catches me off-guard.

- He's one of the air crash survivors.
- Air crash? What are you talking about?
- There was an air crash. The survivors drifted north of the archipelago.
- Not the best place to land, it seems. What the hell: a miracle on Matanceros..." The radio crackled again. Ernesto cursed at it. Segundo had to take the incoming communication under the watchful eye of his passenger. In the receiver, he and Ernesto could hear a distant voice with a strong Spanish accent. It was about surrendering. "Surrender now. It will avoid nasty consequences on both sides. Leave the island, and we'll escort you out of the territory. This is a high security area.

You're not allowed to be here. It's restricted territory." Ernesto was shocked to discover that he knew the voice on the radio. He'd heard it before. But when did Matanceros become a private island? The smuggler grabbed the microphone and said: "Who's this?

- General Benitez speaking. Who am I talking to?
- Benitez! I know you. So you're a General right? Who do you work for?
- I work for an entity you can't even begin to imagine kid. Pull over and release the hostages.
- Rodrigo and I don't negotiate with pigs!
- Rodrigo? What are you talking about, son? You mean Rodrigo Quintado? You're hanging out with Don Tiburon's son?
- May he rest in peace.
- Listen my friend, you have no idea what kind of mess you've stepped into. I liked Don Tiburon, but his son mustn't become a problem for us.
- Let us get off this island and we won't hurt them.
- I hope so, Ernesto. Don't make me send the helicopter.
- So... you remember my name?
- You're Ernesto, Tiburon's son's friend. As you can see, I'm still on Isla Muerta and it lives up to its name. Let the girl and the driver go and we'll let you live.

-   We're not taking orders from no one! And
    the weapons are ours now. Deal with it!
    Adios, 'General' Benitez!"

Ernesto threw the receiver on the dashboard and grumbled in Spanish. His fingers were clutching his gun as if he was about to blow a fuse and attack Segundo. He kicked the glove box and ground his teeth. At the same time, the left side of the truck hit something. Ernesto saw a tree crashing down onto the bumper and the vehicle stopped. Then the tree began moving! It scraped across the front of the truck. Ernesto felt nature raging on the left side of the vehicle, which started shaking. Was it a rock? Ernesto looked through Segundo's window, it was obstructed; something was rubbing against the cabin. Segundo knew very well what it was. He wanted to turn off the lights but didn't want to scare the animal. As they approached the river, Segundo had known they would be entering Baryonyx territory sooner or later. He couldn't imagine a worse time to bump into a Baryonyx. And yet...Ernesto yelled and cursed in Spanish. The startled creature hit the truck with its shoulder. Segundo heard Aileen screaming in the back. The mighty creature was now facing the truck; it lowered its long crocodile head at windshield height. Ernesto was terrified. The giant lizard was standing on its hind legs in the grim jungle darkness.

The headlights glinted off its dark scales and its massive form. The monster opened its jaws to reveal sharp teeth and roared so loud the nails on the truck's metal frame rattled. The smuggler was paralyzed in terrified disbelief and still screaming. Segundo heard Quintado open the back doors; he was going to put Aileen in danger. These men had no idea what was lying ahead. The Baryonyx tilted its head back, ready to jump. It launched itself forward and planted its claws in the cabin. Its disproportionately large jaw crushed the windshield, which shattered. Segundo bounded out of the vehicle while Ernesto was opening fire on the animal, shouting. Bullets pierced the monster's giant mouth. Suddenly it froze and stood up. It was hurt. The Baryonyx spat blood and let out a terrifying howl. It started shaking its head wildly. Ernesto had probably hit the head. The dinosaur took a few steps back and collapsed in a chaos of branches and bark. Quintado pulled Aileen out of the truck by her arm and slung an extra gun over his shoulder. Segundo joined them. The smuggler grabbed the young man by the throat. "What the hell was that?" Aileen snorted: "I told you there were dragons!

- You keep your mouth shut! Nobody asked you. Wait a minute, did you say dragons?
- Yes! And there's one right behind you."

Quintado heard a growl over his head, the breath upon his neck sent shivers down his spine. He turned around, already squeezing the trigger of his automatic rifle. Another animal was attacking him! The man warded it off with a relentless stream of bullets. He could hear the slugs penetrating flesh. The creature had tough skin and a nightmarish mouth, but it wasn't bulletproof. The reptile backed away, hissing. Its flank was covered in blood. What kind of devil was that?

Ernesto too emptied a magazine, shooting at the darkness. He came running and shouting: "Watch out! Run!" Another animal charged and hit the truck with all its might. Standing on its powerful hind legs, it leaned on the cabin and split the door in half with its powerful sickle-shaped claw. It tipped the vehicle with its massive arms until the truck finally rolled onto the jungle floor with a metallic shriek and the sound of shattering glass. The lizard mounted the overturned vehicle, metal bending beneath its considerable weight; the windows exploded and the chassis shook. Standing on the vehicle, the animal let out an ear-splitting screech. Quintado shot at the beast and then ran away from it with his partner and the hostages. The Baryonyx turned around and opened its mouth to roar again. It stepped down heavily from the truck, growling at them. Its claws sank into the damp earth. Segundo was running through the forest holding Aileen's hand. The girl was out of breath, running as hard as she could, wary. Ernesto was following them, focused on his escape, trying to push the reality of what was pursuing them far from his thoughts. He counted Quintado's shots. The man was bringing up the rear a few feet away. He reached for his pocket and peered at his compass in the beam of his flashlight. Segundo was heading south. How would they survive in the jungle without a car, with those vile metal-smashing creatures on their trail? It was dark and Ernesto feared they'd run out of ammo. They left their loot in the truck. They were eager to reach the South harbor but their hopes, like their vehicle, had been crushed.

Tia Porter was rummaging around the trunk of the Ground Tracker. Katherine was shining her flashlight at Tia. The scientist took distress flares and more flashlights out of a fabric bag. She gave one to Katherine and one to George. The vehicle was useless, the tires flat. Only the front right headlight had survived the criminal's bullets. Tall grass stood out in the dim white light, and midges danced around the light bulb. The forest was quiet. Tia was wondering who sent those men. Had they come to loot inGen? This didn't make any sense. The company had reached an agreement with those bullies from Isla Muerta. Were they spies? Why did they take Segundo? Was there someone else in the truck? Had they stolen anything? They had to warn the village as soon as possible. Unfortunately, the radio was dead and so was the dashboard. The bullets had pierced the radiator, right through the too-weak armor. Perhaps the engine was still operational and there was a spare tire in the back, but Tia knew that wouldn't be enough. Two tires needed replacing and the compound wasn't that far. She couldn't evaluate the actual distance - it was too dark - but she knew they couldn't stay here. It wasn't safe. They had to follow the dirt road and walk all the way to the village. She stopped the engine and they found themselves in utter darkness. The flashlight beams swept the tree trunks and shakily scanned their surroundings. Tia told Katherine and George about what she was planning on doing. She led the way, lighting the ground. Katherine was a bit scared: "Are you sure it's safe to walk back? How do you know a Dimetrodon won't attack us?

- Do you remember the white feeding formula made from cuttlefish bone?
- Yes, the crickets we saw where covered in it and they'll haunt my nightmares for years to come, thank you very much.
- This biological mixture is found in the system of the prey eaten by our animals. This mixture is highly addictive. When fed regularly, the dinosaurs don't attack each other and stay on their territories.
- So there's virtually no chance of bumping into them, right?
- If you haven't been sprayed with the solution or sprinkled with white powder, the animals should normally not see you as a prey. They won't be interested in you.
- 'Normally?'
- Some of them fear the light, others are drawn to it. In any case, we're too far north of the site, they stay away from these lands and are sedentary, as I told you already. After all, they're still discovering their habitat!

- Shush!"

George had heard something moving in the undergrowth. Everyone froze. Katherine, frightened, hunched over and hid behind the young man. He was looking at the left edge of the woods with his flashlight. The beam swept across the trees and shone a few yards into the woods. Tia was eagerly watching the area with her flashlight in her hand. They all heard a snap. Then another one. Something was moving close by. Tree tops were swaying, branches were snapping a few yards ahead. George looked at Tia. She knew what it was. "Don't make sudden movements and stay close to me." She softly took the cap off a flare and pulled the plastic tab to fire it. The gunpowder went off with a crack and the flare ignited. The glare from the fire was white and blinding, Kat and George could see as if it was broad daylight. The tube illuminated the area within radius of ten yard. A tree trunk snapped in half; creepers splintered. George and Katherine could now see the animal, they remained silent. It was almost six and a half feet tall! Tia tried to comfort them: "This one fears the light. It's totally unnatural to her seeing daylight in the middle of the night..." Katherine whispered back to her:

"I thought the area was deserted.

- This specimen doesn't have a territory of its own, she's the only one of her kind. The island is her kingdom, she comes and goes freely.
- 'She' looks terrifying and dangerous. Is she a meat-eater?

- Yes. And she's a warm-blooded animal. To survive and keep on growing, she needs to feed on meat.
- Keep on growing. But this thing's huge! Shouldn't we go back to the Jeep? I don't want to be her next snack.
- Stay in the light and keep on walking, she won't attack us as long as we have a light source.
- How convenient. And what will happen when your fire dies? Is this female dinosaur going to pounce on us and rip us to pieces?
- I have more distress flares."

George remained close to Tia and Katherine, all three of them huddled in the firelight. The young man could see the reptile more distinctly now. It was a mighty creature, straight out of another world, of another time; a fascinating, perfectly-shaped machine designed to kill. Its tail was long, at least 15 feet long. The lizard stood on its hind legs. Behind the ferns, George could see its thick-skinned feet moving. At the tip grew small claws, about 4 inches long, digging into the ground. The animal looked like a giant goose, like a reptilian partridge standing taller than a man. Its long veiny neck emphasized the dinosaur's jerky, irregular walk. It was carefully watching the small party move in the darkness. The light from the flare was growing dimmer, yet it was still keeping the dinosaur at bay. The color of the animal was stunning, the scales a brilliant shade of yellow. Black spots, similar to a leopard's, covered its body. The hues were definitely tropical, yet they reminded George of the skin of a cheetah. Long veins ran along its flank and went up in a diagonal along its thigh. It had a thick, purple tail that didn't fail to surprise the young man. The distress flare went out; Tia, Katherine and George were in utter darkness again. Their flashlights were obviously not bright enough to keep the animal at a distance. George pointed his light beam at the dinosaur's head while the geneticist fired another flare. It sparkled. The monster, blinded by the light, took a few steps in their direction, staying under the cover of the trees. Would it venture on the road and leave the forest? Katherine got scared and sped up, pushing Tia up the path; the ground was sloping up and becoming harder to climb. This was quite an unexpected hike for Katherine. What kind of mess had the journalist gotten herself into? This giant chicken-like predator was now observing her, standing a dozen yards away. She knew she mustn't panic, and that the female reptile could easily run and pounce on her in seconds. She would tear Katherine to pieces in the blink of an eye. Katherine could now see more details on the animal's head. It had a plate-shaped crest on each side, covered in the same exotic panther-like pattern. Was it part of some kind of pre-mating mechanism? Joints in the jaw allowed the dinosaur to wrinkle its snout and contract its mandibles. The snout was particularly thin and supple. The young woman noticed a kink below the nostril, an inward curve on the upper jaw. Its teeth were pointy and sharp; as she watched the beast step forwards, Katherine felt her blood curdle in her veins. The throat was white. Its

175

entire spine swayed and its head tilted. The second smoke flare was about to die. The female dinosaur walked toward them with her mouth open; she was licking her lips with her long pinkish tongue.

Tia fired another flare, it was the last one. All three started walking faster. What would happen when they'd found themselves in the darkness with no escape from the dinosaur's attack? Katherine couldn't help but ask the scientist: "Do you think we'll reach the compound before this monster starts hunting us?

- It's not a monster. It's a Dilophosaurus, one of the oldest theropods known to man.
- What difference does that make? Without flares, we'll all end up in its stomach!
- In its tail, to be precise. The genome of the Dilophosaurus was almost complete, so we filled the gaps with DNA from the Eublepharis Macularius. It's a leopard gecko found in Pakistan. It has the ability to store excess fat in its tail to survive starvation and hibernation. When food is scarce, it can rely on this stored fat. This Dilophosaurus copied this anatomical ability.
- And you let it roam free? It doesn't have a pen? That's madness.
- It was the first ever specimen created by inGen. It grew up on the island. It can move around as it pleases. The next litter of Dilophosaurus will be different, their size will be genetically reduced.
- Are you planning on bringing more of these creatures to life? You're reckless!"

Tia Porter fell silent, she knew her flare was about to go out. Paleontologists used to think it was a scavenger species because its snout was too fragile, only fit for small preys. But Tia had seen the female in action, she'd seen her hunting cows and crickets in the forest. She knew what this lizard was capable of and she knew they were next in line. There'd never been an incident on the island. It was no accident that the village was protected by electric fences. This unusual situation could cause their deaths in seconds. Tia Porter had seen the dinosaur grow but, for all that, she knew they hadn't bonded. She was a wild animal who would feast on Tia's insides as soon as the light went out. The flashlights wouldn't stand a chance faced with the curiosity and hunger of this young Dilophosaurus. Tia was walking faster and faster. The others huddled around her to remain in the light; but it wasn't enough to outrun the reptile. It kept on following them, its head bent and its upper body leaning forward, its head hovering above the ground; it was greedily watching them, as if evaluating the situation, assessing the value of the prey before attacking. George brought up the rear, covering both women with his own body, facing the beast. The flare went out; George and Katherine shone their flashlights at the reptile. Katherine went for the eyes with the beam but the animal didn't seem scared at all. It kept on moving closer in the darkness. The ground shook lightly, Tia heard an engine and caught a glimpse of headlights. A car was coming their way! A vehicle emerged from the undergrowth and landed on the dirt road. The engine roared and the white light coming from the Jeep flooded the dark path. Tia squinted, blinded by the headlights; she turned around to face the animal and brace for attack. The Dilophosaurus was gone.

"The car scared her away!" Katherine was laughing nervously and hugging George. "Saved by the bell." She looked closely at the forest, the creature was probably still around. It'd found a hiding spot in a heartbeat. Were they safe now? The vehicle stopped in front of them. Tia recognized Joe Jackson, who had emerged from the driver-side door and was coming her way. The engine was still running. Julia and the other crash survivor waited in the car. Tia jumped into Joe's arms. "Perfect timing! That was a close call!" Joe looked at her gravely: "The village was attacked. Two men left with a truck. They stole our weapons and killed two men.

- Oh my God, that's awful! How did it happen?
- It's my fault. I let them in...
- It can't be your fault. We met those men! They sabotaged the Ground Tracker and disappeared into the jungle." Julia walked up to them. "They have Segundo and Kenneth's daughter. We don't really know what they want but they're heading south.
- It's awful. Do you know if the girl's OK?" Joe answered Tia: "We don't know what they're capable of. We need to find them before it gets any worse. I'm responsible for this terrible mess. I'll escort Mr. Turner into the jungle. We'll get his daughter back.

- Are you out of your mind? It's way too dangerous. Do you even know what you're doing?" Julia spoke again: "We're between a rock and a hard place, I know, but there's no other way. We have to go now. We're running out of time. We can't give you a ride to the village, but you can squeeze in and come with us! We can't lose their tracks!" She gave Turner a glance of support he gratefully accepted in silence. Katherine jumped in, worried as ever: "But they're armed! And this island's swarming with man-eating dinosaurs. It's a suicide mission! We've just escaped from...
- Sorry, but there's no time. You can walk to the village if you wish, it's only 30 minutes away." Katherine snapped back at Julia: "No, thanks. We're coming with you." The young woman climbed immediately into the back of the Jeep where George and Tia quickly joined her. Turner got in too, still silent, and Julia went to sit in the front with Joe. Tia told George and Katherine: "I'm sorry for this unexpected event, it's never happened before. We're not used to traveling across the site at night. But don't worry, Joe and Julia know what they're doing, you're safe with them."

George and Katherine exchanged a dubious look and smiled. They'd just gotten away from the dinosaur's clutches and now they were heading south, into the heart of the action. Above them, they could hear helicopter rotors chopping the air. The night was still young.

The jungle was dark and menacing, the trees closing in on Quintado, Ernesto, Segundo, and Aileen. Creepers were hanging from the branches of tall sequoia trees and swaying in the warm summer breeze. The moon was full and shining bright. The light bounced off the mountain tops and seeped through the trees and onto the path. Aileen was frowning, focusing on her steps, trying to avoid trees in the darkness. The wilderness was quiet aside from bugs singing in the distance. She held Segundo's hand as they walked side-by-side without a flashlight. She was trying to follow Ernesto's and Quintado's beams. Both men were leading the way, and thanks to Segundo they'd found a path. The young man had managed to find his way in the island's darkness; the little party was heading south on a path running parallel to the main road. Segundo had never treaded it before, he was more used to driving on the main dirt roads but he knew it led to a bunker that was the last landmark before the South compound. The smuggler had insisted on taking the shortest way south, no matter how difficult the walk was. Segundo saw cuts on Aileen's arms. The little girl's hair was down and she wore a woman's beige t-shirt and brown tights. Her clothes weren't protecting her at all from mosquito bites. InGen hadn't stocked children's sizes on site C. The girl had to make do with what was on hand.

Aileen managed to keep her temper, she was thinking. She was trying hard to keep the too-big shirt on her shoulders. She treated it like a mission, hoping that would help take her mind off of the terrible situation she was in. She was dizzy with all the smugglers and dragons and she just wanted to sleep. It'd been a hard day, but she knew it wasn't time for bed. She wanted to prove to Segundo that she was big enough to face hardship, that she walked as good as a grown-up and that she didn't whine. She understood how hard the situation was; she had to be strong.

Quintado turned to them and spoke to Segundo: "Come on amigo! Once we get down there, you'll find me a Jeep and some fuel and you'll never hear about me ever again. The kid and you will be free. I don't know when Matanceros became the Lost Continent and I don't want to know anything about it. I just want my boat back. I have no idea what these things that attacked the truck were, but if I have to kill every single one of them to reach the harbor, trust me, I will. Same way I will kill you if you try to trick me. So be a good boy, take me to your camp and you'll live." Quintado suddenly stopped his intimidation act, he'd heard the sound of helicopters flying above the island.

They were close, Quintado thought. He knew he had to reach the compound by any means necessary before things got ugly. Quintado was getting low on ammunition and had to save bullets. Who knew what this jungle had in store for him? Ernesto moved closer to him. "It's Benitez's men. It looks like he's become a "General" since last time. They operate on Isla Muerta and they work for these guys and for the government." Quintado cursed in Spanish. "That's the last thing we need now. Soon the forest will be swarming with his boys. We need to outrun them and hope they get eaten by the monsters before we do. It's dark and they probably have better equipment. Segundo, my friend, you'll need to pick up the pace. We have another compound to raid!" He pushed the young man and the girl in front of him and pressed his rifle muzzle against Segundo's back. The four hikers suddenly froze. Quintado exchanged a look with Ernesto. Both heard the ferns rustle. Ernesto aimed his gun and flashlight at the trees. Branches moved, wood cracked, and it wasn't the wind. Something was hiding behind those trunks. Was it one of these huge beasts again? Should they shoot now, blindly?

Quintado's partner walked to an uprooted tree and took a look behind the mossy stump. He took a few steps into the undergrowth and heard an animal snuffing. Ernesto's finger gripped the trigger, ready to shoot at the trees and kill the creature. Slowly, he walked closer, his eyes fixed on the branches moving in front of him. He gulped nervously and pushed away the leaves with his left arm to expose the monster. The man jumped and screamed when he saw the animal! He lost his balance, fell over and dropped his flashlight. It's bright beam played across the swaying tree trunks.

Quintado aimed at the thickets to confront the threat...and then burst out laughing. He helped Ernesto up and turned around to take a look at Segundo and Aileen. It was a cow! Ernesto had had a close encounter with a cow, quietly grazing in the forest. Nothing to worry about! Quintado teased Ernesto, who felt like an idiot. What was this cow doing here alone in the middle of the night? thought Ernesto.

His question got an immediate answer. An ominous reptilian roar froze his blood in his veins. The smuggler couldn't tell where the attack came from, but a lizard suddenly tackled him from behind, slicing his thigh open. Ernesto howled and opened fire on the beast; it took a few steps back. Gunshots illuminated the forest. Quintado, Segundo and Aileen saw the creature. It pounced on Ernesto's arm and sunk its fangs into his flesh. The man had to drop his weapon, shouting. The dinosaur was more than ten feet long. It stood on its hind legs but had its upper body leaning forward as if it was crawling on all fours. Each limb had three clawed-fingers. The beast looked like a crocodile with a long toothy snout and a slender skull. But it was an orange crocodile; three-quarters of its body was covered in smooth, shiny, bright scales the texture of supple patent leather. Black stripes ran along its back, from the tip of the tail to the thighs and neck. Its tail was whipping across the tall grass. It dug the razor-sharp claws of its right foot deep into Ernesto's ankle; he moaned in agony. Quintado opened fire and riddled the animal with bullets. It let out a screech and, hissing with pain, fell over in the bushes. Quintado ran to his friend's rescue and helped him up. His thigh, forearm and ankle weren't a pretty sight. What kind of lizard species was that? Both men were facing the unthinkable. They were walking up to Segundo and Aileen when a new attack occurred; this time, it came from the side. Two other reptiles pounced on the cow behind them. One of them was sinking its sharp teeth into the animal's throat while the other was mutilating the cow's flanks as it tried to scramble up the bovine's back. The cow lowed with fear as the reptile tore off a piece of its neck, causing blood to gush out of the cow's arteries and soaking the leaves with it. The other orange crocodile brought the cow down with its hind legs. The bleeding animal collapsed, quivering. Two other creatures burst out of the jungle next to Quintado and Ernesto. The crocodiles roared and went after the smugglers, while the two other creatures quickly joined the hunt. Their snouts were covered in blood. Segundo grabbed Aileen's arm and they all started running along the path. But Ernesto's wounds were slowing Quintado down too much. One of the dinosaurs grasped Ernesto's backpack in its jaws and immobilized him. He fell down and rolled over to his side to free himself. The animal tore his bag to pieces; Quintado reached for his partner but another crocodile pounced at Quintado and sank its teeth into his vest. The man shoved the lizard back violently with his gun before shooting. He felt the fabric of his vest ripping up. The lizard snorted and opened its mouth menacingly. As Ernesto rose to his feet, the third animal lept on him and pinned him against a tree. The fourth attacked Quintado from behind; it drove him onto his chest with its forelimbs and drove sank its teeth into his leather boot. Quintado kicked himself free of the animal's hold. He had no other choice but to run away with Segundo and Aileen without looking back.

There were too many monsters; they were standing in Ernesto's way, while he fought them back with difficulty. His flashlight was swinging wildly. Rodrigo Quintado couldn't see his partner anymore. Bullets weren't enough to kill them. These animals were thick-skinned pack hunters that moved around the forest with disturbing ease. The smuggler didn't stand a chance. As he caught up with Segundo and Aileen, he shouted: "Stick to the plan! Get me to the camp!" The three hikers ran down the path, their breath short with fear. They clambered over the forest floor, jumping over trunks and minding their step in the dark. They left Ernesto behind. The four animals were surrounding him, growling. It was dinner time. Ernesto clenched his teeth and pulled back his shoulders. He was petrified, but still retained his survival instinct. He'd lost his gun but he had a spare one on his belt. He drew it from the holster, moaning as his bleeding, ragged arm throbbed with every effort. The monster had tried to rip it off! He aimed at the first animal standing in front of him and pulled the trigger. The reptiles quacked, they sounded like big flesh-eating ducks. They looked like the crocodiles he saw a while ago. But these were smaller and more colorful. Were they big enough to swallow him whole? What was happening on Matanceros? How had the island suddenly become a mutant crocodile's lair? Ernesto didn't think twice and went running into the woods, still shooting. The lizards followed, avoiding the bullets. They were weaving between trees and ferns, surrounding the smuggler who was running breathlessly. Their jaws snapped in the darkness, as they watched him, croaking. His thigh and ankle were in excruciating pain, but Ernesto had to give it his all. He had to find shelter. Getting away from those beasts was a question of life and death. He shot another bullet. It lodged in a tree trunk and splintered the bark. Ernesto held his flashlight against his gun and somehow navigated the maze of young trees. Maybe he would get rid of the lizards. No sooner had the hope of escape entered his mind then one of them sprung at him from the left. Ernesto lost his balance but kept running and shooting at the crocodile. It moved back - it seemed he had hit it in the shoulder. The smuggler ran into the bushes, trampling on branches; he had no idea where he was going. He freed himself from some creepers and burst into a clearing. The moon was shining on the tall grass and the soft ground of the work site. The earth had been moved, the mud had been turned over. Through the damp mist of the jungle, Ernesto caught a glimpse of a construction vehicle. The machine had been left here, in the middle of nowhere. He ran toward the vehicle. Just then, one of the creatures appeared in the clearing, illuminated by the blue moonlight. The vehicle was a small, yellow Caterpillar earth-moving machine equipped with a hydraulic excavator. The operator cabin was protected by black plastic mesh. Two small round lights were fastened to the side bar. Blood dripped from his thigh but Ernesto didn't want to give up; he managed to haul himself on the tire and opened the door, gritting his teeth from the pain. He could still feel the claws in his flesh and he was losing a lot of blood. In the mist, the pack of lizards was getting closer. Ernesto crawled into the vehicle and slammed the door shut. Furious, one of the beasts threw itself against the machine. The metal frame rattled with the force of the impact. The reptile pressed its head against the window to have a look inside. Ernesto gazed into the animal's eye, cradling his gun. The oval green iris was split in half by a black slit. The lizard's eyelid slid up and down its reptilian eyeball; it was concentrating and analyzing the situation. These animals were smart, Ernesto could see it now. Should he shot it in the head through the window mesh screen? Could he get away from these beasts in the state he was in? The crocodile let out a croaky roar. It punctured the tires and slashed at the paint with its claws. It started tugging at the plastic mesh screen with its forelimbs. Its claws cut through the mesh and the monster started pulling at the plastic with its three fingers. It used its thin jaw full of sharp little teeth to tear away a piece of the mesh. The creature slid its bottom jaw through the hole and started knocking on the glass. The vehicle suddenly rocked and groaned as another dinosaur leaped onto the right door. The blow was so strong that the window shattered. The door crinkled and the mesh was pushed in from the outside. The small machine leaned over. The first crocodile pulled harder and ripped away the side protection bars with his jaw; it banged on the glass. Ahead, Ernesto could see two other animals. One of them jumped on the excavator of the Caterpillar machine and bit the hydraulic arm. The fourth member of the pack, climbed onto the vehicle, in front of the windshield. It banged its head on the mesh to destroy it. This creature wanted to get to Ernesto too. It pushed away the hydraulic arm with its tail and leaned on the small hood. The steel squeaked and the Caterpillar machine tilted forward; Ernesto hit his head on the dashboard. The animal standing on the right side of the vehicle stopped attacking the door and joined the other on the left. It pushed the vehicle with its head and shoulders to help its hunting partner. The construction vehicle fell over on one side. It didn't make a noise, as if the mist had muffled the sound of the metal crashing on the ground. The smuggler fell down on the right-side door as it collapsed on the floor. A stabbing pain in his thigh and ankle made him howl. He could feel the coolness of the ground through the shattered window. He was stunned. Those beasts had managed to turn another vehicle upside down! The mechanic arm and excavator dangled into a hole in the ground; the Caterpillar machine lied down in the mist. The lizards growled above Ernesto's head. They tore away the mesh and hit rammed their skulls into the glass. A crocodile snout broke through the door; Ernesto felt the shattered glass fell on his vest and he covered his eyes. Two predators were scratching at the windshield mesh screen with their hind legs. The plastic was falling apart and the glass was breaking. The man was trapped. A crocodile slid its head through the window and tried to clamp its teeth down on Ernesto's skull. Its jaws snapped just above his head. Ernesto was nearly suffocating with fear. The smuggler had no alternative: he aimed at the animal and shot his gun twice. The fearsome flesh-eating duck cringed and stepped back to take its neck out of the machine. A bullet had pierced its throat; it was bleeding into the cabin and on Ernesto's face. A third animal threw itself on the windshield and shattered it.

A glass shard cut deep into Ernesto's shoulder; he howled again. The metal rods supporting the structure of the cabin started bending under the blows of the enraged reptiles. One of the crocodiles tore away the mesh, claws hammering the metal. Mist seeped into the cabin. Ernesto was curled up in a corner. He removed the piece of glass from his flesh, wincing in pain. He grabbed the butt of his gun and opened fire, shouting at the top of his lungs. His friend's stopover had gone sour, nothing else mattered now. To hell with good and bad, to hell with justice and deceit. Ernesto didn't question his lifestyle choices anymore and was now only following one rule. He didn't care about the past or the future, the only thing that mattered was the present. He had to survive.

The mist shrouding the road glowed in the moonlight. The engine hummed just above the hazy ground. The Jeep was slowing down. Joe Jackson recognized the Ground Tracker abandoned in the middle of the road; he stopped the engine but left the headlights on. He grabbed his flashlight and softly shut the door. Julia got out of the vehicle too to take a look at the car. She had a sniper rifle slung over her shoulder and she was scanning the area with her eyes. She approached Joe, who was assessing the damage done to the Ground Tracker. Turner jumped out of the vehicle, holding a gun, and joined them. Katherine, George and Tia stayed in the car, monitoring the surroundings with their flashlights. It was a clear night and the jungle was full of frightening surprises; all three of them were on the alert.

Branches moved to the left. Joe and Julia pricked up their ears. The woman might have looked like a confident, resourceful explorer, but Turner could see that she was worried. Goosebumps covered her neck. She loaded her gun with a tranquilizer dart and switched the safety off. Joe straightened up to gaze into the darkness. They were coming. The forest was alive, and everybody could see silhouettes in the shadows, drawn by the lights of the Jeep. The silhouettes emerged from the darkness and approached the party. It was five men! Joe sighed with relief. "What are you doing here?" The man stopped in front of him and shook his hand. He was a soldier. He had fair skin and short hair, he was clean-shaven. The man was in his forties. Was he a soldier or a mercenary? He wore sophisticated safety gear and was armed to the teeth. He introduced himself to Joe and his party. "I hear you need help on this site. Isla Muerta is here to help you deal with this situation. My name's Davis but everyone calls me 'Scraps' Davis.

- Joe Jackson.
- My men and I are here to arrest the smugglers. We'll identify the problem and solve it." Julia asked: "Are you going to kill those men?"
- Affirmative. But first, we need to find out how many of them there are and what their intentions are.
- You have no idea what you've gotten yourself into.
- Actually Miss, we do. We know about your activities, I told you, we're here to help.
- Do you have any idea of the danger we're exposed to as we speak? Julia said.
- We've never seen the animals with our own eyes, but we know what to expect. Lizard Neck's briefed us. I know we'll have to deal with big salamanders.
- So I guess you know how expensive these "big salamanders" are?
- Expensive and dangerous, I know. We're not on a mission to kill your animals, but the men who threaten them. My orders are clear." Joe Jackson spoke: "The only way

we'll make sure nobody dies tonight is if I'm coming with you.

- I have strict instructions. We're going to track down those criminals and restore the peace. You cannot come with us. Everyone on this island must go to the closest secure compound. Orders, sir. We cannot escort you, but please go back to your Jeep and leave for the South compound." Turner lost his temper. His fingers turned white as he gripped his gun harder: "They have my daughter! Do you understand? They're holding her hostage! I can't give up on her!

- You're not giving up on her Sir. If you get to safety, you're helping us save your daughter. We also know they have Mr. Segundo Leticia. Just let us do our job." Joe insisted: "The others can go to the South compound, but I'm coming with you. I'm responsible for what's happening and I want to make things right. We're on carnivore territory. Only authorized personnel can operate here. If you think you can walk around Suchomimus territory at night without risking your life, you're gravely mistaken. You need me. I'll shoot the animals with tranquilizer darts if we cross their paths, the smugglers are all yours. I'll find Segundo and the girl; I owe this to her father. It's the least I can do." He took the gun from Turner, who

made no protest. Turner nodded gratefully at Joe as he watched him join the paramilitary group.

———

The four men standing behind Davis were wearing night-vision goggles.

Electronic lenses that allowed them to see in the dark. The soldier from Isla Muerta gave Joe a pair. "Very well, I guess we can use a scout who knows the island. But you and only you can come. The others have to get back in the car and leave. You said it yourself: it's not safe here. We need to secure the perimeter so you can get back to your usual activities on this site. Now go!" Davis withdrew with his armed platoon and silently walked into the jungle. Joe followed on their heels; he glanced at Julia and Turner one last time and thought about Tia Porter, who was watching him go.

She was worried. He was too. The canopy hid the sky and the forest stretched before him. He had brought the criminals into the village. Because of him, two people had died. He had to save the girl and bring Segundo back to camp safe and sound. For Turner. For himself. For his work to continue, he needed to prove the staff's ability to deal with incidents. This was a great opportunity to emerge stronger and better and to prove how efficient the company was. Joe Jackson had to succeed. Nothing was lost; Aileen would see her father again soon. Joe held on to this idea, minute by minute.

The more time passed, the more focused Joe became. Scrap Davis and his unit progressed silently; they stepped over trunks and periodically spun around to watch their backs. Mist was now up to their ankles. Joe placed the heavy night vision goggles on his forehead to mind his step. The trunks were gleaming in the night, the bodies of the mercenaries stood out in the darkness; everything was green and perfect visible. Davis turned to him, his pupils greenish and totally dilated; his green skin glowed in the dark and his teeth were white and bright. "While I have you on hand Joe, can you tell me more about the creatures inhabiting this area? What are we up against exactly? Or should I say, what aren't we up against?

- Yes, each specimen is the result of years of very expensive research. We're talking several million dollars for each animal.
- I don't understand why inGen wants to protect those things so bad. I heard you talking about a Suchomimus earlier. What is it?
- A biped, a carnivore. It's about 10 to 13 feet long, almost as tall as you. It's a vicious predator; believe me, you'll be glad I'm there when one of them shows up.
- Is it a deadly specimen?
- As deadly as can be. InGen's Suchos are only three months old. They're a relatively new species, but they're already incredibly dangerous. They grow up fast. Soon we plan to transfer them to site B where they'll reach their full size.
- That's one hell of a factory you have here. Too bad those notorious weapon smugglers are getting in the way.
- Hopefully you're here to take them out of the picture, aren't you?

- That's what we do Joe. Quick and painless. Out of sight, out of mind.
- And everything will get back to normal?
- Everything will get back to normal.
- Six against two, we can handle it!
- We flew over the area earlier. They're not alone. The team's spotted a boat sailing around the island. We don't know how many of them there are on the boat or how many have landed. Part of our mission is to clear that up. Look for broken branches and footprints on the ground! We're tracking four people for now." He stopped talking when he saw another

track on the ground. It was large and clear-cut, a prehistoric print that immediately alerted the soldier. "That's what I call leaving your mark! What species is that Joe? Is that your Suchomimus? I was expecting something smaller.

- It's too big to be a Sucho and too small to be a demon. Those beasts don't venture around here. It's a Baryonyx... I really hope the girl's OK...
- She is. We saw the truck upside down on the road; something happened for sure, but there were no bodies. Well, no human bodies at least.
- What do you mean?
- These men killed one of your Baryonyx, maybe more.
- Hammond's not going to be pleased...
- Is Hammond your boss?
- Yes, he's the billionaire funding this project.

- I'm sure he'll understand. It's collateral damage. You can't make an omelet without breaking a few eggs. I guess he knew there'd be many variables when he came up with this monumental project.
- I'm not sure he 'came up' with everything, as you put it. InGen's bureaucracy is vague and mysterious. Anyway, he does sign the checks, that's for sure."

Joe stopped talking. He'd seen something about 50 yards ahead. Everyone stood as still as statues, holding their breath. The men aimed at the monster that was coming their way. It was a Baryonyx. The dinosaur hadn't seen them. It was busy eating. The huge crocodile with the long predatory jaw was feasting on the remains of a dead animal. But what was it eating? Thanks to the night vision goggles, Joe could see what species the dead animal belonged to. He whispered: "It's eating a Suchomimus." Davis gave him a puzzled look: "Why is that surprising to you? They're carnivores, right? You're the expert!

- The Baryonyx is a fish-eating dinosaur. Growing up, the environment it lives in dictates its eating habits. When fish is scarce, it turns to meat. But I don't think it killed the Suchomimus.
- One of the smugglers might have done it. They killed your creatures to protect themselves.
- And the solitary Baryonyx took this opportunity to broaden its diet and get on

Suchos territory. I have a bad feeling about this.

- Why's that Joe?
- It means the Baryonyx will become more and more dangerous. We need to reassess the feeding process and keep them apart from the Suchos so they won't kill each other. It also means we're on Suchos hunting ground."

All six men were watching the Baryonyx feeding on the warm dead body of the dinosaur. Joe could see steam was coming up from its guts in his night vision goggles. The faces of Davis's men were entirely covered by their black balaclavas and their nights vision equipment. Still, Joe could imagine the look of astonishment on their faces. They were clearly trying to maintain their composure. He knew they couldn't take their eyes off of the Baryonyx. It was the first time these men had seen a dinosaur. When Joe Jackson saw his first dinosaur a few months back, it had left him speechless. Science had brought the most amazing creatures in the universe back to life, and rocketed paleontology to another level. All that power, all that beauty; this animal logic expressing instinctively, in its most natural, ancestral, ancient state. The prehistoric shock still made him smile. It was crazy! What unbelievably wonderful circumstances! Man and dinosaur meeting for the first time, face to face, in secret. A dream that gave men the chills, raised goosebumps and rekindled survival instincts; an unexpected meeting that would change the way people experience the world. Unfortunately for Joe, the men from Isla Muerta didn't particularly want to enjoy the show much longer. Davis signaled them to go around the creature and head east, which they did, slowly climbing up the slope; the animal didn't notice them. It was far too busy licking the bones of the young Suchomimus clean. Joe left the mighty lizard behind him and followed the rest of the commando team. He regularly turned around to make sure they weren't being chased by any of the animals. You had to be on the lookout all the time in this forest - one second of inattention and the night could close in on you forever. Joe didn't see the Baryonyx anymore. The distant mist had swallowed it. Walking was becoming increasingly difficult as they gained altitude. He hoped Julia, Tia and the other crash survivors had reached the South compound in time. If she got there before the smugglers, Julia could snipe them down from the compound tower; she could either shoot them dead or shoot them with tranquilizer. She needed to stop them by any means. Joe worried himself in mental circles. Midges were buzzing in his ears; he took off his cap and ran his fingers through his hair. His sweat was attracting bugs. The grassy turf was gratefully drinking in the surrounding humidity, but his shins were getting unpleasantly cold. A green glow coming from the right suddenly caught his attention. Was it a will-o'-the-wisp dancing behind the tropical plants? The spot was getting closer and bigger in his goggles. Joe whistled to warn the unit; the mercenaries had spotted the reptile too. It was running toward them!

Another animal emerged from the bushes and rushed toward military unit with determined strides. It was getting dangerously close to Davis. Joe shouted a warning: "Suchos!" He loaded his gun with a tranquilizer dart and tried to aim at the animal as it got closer and closer to the merc captain. Joe's night-vision goggles prevented him from aiming accurately so he took them off to press his eye against the scope. He tracked the dinosaur in the moonlight. Joe held his breath and pulled the trigger. The dart flashed through the air and burrowed into the muscular neck of the attacking Sucho. Davis stepped aside and the four soldiers moved back too, ready to shoot. "Hold your fire!" Joe reloaded his gun in seconds and aimed at the other creature. The reptile was swinging its head and forelimbs just over the ground, moving swiftly behind the trees. It opened its crocodile jaws and snarled. The growl echoed into the misty jungle and died somewhere in the mountains. Joe pulled the trigger again, aiming at the chest of the Suchomimus. The dart stuck in the reptile's arm. The two beasts roared, stomping their massive hind legs and piercing the air with their long, toothy snouts. One of the crocodiles hissed and looked away. Then both Suchos weaved a few steps to the left as if intoxicated before pivoting back toward the forest and clambering to safety beneath the leafy canopy. The sedative worked quickly: the animals were already backing off and going to find a place to sleep. Their massive, muscular striped tails disappeared between the tree trunks. Davis looked impressed, he leaned on Joe Jackson's

shoulder as Joe was putting his goggles back on.
"You've saved my life! I owe you one.

- Don't thank me just now. One of them is dead. And there's still potentially two left out there. Be on the lookout. They're pissed.
- You guys heard what Joe said? Watch your ass! We take the path south. Let's go!"

Joe was trying to stay cool. The goggles felt heavy and he was so sweaty they were slipping down his nose. Like every carnivore on this island, he could see in the dark as well as he could in broad daylight. Quite ironic! He owed his life to this miracle of South-American military technology. Joe hoped Segundo and Aileen were safe too. The tracker had seen blood on a Suchos's snout, but he refused to believe it could be Segundo's or the girl's. He couldn't believe the chase would end up that way. He couldn't let that happen to the Turner girl. He couldn't do that to himself. The hostages were alive, so he had to have faith and keep on going. Joe Jackson would bring them back to camp.

The Jeep was tearing down the main road. Julia was heading south fast. Sitting at her left, Turner was biting his nails, gazing into the night through the windshield, more worried than ever about his daughter. Would Joe Jackson and the men from the other island save her from the clutches of the dinosaurs and smugglers? Turner felt useless. It was his role to take care of his daughter, and yet he had let Joe go and be the brave one. His daughter's fate was now in Joe's hands and not in his anymore. But what could he actually do, lost in this green inferno? The night had just fallen and Turner's heart was beating for his daughter. The forest was slowly disappearing around them, the trees getting smaller and smaller. The car drove past a small yucca and the suspension squealed. Katherine, George and Dr. Porter held on to the metal bars; they were sitting in the back with Turner and focusing on the local landscape. Katherine Harrison was watchful, nervously twiddling her thumbs. Suddenly, Turner saw another clearing ahead. Wilderness grew all around and mountains rose in the background like blue pinnacles. Darkness and fog shrouded the palm trees below; the road was going up. Julia sped up on a straight line, she didn't want to linger here too long. The car drove past the trees and went through a little creek going downhill. Julia crushed a few ferns before stabilizing on the flatter ground of the clearing. Turner looked up at the sky. They'd reached the South compound. Tall black gates rose ahead. They were at least 13 feet high and were connected to fences by two massive concrete posts. Tall grass grew at the foot of the facility. Red lights started blinking and the mighty iron gates opened outward. The Jeep drove into the compound and the gates closed. It was much smaller than the North outpost. A tall watchtower stood at the heart of the secure perimeter. Under the geometric thatched roof of the tower, Turner saw a large glass wall, probably a control room. The electric fence lights were off. Was the power down here? There were no cars to be found either, although there were many tire tracks in the mud. A fuel pump had been placed next to the tower; empty jerrycans were scattered on the ground. Julia parked the vehicle near the entrance and stopped the engine. Tia Porter got out of the trunk to head for the building entrance hall. Katherine and George walked with her, looking around. It was unbelievable, another lost facility south of a lost island! Turner stepped out of the car; he felt the sea breeze blowing through the trees. The coast was nearby. The mist was clearing off, blown away by the light breeze. Julia ushered everyone into the tower, her gun slung over her shoulder. With her flashlight, she led everyone to the tower staircase. Suddenly the ground floor flooded with light and they were met by a man from inGen. He was a tall thirty-something redhead with a bulbous nose in the middle of a fat and slightly flat, freckled face. The man had round cheeks and fat lips that drew attention to his buck teeth. Yet, he was tall and skinny. He was wearing a gray baseball cap and sunglasses. His beige t-shirt was smeared with red stains. This immediately caught Julia's eye. The man defused the situation: "Don't worry, it's not blood. Just barbecue sauce... I always eat in the dark, that's a bad habit." He pointed at his brown pants, they were covered in sauce too. Julia turned to the crash survivors as she stepped in. "This is Chad Bradwick. He runs this place with his brother." As she spoke, the latter came down the stairs behind his brother. They looked exactly alike and had the same clumsiness to them, but the second brother was wearing a gray baseball cap and didn't have sunglasses. He wore a gray inGen t-shirt and brown pants. He was eating a can of tuna salad with a small white plastic fork. There really was a striking resemblance between them. Katherine couldn't help but ask: "Are you two twins?" Chad happily answered, pushing his sunglasses back into place: "Tal and I were born a few hours apart, I'm the firstborn.

- Tal? You're called Chad and Tal Bradwick?
- Yes, why?
- No reason. 'Chad and Tal Bradwick'. It sounds... funny.
- We're the Bradwick Brothers and proud of it! We hear you survived an air crash. So? How was it?" Katherine answered ironically: "Well, it was... Epic. An ocean of emotions.
- Epic! I believe you! You must have gone through so much! You've come at a difficult time, but please know that you're welcome here. We have food and blankets, you're safe in this area." Turner was skeptical, he was worried about his daughter. "Really? Are you sure? Why are the lights out outside?
- We have limited power supply on this facility. The generator in the back can't power the fences day and night. We can operate with the power out. We put it back on when we need it.
- And when do you need it?
- When they venture too close.

-   'They'? Who are 'they'?"

Chad gave Julia and Tia a confused look. Julia decided to speak out: "It's fine, you can tell them. These people have already met some of our specimens.

-   Ah. I see. In this case, let's not keep it a secret. We power the fences when the demons get too curious. Five thousand volts up the snout is quite discouraging! Tal and I take turns to watch the area. We keep our tranquilizer guns close to keep the animals at bay. That's the safe solution. We only supply a few rooms in the tower to save power. Think green!" Katherine was puzzled. "What demons are you talking about?" Julia answered her, looking at Turner: "Demon is the code word we use for the biggest dinosaurs on the island. They happen to be the hungriest ones too.

-   They're the carnivorous kind, I guess?

-   The very carnivorous kind..." Tia provided details: "Carnotaurus. That's the name of the species living in this area. It means 'meat-eating bull'. It's a Saurischian dinosaur from the superior Cretaceous period. The specimens have been cloned from amber and fossils found in Patagonia. They easily adapt to this environment, as they originated in South America.

-   How many of them are there?

-   Two males. They're three months old and they're growing fast."

Tal added: "Conway wants to move them to site B before they become uncontrollable here. They're getting more and more curious and they come prowling around the facility. Turner was running out of patience: "You settled on the territory of two huge predators and your fences are not electrified? What's inGen thinking?

- It's fine. We've only been here a few weeks, but we got this, right Chad?
- We do.
- My brother and I have everything we need to survive for weeks here, and there's room for everyone. Downstairs, we keep fuel, batteries and a few weapons. Upstairs, there's a small lab. That's where we keep the embryos of the species from site C. The lab is equipped with refrigerated boxes and tubes to transfer genetic material from one site to another. We don't create dinosaurs here, so to speak. We just keep their DNA.
- On the top floor, there's a communication room looking out to the perimeter. There's a shower cubicle in the kitchen if you want." Chad said. Katherine snorted quietly to herself: "Showering in a kitchen...great."
- "Come with me, I'll show you around. You can make yourself at home upstairs." Katherine started speaking to herself, smiling. "So Chad and Tal... you don't have a triplet called Brad by any chance, do you? Chad, Tal and Brad Bradwick... Brad Bradwick. Brad, Tal and Chad. The Bradwick

Brothers! That'd sound great." Tia was listening. She smiled at Katherine and climbed the stairs of the concrete watchtower. She knew they were safe behind the fences of the South outpost, but what about Segundo and Aileen? Were Joe and Davis's dream team making any progress? Tia had to get in touch with Chua on site B. Lives were at stake.

Cicadas were singing in the night, and the air was getting thin. Rodrigo Quintado could feel it. He was moving slower. Getting tired, too. They'd been walking in the forest for hours. He was surprised the girl was holding on so well. She was a key asset in his strategy. Holding a ten-year-old girl hostage meant victory. No one would risk a child's life. The new guys on this island would have to comply, they had no choice. It was the power of childhood faced with violence. He could spare Segundo though. He would get rid of him in a heartbeat to suit his ends. Just one more dead man on his list. Segundo had gotten them out of trouble and taken them away from giant lizard territory. Those blood-thirsty reptiles now seemed far away. They were still walking uphill, under the palm trees and creepers. Quintado had left his friend Ernesto behind to save his own. After all, he still had a mission to complete. He'd send Ernesto's family his kind regards along with twenty five percent of his share. That would pay for his sacrifice. Matanceros had eaten his partner and the criminal knew the forest wouldn't give him back; he had to keep on going, step by step, no matter what. Quintado's patient determination was rewarded; ahead of Segundo and Aileen, he saw a bunker on the side of the mountain. A large iron door blocked the entrance. Pour-lines criss-crossed the flat concrete facade. Two lights shone bleakly in a pale and gloomy vertical rectangle. A line of yellow paint ran horizontally above the door. Above, a bright white stripe bore a warning in Spanish. A triangle, indicating danger, was printed on a metal sign left of the entrance. Red lights shone on the ferns that grew up the hill and covered the pipes with their spiral leaves. Quintado didn't give a damn about the bunker, he had no time to spare. Yet, this topographic landmark was a good omen; what Segundo said was true: they were actually heading south and they'd reach the facility soon. This wasn't the time to give up. Behind the concrete hill, clear water was falling from another mountain. Clouds hiding the moon were clearing, revealing a steep green peak at the heart of the island. Water was quietly falling in the distance, sparkling like a diamond though the mist. Nature's coat grew on huge rocks on the horizon; Quintado was getting close to the coast. But something in the air was making him uneasy, a distant sound, like a sixth sense telling him danger was closing in. He took a deep breath, listening to nature surrounding him, he didn't look back. He knew something was off. He pointed at Segundo and Aileen with his gun and whispered: "Move. Walk to the bunker, I'll watch the door. Stay still, I'm watching you, stay in the light." Segundo and the Turner girl walked to the front door as Quintado climbed up a baobab tree. He ascended the big roots and pulled himself up on sturdy branches. Like a cat, he went up the tree, sat on the gnarled, knotted bark and hid behind dark green leaves. Segundo watched him from below. The young man wondered if he should take this opportunity to run away with Aileen. If they ran fast enough they could lose the smuggler and find shelter. Or maybe he would be too quick and kill them as they ran. The man was strong and resilient. He would probably come looking for them and get revenge. On the road, he'd make them pay for this outrage and might become even crueler...it was too risky. Segundo couldn't put Aileen's life on the line. He had to remain calm, comply and wait under the red light.

If a Suchomimus came to attack them, they'd be vulnerable. And Quintado knew what he was doing when he climbed this tree, something was coming their way. Aileen huddled up to Segundo. A voice broke the deafening silence. "Are you two OK?" A soldier and his response team came out of the bushes, the man walked up to them. Segundo didn't get the chance to see his face or warn him. He immediately understood why the smuggler had gotten up that tree. Gunshots flashed in the dark canopy. Hot lead hit Davis in the chest and in the shoulder. He gasped before a third bullet went through his head. Blood splashed on the floor and the man fell flat on his back. Aileen screamed.

Segundo put his hand over her mouth to muffle her cried. Tears of horror ran down her cheeks. Perched in his tree like a crow, Quintado was spraying the platoon with bullets. A burst of gunfire killed two men instantly. One of the soldiers spun right, his head facing the sky, a bullet in his head preventing him from shooting. The fourth man tried to identify where the gunshots came from. The lens of his night-vision goggles had focused on Segundo and Aileen and he hadn't seen the bright spot hiding above. Quintado shot him in the lungs and kept on firing. Bullets whizzed through the jungle, through the bodies, through the leaves. In the dark, Quintado noticed Joe Jackson's red cap below. The tracker was running away; he was hiding behind the bushes. Quintado aimed and pulled the trigger. Another burst of gunfire destroyed the trees near Joe. The tracker saw bullets piercing yucca leaves mere inches from his eyes his eyes. Gunshots echoed in the jungle until the gun jammed. The criminal was out of ammunition. Joe took advantage of the lull to crawl to cover; his gun was beating against his side. He withdrew into the undergrowth, holding his breath. Playing cat and mouse had just cost five men their lives. "Scrap" Davis had died in appalling conditions. The squadron from Muerta was gone, all because of one blood-thirsty criminal. If only Joe could aim well and shoot him with a tranquilizer dart. Quintado had used the element of surprise to end the hunt before it actually started. Now it was time to close the trap. Quintado climbed down the tree to pick up Davis's gun and ammunitions.

He threw his own gun in the mud, useless now. The soldier's looked much better to him. Aileen was crying in Segundo's arms, the young man was voiceless. The criminal's victims were lying on the ground, the mist covering them like a blanket. Quintado took a look around and threatened his hostages with his new gun. "I've got supplies now. Let's go. Segundo, please lead the way. I can feel the call of the sea. We're almost there. You and I will soon go our separate ways, amigo. Take me to the promised land!" Segundo and Aileen, stiff with shock, stumbled before Quintado into the jungle.

Bradley Conway's voice was crackling on the radio. Julia and the Bradwick Brothers were carefully listening to the instructions on repeat. They couldn't broadcast, the frequency was too short. The rest of the party was looking out the watchtower glass wall. They were watching the forest through the misty window. Turner was listening to the conversation, scanning the ground; he was worried sick. Conway's voice made the radio tuner throb. The device was vibrating on the desk. "All activities are frozen on site C. The site is temporarily compromised. I repeat: the site is temporarily compromised. Helicopters have no authorization to land until further notice. Please proceed to the North or South outpost. A team from Isla Muerta is currently operating on the site to restore the situation. For safety purposes, personnel on the island must be evacuated in the morning. This is Conway speaking. There had been an incident on site C. Personnel of the South outpost must be on the South dock at 6 a.m. They will be evacuated by boat to site B. Meet up at 6 a.m., South harbor. Helicopters from Isla Muerta will pick up the personnel from the North village at 7 a.m., please get ready for evacuation. All activities are frozen on site C. The site is temporarily compromised. I repeat: the site is temporarily compromised."

Julia asked Chad Bradwick: "How long does it take to get to the harbor from here?

- It's a fifteen-minute drive. But all vehicles are currently requisitioned for an operation on Sorna. And everyone won't fit into your Jeep. I'd go for the tunnel.
- The tunnel?
- Yes, they've started building an underground path beneath the facility. The concrete girders are set, and there's an entrance in the basement. The tunnel leads to a road that leads to the harbor. It'll soon be asphalted. It'll only take 30 minutes to reach the docks.
- Got it, it's good to know there's a way out when we need it!
- You're right, Julia. I'll leave the power on in the lab so the genetic material won't deteriorate. We can't be held responsible for

any loss during this period of inactivity. At least the embryos will stay fresh while we're away. I really don't want to lose my job. InGen could blame me for this!

- Look outside!" Katherine Harrison yelled. The

young woman had seen something below. A group of three people was approaching the gates of the secure facility. It was Segundo and Aileen. The terrorist was with them, he was pushing them with his gun! Turner ran to the window and pressed his hands against the glass. It really was his daughter down there! Turner shouted: "Aileen! Aileen!

- She can't hear you," said Tal Bradwick.

"That's my daughter down there, we have to save her!

- I suggest we wait a little more. We can't let this man in."

Quintado stood before the electric fence. He took a few steps to the right, following the black cables. Rectangular warning signs indicated danger. "Warning. High Voltage. Keep Away." But that didn't put Quintado off; he was eying the tower skeptically. He started walking around Aileen and Segundo with a spiteful look on his face; he turned to the watchtower and shouted: "Is that all you got? No guards? As you can see, I have something that belongs to you here. A hard-working guy and a starving little girl who needs her vitamins! Poor little one, I had her walking for a long time. Open the gate and give me what I want and it'll all end peacefully. What do you say?"

Inside the tower, Julia and the Bradwick Brothers looked at each other, worried. Katherine, George and Tia could feel the tension building in the room too. From the top floor, they could see the smuggler was losing his temper, pacing back and forth along the gate. "I lost a very dear friend today. By now, your giant iguanas are feasting on his remains...so you're going to open this gate and let me take your vehicle and fuel. That's all I'm asking for. If you don't comply, I'll have to kill the girl. She might be another one on my list. I don't care much either way. And I could kill them both and get in anyway!" Chad Bradwick was shaking: "I thought Isla Muerta took care of the terrorists. What are we going to do? We can't turn the fence on, he'll know something is off.

- And it'll make him even madder. Where on earth is Joe?" wondered Julia.
- I hope they're fine." whispered Tia.
- "We can't let them in. It's too risky. There might be another way." Chad was thinking. Turner asked him: "What are you thinking about?
- Well, we can try to snipe him with lugubris.
- Lugubris? What are you talking about?" Tia answered his question. "Phyllobates Lugubris It's a species of poison frog from Costa Rica. InGen uses the toxic poison it secretes as a sedative.
- That's right, we're supposed to use it against the demons when everything else has failed, Chad said. The toxin can knock you out pretty quick I heard. We keep a loaded gun

downstairs, just in case. Maybe we could shoot the smuggler and..."

A gunshot echoed in the silence of the jungle. Quintado was running out of patience; he kicked the fence, shot his gun again in the air and walked up to Segundo. He kicked the man in the back of his knee to knock him down to the ground. Aileen started crying. Segundo gritted his teeth and squeezed his eyes shut. The smuggler punched him and pointed his gun at him again. But this time, he didn't hold his fire. Segundo howled in pain; the bullet went through his foot and clumps of dirt flew into the air. He curled up on the dirt in agony. Aileen cowered near the gate with her hands on her ears. Through the watchtower window, Turner and the others were helplessly watching the awful scene. "Open the goddamn gate!" shouted Turner. "Do as he says." seconded Julia. Chad Bradwick pushed a big red button on the control panel. "The gunshots may have attracted the Carnotaurus. If they get to us, that'll be your fault." The black iron gate opened slowly; the yellow warning lights blinked. Quintado smiled. "That's about time! I thought I'd have to blow the young lady's head off. But you've wasted a lot of my time. I'm now behind schedule because of your bullshit. I'd be sipping a cocktail on my boat with my man Smokey if it wasn't for you refusing to open your stronghold. I think I need compensation for my time. Your colleague's lost a foot, look at him, bleeding like a pig. I want to shoot the girl in the foot too. We want everyone to be the same in the army, right? It's non-negotiable. Sorry sweetheart, but we're at war." Quintado aimed at Aileen's leg, his finger gripped the trigger. Suddenly, he felt something like an electric shock in his neck. Something had stung his arm. He looked down through bleary eyes. A dart. The smuggler felt a weakness in his right arm and his vision blurred. Had he been shot? Was he going to die? He stumbled back. Aileen ran to Segundo, crying. Quintado could feel his whole body shutting down. His eyes wouldn't focus and shapes were becoming distorted. He'd been shot with a poison dart! He felt so sleepy. He walked away from Aileen and Segundo and followed the fence, limping. That's when he saw Joe and his red cap behind the trees. The smuggler shot his gun in Joe's direction but missed. The tracker had finally got him. Quintado was about to faint. He needed to find some place to hide before passing out. He mustered his last strength and ran into the forest. He emptied his magazine on the way. Bullets whizzed in Joe's ears, who was trying to catch him. "Let him go, he won't get very far with your dart. You saved the girl!" Tia Porter laughed. The scientist appeared on the threshold with Julia and Turner. "Are you OK?" Turner took his daughter in his arms, she burst into tears against his chest. "Thank God, you're OK.

- The bad man... Is he gone?
- Yes sweetie, he is." Turner watched the plants

swaying in the sea breeze, the mist was clearing up. The blinking yellow lights shone on the trees and tall grass; the forest had swallowed up the thug. The flora had drowned him in darkness. Turner gazed at the mossy creepers moving back and forth in the wind. "It's over baby. He's gone."

It was a mild night. Mist surrounded the island, steam and froth clung to the rocks. Smokey ran his hand over his bald head and wiped his sweaty on his combats. The man had eaten his last chocolate bar and he was still hungry. Worse, he was worried about his partners. Quintado and Ernesto had left him alone north of the island. He'd followed orders and sailed to the south with the dinghy; he'd even moored a hundred yards away from the docks for more discretion. But he hadn't heard from them yet; he couldn't reach Quintado. None of them would answer his calls. Did they both lose their walkie-talkies? Was the signal spotty because of the mist, or the ocean? Smokey had never been here before. He didn't know the island or the archipelago. He knew Quintado was a tough cookie, but a bad feeling was creeping up on him. Why hadn't they reached out to him already? Time wasn't up yet but the mercenary knew something was off. Should he take a look around while he waited? He could patrol and refuel the go-fast before they came. Surely it was fine to leave the boat and the precious loot unattended for a few minutes.

Mist was so thick on the southern coast, nobody would see him or the boat. As if anyone would sail here in the middle of the night. Smokey was confident. He was just going to stretch his legs until his partners arrived. Maybe he could even meet them halfway. Something knocked against the hull. The man stepped out on the deck and looked ahead at the prow. Was it the waves, crashing noisily on the boat? Or a piece of driftwood? The smuggler adjusted the strap of his gun and scanned the sea with his flashlight. Smokey jumped back in disgust and swore in Spanish! It wasn't a log knocking on the hull, or a big fish, but a corpse! A human body washed away by the sea was banging on the hull. The mercenary took a closer look at the dead man. He was floating face down, wearing shorts and a Hawaiian shirt, both in shreds. His body was torn apart. Part of his blond scalp had been ripped off his skull; his blueish, bloated skin floated on the water. The drowned man had been eaten by fish. His lacerated limbs were covered in seaweed. His head banged harder on the hull. "Another victim of the seas." Smokey thought. Probably someone who got lost at sea and washed ashore around here. Or maybe he was killed by South-American pirates. These islands were unmapped, no one would come here and claim the body. The island itself would officiate the funeral; the man would go back to the volcanic depths. He'd join the pirates and victims that came before him. Just one more ghost haunting the archipelago. Coral would grow on his bones; it was the harsh reality of the sea. Smokey shone the beam on the back of the corpse. The poor man had a hole in his back, revealing rotting flesh and ribs. A crab suddenly crept out of his chest and crawled on the bones of the traveler of the high seas. Smokey frowned and cursed at the crab, taking a step back. There was no way he'd spend one more minute on this stupid boat, he wouldn't be another man lost at sea! He was going to take a look at the docks and find his partners. Smokey tied his laces and spat into the sea before stepping down onto the beach. Sand mixed with dried palm leaves crumbling on the shore.

He glanced at the boat and went up the pier and up the sandy dunes under the moonlight; the mist escorted him on his climb. His stomach was rumbling. Unfortunately, there was no snack vending machine in the harbor. Smokey walked on the wooden dock, his boots squeaking on the wet wood. The beach had been fitted with metal platforms facilitating loading and unloading operations. They looked new. Large mesh containers in a variety of colors were stored on the sand. A Caterpillar construction vehicle was turning to rust next to a wooden shack. This cabin looked older, the dark wood saturated with water. Fuel drums were piled up under a corrugated iron roof. Used military netting was fluttering in the tropical breeze. There was enough gas to refuel the go-fast, leave this island and reach the continent. Smokey would fill the tank later. For now, he was treading on a marked dirt road. A metal post hidden behind the ferns indicated the way to the "South Compound". The man stepped onto a trail leading up into the mountains. The moonlight got dimmer, and the pale glimmer on the stringy trunks of the palm trees disappeared. The salty breeze swept across the shore and through the jungle; the tall grass bent sideways, in harmony with the whistling of the wind. The mercenary held his gun tight against his stomach as he trod on the path. Everything was quiet, but it was better to be safe than sorry. Smokey wouldn't be the town idiot, as Quintado liked to call him. He could be efficient and helpful too. His partners might be injured; meeting them halfway would help them pack up and leave faster. For several minutes, he walked under the pine forest canopy. Pine needles filled the night with their intoxicating scent. In the beam of the flashlight, the ground was red and spiky; dry reddish needles covered the path, which looked like a river of blood in the darkness. Smokey pointed his flashlight at the trees and saw gigantic roots on the side of the path. They led to a colossal baobab tree! A sacred tree in many cultures, a large tree that must be respected. Roots intertwined and rose up to the starry sky. A long dark shape was partly concealed by the branches. Smokey saw steel under the bark; he shone his flashlight directly at it and slowly climbed onto the roots. It was a plane! A plane was stuck into the tree; it was unbelievable! The aircraft was old and rusty. It was a WW2 American fighter plane. Smokey identified the plane type from the faded colors and the star logo. A North American P51 Mustang. His little brother had a model when they were kids. The famous warplane must have crashed here about forty years ago, and the baobab tree had grown around it.

The sturdy roots wrapped around the aircraft, and only the wings stuck out. The fighter plane was trapped in wood and leaves, stuck upright among gnarly branches. Young shoots sprouted at the very top and grew all over the tail. But what was a P51 doing here off the coast of Costa Rica? South America had stayed outside the Second World War, no fighting, no destruction. Very few men were enlisted, only a couple thousand Mexicans and Brazilians. How could an American fighter plane land here, so far away from the war zones of the time? Was it on a secret mission at the margins of the war? Or did it run out of fuel and drift away on the Pacific Ocean? The mysterious plane was buried under the foliage. Smokey stepped closer to the cockpit, only to discover a body still inside! The skeleton had been there for ages, sleeping in the war machine. Branches had grown through his ribcage and neck. Young roots crept through his open mouth, intertwining with higher branches. Life sprouted and grew from the jaw of this man; it was both an abomination and a thing of beauty. Life had reclaimed this plane. In a few years, the pilot would be but a fossil, dust, the mark of a human past in a forever untamed jungle. Had no one noticed this plane before?

Why had they left it here? Was it some kind of local curiosity? The smuggler then remembered the stories his grandfather used to tell. How he complained about the government back then. A few anecdotes came to his mind. In the 40s, some drug smugglers from Central America shamelessly used P51s to export merchandise. The Mustang was blatantly copied by drug lords hiding behind the heroic logo and making the most of the war, inconspicuously. Could the corpse lying under the leaves belong to a smuggler from the 40s? When war was raging, some of them used unused air lanes to carry cocaine out of the country. Was the pilot a war hero or a crook? To find out, Smokey would need to go through the shipment and search the plane for drugs and money. Could this rusty old wreck actually be a treasure chest? But the baobab tree had swallowed it up along with all its secrets and no one would ever find out. Smokey heard twigs snapping to the left.

The man came down the rooty steps and went back to the trail. He felt a presence a few yards away from him. He shone his flashlight around, but saw no one. Was it Quintado and Ernesto? He couldn't help but call them: "It's Smokey! Guys, is that you? Rodrigo! Ernesto! Can you hear me?" The smuggler was looking for his partners, trying to find his way in the dark. The baobab tree moved. The roots disappeared behind the branches in the obscurity. A thick dark shape made the trees quiver. Was it a trunk? Smokey could see the foliage shivering above the baobab roots. The tree was shape-shifting. Was the bark actually changing color? A long shadow blended into the forest; it was standing right in front of him. Was it a baobab blown away by the wind? Spontaneous uprooting? The mercenary lost visual contact with the moving rock and felt something breathing down his neck. Nature was breathing behind him. Smokey turned around in fear, his hand grabbing his gun. Slime dripped on his bald, shiny head. It couldn't be rain, it was stickier. Drool, maybe? Smokey shrieked in terror when he saw the animal. A huge creature was facing him, leaning on the roots of the baobab tree. Like a chameleon, it had camouflaged into its wooded surrounding to approach the mercenary. It was fearsome, a fiendish harpy, an evil beast so hideous that the man thought he was having a heart attack!

The devil was ten feet high, its several feet long tail disappeared in the bushes. Its thick and sturdy repulsive skull contrasted with its thin lower jaw. It opened its pink mouth, revealing rows of sharp teeth. Smokey could smell the creature's foul breath on his face as he yelled in fear. The horned creature roared and ran toward the smuggler. Smokey ran for his life up the path, crying in terror. The carnivorous shadow was after him, ready to close its jaws on him.

"Lay him down on the table, make room." Turner sat Segundo down in the small lab. Joe took his shoe off; Julia removed his sock. The young man moaned. Little Aileen asked her father: "Is he going to be OK?

- Yes darling, he is. Why don't you join Katherine and the others upstairs? It's late and it's time for bed. Go upstairs and I'll come see you as soon as I'm done here." Turner then spoke to Chad Bradwick who had come back down from the watch room, coffee in hand. "Do you have surgical scissors and tools?

- There's a small surgical kit box on the desk." He handed the box to Turner who opened it and grabbed a hemostat and gauze swabs. Julia was worried. "Are you sure you want to do this, Kenneth?

- Segundo can't wait for the rescue squad or he'll lose his foot. I need to remove the bullet, it didn't go through. It's still in the bone." Tal Bradwick joined them: "I'm not sure we have the proper equipment to operate.

- Segundo saved my daughter's life. He managed to bring her here. I owe him. Do you have alcohol?" Joe found a bottle of Centenario on a counter. "Does rum count?

- There's rubbing alcohol here!" Julia handed Turner a bottle. The Bradwick Brothers watched Turner digging the surgical pliers into Segundo's bare foot as the young worker screamed and bit into a piece of fabric. Turner focused on the crude surgery, bright red blood staining his white plastic gloves. Segundo couldn't take the pain anymore. He passed out as Turner took the bullet out of his aching extremity.

"I'm afraid the extensor digitorum longus is damaged. The tibialis anterior doesn't look too good either. It'll take months of physiotherapy to get better and the middle cuneiform needs to be filled up, too. I need to suture. Do you have thread?" Chad handed Turner a spool and needles. Julia cleaned the wound. "He's lucky you're here Kenneth, I'd never have dared. I'd have been too scared to ruin his foot.

- If he heals fine, he'll walk again. But he'll permanently lose some motor functions. The terrorist who did that to him needs to pay!
- I can't wait to kick his butt myself!" mumbled Joe.
- You did the right thing, using this tranquilizer dart Joe. He's probably sleeping under a tree by now! People from Isla Muerta will deal with him." said Julia. "But not the ones I came with. I watched them die. The smuggler murdered them." Joe took off his cap and put it on the counter. He scratched his head, gazing at the table, and said: "The serum will work for a few hours. I just hope a dinosaur will eat him in his sleep. That'd settle the issue.

- Speaking of dinosaurs, come, quickly!" Katherine yelled. The young woman came running up the stairs and told everyone to meet her on the top floor. They'd seen something! Chad and Tal joined Tia, George and Aileen upstairs. Both redheads stood in front of the control panel to look out the watchtower window. Below, left from the door, a heap of creepers and roots was moving along the fence. Chad stared anxiously at his brother. "It's them." Tia turned to Katherine and George: "Their genetic code was filled with chameleon DNA. The Carnotaurus can camouflage, which makes them extremely dangerous.

- Maybe you should power up that fence!" Katherine asked.
- "You're perfectly right, I'll activate the generator. I need to enter all data into the computer code to..." Chad was suddenly interrupted as a frightening metallic squeal covered his voice. An animal was attacking the fence. It pushed one of the thick black bars of the stronghold and the horizontal wires bent and twisted under the mighty limb of the young creature. They couldn't see it because it had camouflaged itself, but they all knew the threat was real.
- "What are you waiting for? Put the perimeter back on!" screamed Katherine. You should have warned me earlier! The computer needs time to process data!"

Chad was typing hard on the keyboard of a big white monitor built into the control panel. He typed a line of code and hit "Enter". A dozen white lines of code scrolled down the screen; Chad entered a new code and confirmed. A button lit up on the tower dashboard. Small light bulbs blinked on the walkway outside the window and on the fence columns. Sparks spurted from the damaged fence. Blue electric currents arced off the steel and pierced the ground below. The nocturnal beast roared and jumped back, surprised by the electricity. Its shriek sent shivers up each survivor's spine; it was croaky and coarse and terrifying. The mighty dinosaur lumbered back into the darkness and melted into the landscape. The fence lights all went out at the same time and smoke rose from the damaged fence and from the generator at the bottom of the building.

"The power's out!" yelled Tal. "The demon's attack tripped the power supply. It seems that some fuses have blown; we need to get down there and restart the generator manually!

- Are you sure you want to go outside? Look!" Katherine pointed her finger at the window. Outside, the dinosaur was back and ready to charge again. Aileen screamed and hid behind George. The huge lizard charged into the fence. As the barrier collapsed inward, the Carnotaurus stomped on it with his hind legs. Cables snapped, and the beast tore away the irritating wire mesh with its massive jaws. Then it entered the perimeter. Its large clawed feet sank into the mud next to the secure watchtower. Under the yellow lights of the tower, its skin changed color. It went back to its original hue, as if the artificial light had revealed it. The biped was 10 feet high and 23 feet long; it was a mighty, evil-looking, blood-thirsty reptile. Its cruel yellow eyes were set in front of its skull. The head was covered in thick skin with small spiky scales, and two horns grew above each eye socket. The animal looked like an actual demon. Its tiny arms and body were as black as soot. A whitish abdomen contrasted with the other colors of the carnivorous beast. It bore red markings on its back and upper thighs. Its nightmarish posture spoke of prehistoric strength; this monster was coming right from Hell. Its lower jaw was thinner than the rest of its large and sturdy head. The terrible demon stepped closer and sniffed the Jeep. Then, it looked up and stopped moving. The Carnotaurus was watching the people in the watchtower. It went to the building door, head down, sniffing the ground. All were voiceless as they watched the dinosaur freely explore the inside of the outpost. The electric fence was useless. The theropod pressed its snout against the ground floor door and rubbed its head against the wall, pushing. The watchtower shook. The demon let out another evil screech and threw itself against the tower, scratching at the concrete. Pieces of cement littered the grass as the animal dug its claws into the tower wall. Its long tail whipped through the air, knocking over jerrycans. The reptilian devil was trying to climb the tower to get to its prey.

Tal stepped out on the top-floor walkway, grasping the guardrail with all his strength. The man walked to the building searchlight. "I'll try to blind it, someone go get the Lugubris! Now! We need to put Hades to sleep!

- Hades? You gave them names?" Katherine was puzzled.

- "Of course! This is Hades and the other one is Pluto. They might be young, but they're already gods." Chad Bradwick smiled at the journalist and at George and left the room to get the gun. George couldn't believe his eyes. Tia, for her part, was silent. She'd never been so worried in her whole life. The Carnotaurus closed its jaws on the Jeep; it bit at the iron cabin bar and tried to lift the truck. The vehicle hovered in the air for a second and the animal let it go. It landed with a deafening crash.

The dinosaur banged its head on the right fender, the small horns squealing on the metal. It raised its head and tried to go up the tower again, clawing at the concrete. Tia whispered: "It sees us. It won't let go. It wants to get to us...

- Let it try!" said Chad as he stepped into the room. He switched the tranquilizer gun safety off and stepped onto the walkway behind the window. "I've got just what it needs!" His brother was shining the large white spotlight at the dinosaur. The creature was blinded by the light. Chad bent over the guardrail to shoot the dinosaur below. He took his time to aim at the neck while the beast was standing still, squinting. Suddenly, the brothers heard human screams. Someone was running at the hole in the fence. It was a bald armed man wearing a muddy shirt. Was he someone from inGen, or another smuggler?

The man was yelling: "Please help me! There's a devil after me!" He turned around and shot at the darkness. The gunshots drew the lizard away from the searchlight to get to Smokey. The man cursed in Spanish when he saw the specimen inside the compound! He thought he could escape the monster following him by entering the perimeter. Never had he expected to find another inside the gates! Chad Bradwick shot Hades, but it was too late. When the Lugubris dart stuck into its back, the animal had already caught the smuggler in his strong, sharp jaws. Smokey let out a hopeless gasp as he felt the long teeth slice through his skin like tissue paper. The animal's bladelike teeth tore through his organs; the monster lifted the mercenary in the air and shook its head violently from left to right. Smokey's ribs, guts and lungs were torn to pieces beneath the deadly jaws. The man stopped screaming. He wasn't thinking about his family or his life. Only about what had just happened. He'd left the boat behind him and he wouldn't be back to watch it. What was going to happen to the precious loot? Did Quintado and Ernesto die in the jaws of these terrible creatures? Why couldn't he feel his legs anymore? Who was going to enjoy this unclaimed booty? Smokey and the treasure belonged to the island now. The man had become the animal's toy. He accepted his fate. Blood flooded his lungs. The surrounding lights became blurry, his head dizzy. Pain turned into the darkness of death as the mercenary's skeleton snapped like a twig. Blood spattered the theropod's mouth.

Was there a god? Was there life after death? The time had come for Smokey to find out.

The Carnotaurus shook the poor man's shredded body and threw it with all its might at the tower. The corpse crashed through the window, which shattered under the violent impact. Shards of glass knocked several half-full coffee cups onto the control panel, and their contents doused the delicate machinery with liquid. The snaps and squeal of short-circuiting machinery filled the room and the power went out. Smokey's body finally tumbled to a stop against one wall, his legs only connected to his chest by a few bloody muscles. There was blood and glass on every desk.

Katherine and Aileen screamed and sobbed hysterically in terror. Below the tower, the animal that had been chasing Smokey emerged from the dark forest and snuffled in recognition as it joined the other. It sniffed the gates and the destroyed fence, then looked at the other Carnotaurus and roared at the moon. Its fellow turned his back on the tower and lumbered beyond the perimeter of the compound, swaying its tail; the Lugubris was affecting him, and the animal probably wanted to find a cool place to rest too. The two dinosaurs melted back into the surrounding forest, their skin changing color yet again. Stunned, Katherine and Aileen went down to meet Turner, Joe and Segundo. Chad left the walkway to warn George and Tia. "They're going back into the jungle, they must have heard a cow! We're going to wait till they come back and shoot them with tranquilizer darts if they attack us again. Given the current situation, it'll be better for you to spend the night in the basement. Get ready to leave camp by morning." Standing behind the control panel, Tal was examining the smuggler's corpse. He suddenly felt sick. He turned around, grabbed the guardrail and vomited his coffee onto the ground below. He turned back to the body, wiping his mouth; Tia and George joined the others. They each silently acknowledged that the unthinkable had happened. Thinking back on the events of the last twenty minutes, Tal suddenly realized he was at the bottom of the food chain. His fragile body was just a toy to be played with in their evil games, a rotting carcass they would swallow in the blink of an eye. The island was huge, a ferocious, inescapable, cold-blooded predator. It was indifferent, inflexible, full of merciless midnight devils. The mountain breeze blew the mist down; clouds hung above the trampled piece of fence. The night song of the silver-throated tanagers welcomed the first light of day.

Sunshine was piercing through the clouds, though the jungle was still shrouded in darkness. A dense canopy covered valleys and clearings. Riverbeds snaked wildly through the forests, trees followed their courses across the island and lined the mountains as far as the eye could see. The dark sea was taking an orange hue as pale moonlight gave way to fiery sunrise. Dawn glinted off the clouds, blowing over the land and through the trees to follow streams. Air was scarce at this altitude. Ernesto had to take it easy. It had been a long night. He was gazing at the red dawn flowing into the mist between the wild summits; it looked like lava was spreading on the island. Matanceros was falling victim to a raging and magical volcanic flow coming from the heavens above, exalting the magnificent beauty of life. Ernesto hit the road again, watching this magnificent illusion; he had to reach the south. Was he still alive? He wondered to himself, dragging his wrecked body. The last hours had been a key moment in the smuggler's destiny. What had happened to his friend Quintado? Did he make it with the hostages? Answers didn't really matter anymore. With each step he took along the cliff, Ernesto felt that he was digging his own grave a little deeper. He was exhausted, drained. His wounds hurt and he had lost a lot of blood. In this waking nightmare, he'd managed to apply a tourniquet to his arm. But the bandages on his thigh and ankle only soaked up the little blood he had left. The kid from San José was going through hell. The tedious night was wearing on. Using the last of his ammunition, he had managed to get rid of these appalling lizards and run away into the forest. He escaped the construction vehicle without dying, but he didn't own his freedom to his fighting skills, even though he had killed one of the creatures on his way out. He owed his life to fate and nature; the mighty predators had suddenly rejected they prey. They'd walked away from Ernesto to chase another victim. The orange reptiles had suddenly stopped hunting him, as if lured by a sound only they could hear. They'd communicated with a few yelps before leaving. Their grisly croaks still echoed in the smuggler's head and made his arm hurt more. Ernesto was sweating and shaking as he staggered along the pipeline. After a few hour walk in the darkness of the island, he'd found this old rusty pipe. He'd had good fortune amidst his misfortune, this old pipeline could help him find his bearings, the best way to know he was heading south to Smokey and the boat; easy does it. If he didn't collapse before he got there. The old pipe ran along the south-east coast of Matanceros, "the killer island". It'd been built in the 60s to carry all fluids found underground: mainly petrol and gas. Ernesto didn't remember exactly, he was just a kid at that time. Yet he remembered walking along this pipe with Quintado when they were younger. When all the natural resources had been drained from the island ground, the pipeline had probably fallen into disuse. Yet it was still there, still standing. Its brown rusty steel stood out from the bright green bushes, stretching out into the horizon like an ancient relic. Numbers written in white chalk on the reddish metal of the cylinder indicated measures every ten yards. Ernesto had braved the night and its monsters, but he didn't know how long he could keep going before collapsing. Would anyone come to his rescue or would he die here, alone, on an island he barely recognized? On his right, the man noticed a banana plantation. The terrain was rough and there were not so many palm trees up there. Still, fruit trees grew and thrived in the mountain. There were bananas in those trees, and Ernesto was hungry. He needed sugar to survive; he had to eat. Unfortunately, the trees were far too high and their trunks too spiky. Ernesto couldn't climb. He could barely stand. That's when he saw a thicket with a round banana tree growing below. The bananas looked fresh and sweet. Despite the pain he felt crawling down the hill, his mouth was watering. He was looking forward to binging on fruit. He kept the meager reward in mind as he supported his busted limbs with branches on the slope leading to the canyon. The tree was growing on the side of the cliff. If he fell, he would most definitely die. He secured his right foot on a sturdy dry clump of soil to get closer to the little tree and knelt on the horizontal trunk. Bending over the edge of the rocky overhang, Ernesto grabbed a fat yellow banana and ripped it off the tree. He sat down, peeled it and stuffed it into his mouth. His stomach was growling, and he couldn't feel his arm. He needed help...but for now, he'd recuperate and try not to pass out. He avoided looking down into the canyon so he wouldn't feel dizzy. He bent over once more to pick another sweet banana from the tree and ate it whole. He threw the peels in the emptiness and lay down on the hilly side. The banana was delicious and the landscape was beautiful. So beautiful it took his breath away. It might have been down to the beauty of the island or the lack of oxygen maybe... he had no coca leaves to chew on, but bananas would do the trick. He moved closer to the bunch to grab another one. Suddenly, a huge spider jumped on Ernesto's hand. He stood up, screaming.

The large arachnid ran as fast as lightning up his arm to his neck. It was a banana spider! Originally from Brazilian banana plantations, it was known to be venomous and aggressive. The repulsive arachnid clambered over Ernesto's skin with its four pairs of spiky legs. The man tried to get rid of it with the back of his hand and spun around to get his chin away from the deadly spider. The little banana tree trunk lurched forward, roots emerging from the ocher soil. The smuggler lost his balance and fell over. His felt the fangs of the arachnid sinking into his throat and he howled in pain. His hand brushed against the bug as it scrambled down his vest. Ernesto felt the venom entering his nervous system through his neck. His muscles stiffened and he slipped on the soil as he tried to hold on to the edge of the cliff. Unfortunately, the roots were too young and they gave out under his weight. The man yelled and plummeted into the abyss. He'd been too greedy! In his fall, Ernesto managed to grab a creeper, then a plant. He mustered his strength to catch hold of a large agave leaf to stop his deathly fall. His right arm snapped taut with the strain of his entire body weight and he yelped as his shoulder popped out of its socket. His legs dangled over thin air, his hand gripping a bundle of serrated leaves as hard as he could. The spiky, stiff gray-blue shoots of the agave pierced Ernesto's skin and made his hand bleed. His entire life hung on a thread covered in stabbing thorns. Blood ran down his face. The pain was unbearable. The man felt the spider toxin flowing through his muscles. Was the bug still on him? He didn't care actually. Ernesto looked down at the canyon below, orange clouds washed over him like a flow of lava, hiding the canopy. A wonderful fluffy ocean was awaiting him. His arm was getting weaker, the plant ripped his hand to shreds. Ernesto let go of the leaves and fell down without a sound. He held his breath as he disappeared into the clouds. He felt his stomach heave and he wanted to shout. His skull cracked open on a rock and his broken body landed on a wet ledge a hundred yards below.

The sun smiled on Matanceros' sentence, shining its warm morning rays upon the hills. Rocks swallowed yet another fossil. The trees agreed unanimously: the Earth's judgment was irrevocable.

Sun was rising on site C. Segundo Leticia would be at the rendezvous point soon; he was slowly recovering from his hellish night. His foot was tender, but it didn't hurt that much, probably because of the morphine Kenneth Turner had given him when he sutured his foot. Would he be able to walk normally again one day? Or did this crook Quintado steal his foot in his escape? For now, he was leaning on Joe's and George's shoulders. Like them, he was getting ready to evacuate to site B. He was hopping on one leg to preserve his wounded foot. Earlier this morning, the party had left the South compound to reach the coast through the tunnel. The Bradwick Brothers had been leading the way with burning torches for about twenty minutes. They fed the fire with white liquor, squeezing a plastic bottle to saturate the pieces of cloth; the fabric was burning around a makeshift wooden handle. Segundo had never stepped foot in this tunnel, nor had he participated in the building process, which was far from complete. Hopefully, the party had found a recently refurbished path.

However, at a second glance, the road looked more like a rough and wearying trail. Each step leading to the harbor was more than 20 inches high! The young man's leg was numb, his mind was racing as he watched the ferns. Leaves were drying up on the orange ground and on the roots; the sea breeze was getting more breathable and nice. The drug helped him walk. Behind him, Turner carried Aileen on his shoulders. The little girl was asleep, her head resting on her father's. Turner was worn out and struggled on the path. Tia and Katherine were walking behind them, bringing up the rear. Both were silent. Segundo still couldn't process what had happened last night. This awful adventure was real. And fate had taken him to southern territories. It'd led him to the demon's lair. This compound was where they kept the embryos and DNA samples of the Carnotaurus. This exhausting journey had taken him to the tower lab. He'd seen the electric pillars and the DNA capsules, and he'd even caught a glimpse of refrigerated micro-boxes while Turner was tending to his wounds. Glass vials were what the mystery man on the phone had asked for.

Glass vials that could fit in a pocket. The mystery man wanted those samples, and had in fact already paid for them. This treasure with the name "demon" written all over it could only be of interest to another bio-genetics firm...by stealing them, the young man would be crossing the line into industrial espionage. Still...he had found himself where they kept the embryos, and it wasn't a coincidence. It might have been fate. A Godsend. A reward for everything he'd gone through. After all, he had protected Aileen without a care for his own life...but there was nothing noble in stealing those vials. With the strength they had left, Joe and George reached the beach. Segundo thanked them and relieved their shoulders of his weight. The choice had been a difficult one to make; Segundo was tired, he felt like he was floating. He started wondering about the night's events. Did he survive the Suchomimus? Was he shot in the foot? Did he take micro-boxes from inGen? He made a fist against his chest and felt his vest. The sky was getting clearer, the palm trees were basking in the morning sun. Segundo was out of breath, but they'd made it to the beach. A few yards below, men from inGen were heading their way. A boat was moored to the beach. It was a landing craft, an armored vessel towing large flat-bottomed floating platforms. Frothy waves broke against the iron. The platform carried cages, vehicles and equipment. The convoy of boats sailed between the islands of the archipelago. Segundo had already parked machines and cranes on one of those ships. He saw Bradley Conway standing behind the paramilitary soldiers, giving orders. He got them all on board. The sound of the waves crashing on the volcanic reef covered the soldiers' voices. Dark clouds were clearing and the vastness of the sea blinded the crew. Silver waters glinted off the hull of the boat. The Bradwick Brothers threw their torches into the water when they saw Raymond Chua on the boat. He waved at the passengers and invited Segundo into the cabin. The men from inGen were striding along the yellow beach, they were coming and going in the sand. The engine of the ship was humming. Conway called out to two soldiers and asked them to brief him before they sailed off to site B. The two men stopped in front of a tall palm tree to give him an update on the situation.

Hiding behind the bushes about two yards away from them, a dark shadow was lurking, ready to step in. Cold wind coming from the sea swept the dunes. Quintado wiped his face with the back of his hand, a grain of sand had gotten in his eye. He was lying on the floor, motionless, like a snake ready to spring on its prey. He was listening to one of the soldiers. "We've found a ship a little lower. No one was on board but we found a really big chest. It's probably the smugglers' boat." Conway answered: "These guys have no clue what they've gotten themselves into. Tow the boat to site B. We'll sink it once we get there, but first we retrieve the shipment. Their loot is ours now; take care of this and get ready to board."

Hiding behind the tall grass at the soldiers' feet, Quintado couldn't believe what he'd just heard. These men were going to take his weapons and drugs away from him! This once-in-a-lifetime contract was going to vanish into thin air. His precious money, lost forever on a strange island. The smuggler just couldn't stand the thought of it. After being shot with Joe Jackson's sedative dart, he'd fought sleep and had hidden in a sequoia tree trunk where he'd finally passed out. After three or four hours of deep sleep, a big centipede had woken him from his troubled, chemical dreams. The bug had crawled under his vest. Tired and disoriented, he'd put the energy he had left to make a move south. He'd left Ernesto and it seemed that Smokey had gone missing too; the boat was empty. What should he do? He heard Conway and the guards walking away on the shore. The smuggler was feeling sick, his limbs were weak and he could barely look above the ferns. He felt groggy and exhausted - the sedative was still in his system. He got up, feverishly leaning on his gun. He still had some ammunition left and he was determined to use it.

The convoy was about to sail away. He had to act fast. Quintado noticed the empty cages on the platforms. Stooping, he walked along the path to one of the barges and came out of the bushes, treading slowly and calmly to the ship. He got on board without anyone noticing. It was easy to blend in with all these armed men and that effervescence. He stepped closer to a container. It was empty and had no lock. He inconspicuously slipped inside, leaving the door open. Quintado couldn't launch his attack now, there were far too many men and he wanted to get away from the horrible creatures living on this island. He crouched inside the cage and scraped the straw with his gun. He'd take his loot to the continent even if he had to kill every living soul onboard. Quintado was tired, but he was determined. He'd make Joe pay for what he did. He was capable of anything and ready to prove it. His revenge would not be merciful.

The platform was rocking. Tia was listening to the lapping of the waves on the steel, gazing into the distance. She was leaving site C and wasn't really paying any attention to what Chua was saying. He was sitting on a beam behind her. The man was smoothing his thin black mustache and nervously playing with the cap lying on his lap. Sweat made his glasses slip down his little nose; his cheeks shone in the morning sunlight. The heads of inGen were talking to Tia away from prying ears. "We are so relieved to find you safe and sound Mrs. Porter. You'll be safer in your new facilities, before everything on site C is settled.

- How long do you think it'll take?
- That's a tricky question. After last night's events, inGen thinks site C isn't safe anymore. Moreover, it raises a lot of serious issues concerning the handling of our activities. None of this would have happened if we had held our ground.
- If Conway's men had stayed on site C, the two workers would still be alive.
- True. But with ifs and buts, we could change the world Mrs. Porter.
- Isn't that what we're doing already?
- Yes, we're changing the world, bringing it back to life, it's amazing. But everything has a price...and that's why we've decided to stop our activities on site C.

- What? Are you closing the island?" asked the baffled geneticist.
- "With everything that happened and those smugglers roaming around, we have to stick in one place. We'll concentrate our facilities on site B.
- What will happen to the cricket factory?
- We've decided to close it. When we get back to the island to demolish the buildings and transfer the dinosaurs, we'll let your insects go, or we'll incinerate them. Then, we'll move the lab.
- And what about the calcium formula and the food-processing plant?
- We'll give it to the cows and goats we're keeping in the farming facility. Matanceros will become our pantry and maybe, someday, the world's. But for now, we need to improve the finances of inGen Mrs. Porter.
- The company is constantly injecting money but never bailing itself out, am I right?
- You are. This is a substantial investment. We're talking 10 million dollars just for amber purchase.
- I guess the international amber industry isn't letting inGen do the dirty work. Amber is used and coveted everywhere, it's no surprise priests in ancient Egypt used it to seal sarcophagi Mr. Chua.
- Its chemical structure absorbs water molecules and because of its antibacterial properties it can be used as a prophylactic ointment and to prevent decay. I know.

Amber is great but it costs the company millions of dollars. We're developing a super computer that'll make cloning safer.

- It is already safe. Haven't you seen dinosaurs walking around on site C? What more proof do you need? The device works.

- Are you sure Mrs. Porter? During all attempts until now, 99% of all specimens died. Our new computer will reduce this rate and make DNA extraction easier.

- Site C computers weren't good enough for you Raymond? Too slow maybe?

- Our blocks of amber have clean air. They contain all kinds of microscopic particles: pieces of pollen, of flies, of petals or twigs. Each element has its own DNA. If your lab assistants don't use the needle with precision, they can collect genetic material that has nothing to do with dinosaurs.

- It's very time-consuming, confirmed Tia.

- And let's not even mention mosquito DNA. If you go through the abdomen, you'll get through the skin and muscle.

- So, what do you suggest? A new computer capable of sawing amber in half? I hope you know what you're doing, because once it's out of its protecting envelope, the insect will be exposed to any airborne DNA particle. It'll be exposed to viruses and bacteria living on your skin or in your tuna sandwich.

- That's right. But the embryo department we're building on site B is perfectly sterile. You'll work there and you'll forget all about your little factories. We're using Plexiglas cases equipped with gloves and UV lamps.

- UV light destroys DNA molecules.
- Precisely Mrs. Porter. It sterilizes the pressurized box. Clean air is filtered and injected into the box at a slightly higher pressure than atmospheric pressure. The box remains closed at all times. Beforehand, amber is immersed in liquid nitrogen to make it easier to work with. Then, the mosquito is dissected using an electronic microscope and then placed into vials.
- That's more or less what we already do on site C by collecting the stomach.
- Yes, but what we're interested in are mosquito cells. To access DNA, we need to open the cells with a solution that will dissolve the membranes.
- My formulation is quite effective already, we don't need to go to site B to practice this kind of procedure.
- Your detergent, Mrs. Porter, was pretty efficient on lipids, that's true. But our new enzyme will neutralize the proteins attacking DNA. Then, we'll isolate it with a powerful organic solvent.
- If you're talking about carbolic acid, it causes skin burns and even liver cancer!
- Yes but, to be fair, it isolates DNA much more efficiently. DNA molecules will rise to the surface while the carbolic acid burns the cell membranes. In the meantime, proteins that

aren't soluble in water or carbolic acid will form a precipitate.

- And to isolate as much DNA as possible, you shake the tube and get a homogeneous mixture. I know that already Mr. Chua. I don't see how your new facilities will improve the procedure.
- The new centrifuge separates water from carbolic acid, Mrs. Porter. You get three layers in the tube. On top, water containing DNA, then the milky precipitate with all the proteins and finally, the carbolic acid with all we can discard! You just have to collect the water with a pipette to get a little DNA.
- And have your scientists on site B found a solution for the liver?
- The liver? I'm afraid I'm not following, Mrs. Porter.
- A lot of the DNA we collect on this archipelago has no particular function and can differ from one species to another. This procedure's proving particularly challenging because it's almost impossible to find the DNA sections responsible for the development of the liver.
- Why the liver? Sorry, I'm just a medical doctor and a scientist, not a geneticist like yourself...
- It's a main organ fulfilling a lot of metabolic functions. A tiny gap in the genetic code can be fatal to the future embryos. I hope your lab assistants can align A, C, T and G correctly.

- That's why I want you to be the head of the department, to help them. When our new mixture reaches 160°F, inGen enzyme become active. Our enzyme, DNA polymerase synthesizes the missing strand of DNA and multiplies it. We can fill the sequence more easily and complete the double helix. If the polymerase has a T, it'll find an A to face it; and same thing...
- With a C and a G. I see.
- Come supervise our teams on site B Mrs. Porter. I'm sure you'll enjoy your new job.
- You've just basically fired me from my job on site C, I can't carry on my research...do I really have a choice?
- Well if you wish to continue the adventure with us, I'm afraid you don't.
- That's what I thought. I'm surprised you want to leave site C, what happens to developing your anti-diabetes vitamin?
- It's not really a vitamin...and to be honest, I can work wherever. To tell you the truth, it's a dream opportunity, the lab I'm telling you about is technically spectacular. When it's fully operational, we'll finish building the other one on site A and we'll sell computer and bio-chemical licenses to our future partners and we'll get the money flowing. We need to be quick and sell fast. Especially since the company's invested a lot in PCR to build this new lab.
- PCR? What is it?

- Polymerase Chain Reaction. As the machine raises and decreases temperature, the multiplication process repeats. The initial duplication gives two DNA molecules, the following one gives 4, then 8...after thirty cycles, or about ten hours, we get one billion molecules. We bought the patent for this method called "DNA amplification method" from Kary Mullis.
- Mullis? I've heard about him; he's a famous biochemist.
- inGen bought the patent last year. Soon, we'll make it available to every lab in the world and we'll make a lot of money Mrs. Porter.
- I won't be surprised if Mullis won the Nobel Prize for such an accomplishment.
- Come work with us on site B and you might win a Nobel Prize too.
- One can dream. Fine, I'm intrigued by your new equipment and I won't stop now!
- Or you'd be unemployed.
- I would." Tia looked at Katherine Harrison who had her back to the metal wall. She was sleeping under a blanket. "I gather that you're trying to avoid information leaks and clashes with the crash survivors. It turns out, Raymond, that I have something in mind concerning one of them..."

The boat slid easily across the sea. Everyone was tired. It would be hard to recover from last night. The night visit of site C had caught George's attention. He was dreamily gazing at the sea, the golden waves playing with his imagination. The young man had met dinosaurs. Dimetrodons basking in the sun by the river, the female Dilophosaurus chasing them... these creatures were real and they eclipsed all of George's other memories. "George"... he was trying to persuade himself that it was his name, and he was beginning to answer to it. Frieda's treason, his running away from the FBI, abandoning his father and his values, everything was fading from his memory. He could only think of the present and of this island he was leaving. Katherine was sleeping next to him, the sea breeze blowing through her short hair. The blanket was flapping in the wind; George pulled it down to cover her naked thighs. He didn't want her to get cold. The small sea convoy was getting close to another coast. Had they reached their last stop before going back to the continent and being on their way? The ship sailed past the bank and headed south; the sea was calm, merciful and friendly. The yellow sunlight pierced the water and shone onto the colorful ocean floor. The water was blue and clear; it moved gently and slightly stirred the pale sand as the ships went by. When would George land? His thinking was interrupted by Joe who was coming from the left. "It's not site B. We haven't reached our destination yet.

- Which 'site' is it then?
- That's not a site. That's Isla Muerta. This island isn't company property. It's an old hub for smugglers and former paramilitaries. They work with inGen and the local government now.
- The men who were deployed on the other island came from here...
- That's right. I've never been there and I really don't feel like going. I think I prefer the company of animals more than the company of men these days.
- Especially those men.
- Yes George, I don't really want to collaborate with them anymore. It didn't go well last night.
- Everyone died. That smuggler must pay.
- And he will be held accountable for his crimes. By now, he's probably in a Carno's stomach. This kind of incident won't happen again, I'm sure.
- What do you know about site B?
- I've been there a few times and I really like it. The jungle's beautiful out there.
- What else?
- It's inGen's second island, the biggest one. To tell you the truth, the company only owns two islands out if five here. But it's investing in another site, up north, site A.
- It's another island, isn't it?

- Yep. But it's not part of the five dead, it's much further away. It takes a long time to get there.
- What do you mean "the five dead"?
- That was the name of the archipelago before we even got here. Before inGen set the facilities up here, it was a meeting place for all kinds of pirates and other unsavory people. They came from San José. It was the perfect hideaway, the archipelago being unmapped and all. And it still is. No one knows these islands exist. The government cleaned the sites and installed its pseudo-elite on Isla Muerta to help inGen.
- The Mercenaries came with the islands!
- A real bonus!" Joe smiled. "These men call the island group "The Five Dead", since each island has seen its share of dead bodies. I bet the company managed to get a discount! But the natives from Isla Muerta, the older ones, they call this place something else."

Joe pointed at the reefs lining the glittering coast. Behind the vapor coming from the swamp, George saw people fishing quietly. They were lightly clad and wore paint on their chests and cheeks. One of them was wearing a patched-up yellow t-shirt and a bow on his back. Joe waved at him. Sitting on a rock splashed by the waves, the man waved back.

"These are the last of the Chorotegas, the real native inhabitants of Isla Muerta. They've carried on living their lives in this remote place. Enterrado en la Isla de Muerta que sólo unos pocos pueden encontrar.

- I don't speak Spanish.
- The Island of Death that only those who know can find. That's the way they see this island, and since they don't exist for the rest of the world. They live like ghosts, invisible to others That's why they call the archipelago "the dead islands". People dying on dead islands. A fat lot of good that does us!
- Do they know you're raising dinosaurs on the neighboring islands?
- No, they have no contact with the other sites, they only fish on the coasts of Isla Muerta. They do their thing, we do ours. They don't seem to mind our cages for now. This tribe descended from the Mayas and Amazonian natives. There's a good chance they'd start honoring the specimens like gods! These men were once enslaved for a very long time. They feared outsiders and they'd kill anyone trying to venture onto their island. These days they tolerate us, so our teams aren't in danger anymore."

Wooden and bamboo huts stood in the mist and disappeared into the forest. Small houses were built on the reefs. A native was cutting up a wild boar on his doorstep; women wearing traditional costumes were washing fabrics and vegetables in the brackish water. The sea breeze cleared up the mist and a small worm-eaten dock appeared. The fragile structure, covered in moss and sea-shells, led to a huge barn. The wobbly building extended into the water on stilts and bent into the sea. Dark and broken boards had turned into a playground for plants and roots. Trees grew on the old facade and the roof was caving in. A shirtless old man was sharpening a wooden knife, looking at the convoy. His eyes met George's. The ship sailed on south along the coast of Isla Muerta. A few canoes moored against the bank were banging on the sea-polished rocks. George couldn't see how big this island was. He was too close to the shore. Seagulls were flying above the palm trees, heading for the mountains. In the distance, beyond the ocean, loomed a mighty, majestic silhouette. A third island appeared on the horizon, green and magnificent. Like a well-kept secret, Isla Sorna displayed its beauty under the bright blue sky. The legend rose proudly to the sky, piercing through water and clouds. Site C and Isla Muerta had disappeared behind the waves, a new dawn was breaking and the archipelago had revealed its splendor. What kind of surprises did site B hold? And what was this mysterious site A on the fringe of the dead islands? The sea pushed the barges south as they motored closer to the legendary and colossal Sorna.

DAWN OF DAYS

The engine of the Jeep CJ-7 stopped; the car stood still and Aileen woke up. The green branches of the trees were dancing to the sing-song of the birds. Her father was holding her hand under the blanket. Deep down, Turner hoped she'd forget last night's events and repress all memory of the terrible experience as if it was a distant nightmare. They'd both made it this far. It was a new day and they were stepping away from this bad dream. The nature surrounding them was nice and peaceful. The boat had moored on the northern coast of site B. Trucks and Jeeps had come to pick them up. Equipment and a few cows had been transferred to the center of the island. Like all other survivors from site C, Turner and his daughter had been taken to the inGen village several miles inland from the coast. The island seemed huge; countless green mountains stretched as far as the eye could see. Dirt roads were as bad as on site C. There was only one road leading to the center of the territory. The CJ-7 had made its way with difficulty through the forest, but they'd finally reached camp safe and sound.

Julia was riding with them. She slammed the door shut and said goodbye to the driver. Turner watched her walking away and disappearing behind a giant fern. The village was surrounded by electric fences. Turner noticed the same rectangular warning signs he saw on site C. "Danger 5000 Volts". He stayed away from the fence, wary of getting electrocuted. But the 50-foot-high concrete columns and the stronghold seemed impregnable from the outside. His daughter and he would be safe 'til morning. Conway had promised them they could leave for Costa Rica by helicopter. Tomorrow, they would leave and this awful adventure would be behind them. They could go surfing at home in Australia, lie on the beach in Bundaberg, come back to the world of the living and indulge in frivolous activities for a while. Turner needed a vacation. Again. InGen's project was mad and dangerous, and definitely not a good place for a kid. He and Aileen needed some more bonding time together. Turner didn't want them to grow apart because of this experience. Aileen had seen the unthinkable and gone through hell. He had to stick with her and be by her side all the time; she was all he had in this world. Turner took his daughter to the military quarters. Three off-white barracks were aligned under a baobab tree. Their curved roofs reminded Turner of those tennis bubbles. A small door painted the same color and two black mosquito nets aerated the semi-circular facade. The workers lived in the military barracks, which were about 50 feet long each, under the creepers in the shade of the tree. Girders stored on the ground were collecting dust by one of the barracks. A camouflage painted Land Cruiser was parked nearby. On the right, workers were standing on a scissor lift truck. The accordion engine unfolded into the sky; on the lift platform, two men were fixing cables on a concrete wall. Another Land Cruiser was parked next to the elevating work platform. Turner noticed a huge heap of red containers behind drums and pallets. Behind the empty cages, other elevating machines were lifting workers into the trees. Beyond the barracks and the construction vehicles, he saw other foundations. The camp was growing fast - construction was in full swing. On his left, two armed men were guarding a sandy-colored bunker. Two Camo Quads were parked on the side. Turner caught a glimpse of a familiar face. A face he hadn't known too long but still...it was Cole Prescott! The Irishman had left the marquee and was walking in his direction. He had the new crutches Sebastien had made for him. The young cook had crafted them from bamboo. He was walking alongside Prescott, smoking a cigarette. Prescott moved closer to Turner and Aileen and hugged them. "Thank God, you're alright! I was worried sick! Evacuating in the middle of the night was terrifying. They say there are dinosaurs on these islands! Did you know about it? The little one was right!" Turner was exhausted. He said:

"Yes, we knew. And we say some others learn the hard way, unfortunately.

- We're leaving tomorrow, I already signed a contract... Some kind of non-disclosure agreement and I'll get the tidy sum of 50,000 dollars when I get back home. You should sign yours as soon as you can Kenneth! It's not that bad after all!
- Segundo got shot in the foot. Some men died.
- I know...what a nightmare. How's the little one?

- It'll take time, but she'll get over it.
- Anyway, this compensation is welcome if you ask me. This place is unbelievable." Someone was coming. "Tell me about it! And it'll be even more unbelievable when we're done fixing all facilities in a year or so."

Prescott recognized Fahran Nurdinah, the Indian engineer and architect. He was wearing gray shorts and a white shirt under a black sleeveless vest. Fahran was writing something on a note pad with a pencil, he said "Glad to see you again, we feared the worst when we heard what happened last night. Have you just gotten there?

- Yes, Kenneth and his daughter landed in the south. Sebastian, the workers and I waited for the rescue teams up north. This construction site is totally amazing - my real estate projects are quite insignificant compared to such investment!
- I'm very proud of what we're building here. All my plans are respected down to the millimeter. Do you want me to show you around?" Julia Barret suddenly answered for everyone. "They'd love that." She smiled at Aileen and walked up to her: "Are you coming Aileen?" I'll show you where you can make yourself comfortable. There's a nice bed with clean sheets waiting for you if you want to finish your night." The little girl rubbed her eyes and followed the young woman into one of the barracks. Turner looked tenderly at his daughter: "Take care!"

Aileen deserved a good night's sleep and Turner had nothing else to do. He just had to wait until he left the island. Fahran took them to a little concrete staircase. The steps led to a small concrete building, partially covered in light wooden boards. Large glass panels gave the building a more modern look. The structure was extended by a concrete bridge snaking into the forest beyond the perimeter. Columns supported a thin platform on which a rail was attached. The architect turned to Prescott, Turner and Sebastian. "This is our latest project: the monorail!" Prescott and the cook seemed very impressed. Prescott was looking at the little station with admiration. "I can't believe it! Are you going to travel in the jungle by train?

- That's absolutely right Cole! It's a viaduct too. It stretches on south-east for about 6 miles. With our automated sealed railway wagon we can carry men and equipment to the heart of the island. It's a state-of-the-art streetcar and it doesn't need a driver; we're still testing the Beta version. We hope we'll be able to build another section next year, probably leading north-east. Eventually, the monorail will stop on every activity base on site B; pens, geothermal power plants, the four harbors.

- Sounds like you have some long years of hard work coming your way. This island seems huge, noted Turner.

- It is. It'll require a lot of concrete and men, but one day this gem of a train will travel across the future city of inGen; above rivers and hills...

- How many stops are there at the moment?
- Just one. And there's nothing there, only a few empty containers and drums. But our work here is only beginning. Let me show you something that, I think, you'll find much more breathtaking."

Fahran went up another staircase, made of iron this time. Sebastian helped Prescott up the walkway. The wire mesh path stood on top of 13-feet high concrete walls. "We've built the secure pen for inGen to study their specimens." Turner suddenly felt anxious when he saw electric fences bending over the walls. "What kind of specimen is it this time? It has some impossible name, I imagine?

- I'm just the architect, this isn't my area of expertise. But I know we built this for predators. I call them Darinda in Hindi. InGen calls them 'Velociraptors'. 'Laalachee', birds of prey. They're young, but they're skilled hunters." Branches shivered below.

On the other side of the walkway, a man was holding a chicken. The bird was wriggling and cackling. The employee threw it over the fence. The chicken clucked when it fell on the leafy foliage. The vegetation was dense inside the pen. The bird spread its wing and darted around into the ferns before disappearing behind the foliage. The yucca trunks moved back and forth, the bushes were shaken by three reptilian shapes. They were all watching attentively. Sebastian stopped chewing his gum. The three-foot-tall bipeds pounced on the chicken and tore it to pieces in a few seconds. Jaws snapped and white feathers flew in the air. These didn't belong to the lizards, of course; their bodies were covered in a sleek hide. One of them looked up, its snout covered in blood. Its skin was both thick and supple and had magnificent stripes. The birdlike reptile had bright scales, the snout and lips two different hues of orange, the eyes and throat a beautiful deep yellow. Its head was rough and thinner in the front like a dolphin's. Muscles showed on the skull and jaw; two small black holes at the extremity of the snout were the nostrils. The serrated scales lining the sides of its winding mouth were brighter. A maroon border underlined the curves of the forehead bones. The same hue was found underneath the eyes of the dinosaur, which made its gaze darker. The creature glanced at the little party. Sebastian shivered; Turner could tell his gum was suddenly flavorless. The eye of the velociraptor was bright yellow with a black slit as a pupil. Brown stripes embellished the top of the brow bone and the same pattern spread on the back, warm colors mixing to the tip of the tail. The animal drew back its lips and revealed bloody gums, growling. A chicken feather was stuck to the pink membrane at the corner of its mouth. Turner and Prescott couldn't see how big the teeth were but they could tell they were as keen and sharp as razorblades. Prescott was stunned, his breath short with fear and disgust. "I think I'm going to have a heart attack!

- Me too. This lizard's freaky!" Said Sebastian. The sight shocked Prescott, too. It was a lot to take in for his fragile fifty year-old Irish heart. The creatures must have been five feet long and it was obvious they'd become fearsome predators. Prescott was in schoc, he couldn't imagine spending even one second with these carnivores. They'd gobbled down the chicken as if it were a canapé. They must have been twice as fast as him. Their claws were sharp, the ones on their feet especially long and curved. The three long, sinewy fingers on their hands moved delicately, as if playing the piano. But the only music Prescott could hear was the symphony of death. Fear triggered the stabbing pain in his leg. His wound throbbed. What an abomination! Turner, on the other hand, was fascinated; he watched the bipeds walk to the center of the pen, the young Velociraptors hiding under the palms in the middle of the concrete square. Fahran put an end to his contemplation: "What if dinosaurs were alive? You're all going to sign an agreement if you haven't done it yet. I guess I can show you the highlight of the facility. That won't make any difference now." The engineer went down from the pen, munching on his delicious Malaysian jerky. He offered Prescott a packet. Prescott gratefully accepted, and immediately ripped the seal to begin snacking. "This is just exquisite!" He said through a mouthful of cured meat. Next to the Velociraptor area were several concrete ditches, thirteen feet deep and separated by an electric fence. Red beacon lights blinked a warning from the top of the posts. There was something down there. "Come closer - don't be scared. I designed this pen. We poured concrete into the ground instead of building up walls. Walkways are too expensive. This Darinda's pen was built underground. It can't possibly scale the ditch or penetrate the electric fence." Despite these reassurances, Prescott was a bit frightened. He combed his fingers through his grayish blond beard. "Are you saying there's another... Velociraptor in this hole?" he asked. "I think I've seen enough of them!

-       There's very little vegetation in this pen and it's a closed space. Just look down and you'll see the dinosaur. I get cold sweats running down my back each time I look at him." Fahran smiled at Sebastian. The cook leaned over the guardrail to look down. The slope was dark and, just like the others, the young man couldn't see much. Sebastian grasped his medal in his hand and searched the darkness below for a splash of color. Suddenly, the monster slammed into the fence just steps from his face. Sebastian caught a glimpse of claws behind the spray of sparks, then the creature backed off under the electric shock. Its sharp claws scraped and scrabbled at the concrete looking for something to sink into, but the unlucky creature slid down to the bottom of the pit. It shrieked in what must have been frustration. It was a chilling noise; something between a turbine and a porpoise. The dinosaur was bigger than the two others. Why had they trapped it in this sad, barbed-wire pit? Fahran laughed at Sebastian and Prescott when he saw their faces. They both looked stunned and dizzy. "Gets me every time! Nice surprise, isn't it? I wonder how the science people from inGen managed to bring such a thing to life! My wife and mother would call it a Daraavana, a bogeyman. But I'm pretty sure they'll never see this monster."

Turner stepped toward the fence and stopped before the black and yellow stripes to take a better look at the dinosaur below. Hidden in the shade of a little palm tree, it was licking its wounds. Turner was struck by its color, or rather the absence of it. The dinosaur was one of a kind, even for a prehistoric species brought back from the dead. This new dinosaur was different from all the other carnivores: it was a big Velociraptor, probably an adolescent or an adult, and its body was as black as soot. The reptile was death itself. Its long tail was swinging and whipping the yellow sand. Standing on its hind legs, the terrible "Darinda" took out its frustration on the asphalt; it was scraping the ditch with its clawed hands at unbelievable speed. The black lizard jumped once again, roaring, stopped right before the fence, and landed on the wet soil. The reptile clucked and showed sharp teeth as long as pocket knives. The animal was hissing and snuffing as it dipped its neck to sniff the wooden chips. Its iris was a dull shade of green cut in half by a soulless black pupil. The stomach of the animal was grayish. The smoky coloration made it diffcult to discern any musculature beneath the skin, but the thing practically radiated taut, predatory hardness. The creature was pacing the 32 foot square pit like an evil spirit trying to escape hell. Its mouth was dark pink, The membrane at the corner of the mouth almost red. The inside of the mouth contrasted with the darkness of its reptilian body to emphasize its snout and teeth. Or was all that red just blood? The enraged black Velociraptor drooled and sniffed around, banging its head into the concrete. Turner was speechless; this lizard was absolutely staggering. "Why is this one black?" Fahran answered with a smile: "Who knows? I don't know what they've done. But everyone here knows it was the first Velociraptor they cloned. It was born here on site B. They experimented on it while it was growing up. This dinosaur is only 5 months old and it's already a killer. They then cloned the other three from this one. They meddled with the genetic code, I don't really know how...but the result is giving me the chills. It's the very first Darinda, an all-black male. Hopefully, there's no chance it can get out of this super pen. It won't contaminate the other animals.

- What do you mean? Are you saying it's sick?
- It is, like all of the others. Other dinosaurs sometimes have bumble foot, an inflammatory condition of the foot. They have digestive tract diseases, stomach poisoning, the flu or tick infestations. Scientists and medical doctors from inGen spend their days caring for them. Who'd have thought these creatures were so fragile?
- This one doesn't look wounded or malnourished though, but it looks...
- Rabid! That's right Kenneth. That's why it's quarantined. The geneticists could tell you more about it than I can! I create the

facilities for the dinosaurs, but not the dinosaurs themselves!"

He invited the little party to step away from the pen, laughing. Turner, Prescott and Sebastian were stunned and filled with dismay. These new encounters were quite violent! The four men bumped into the Bradwick Brothers as they were walking back to the barracks. Tal nodded and waved at them. Chad was carrying a jerrycan and heading for the generator. "It's high time for a nap. It's been a long day, we need rest to be refreshed. Isn't it a nice afternoon for a nap?" Prescott, who was regaining his composure, said happily: "Fair enough! I'll go and get a tan! The weather and nature are quite nice today." Sebastian was still speechless. "Nice? Really? There's no way I'm going back to see those carnivorous creatures. I'd rather be cooking. I wonder what kind of cookware they have at this site...

- I guess you'll have to find the kitchen!" chirped Prescott, brandishing his bamboo crutch. "I wouldn't say no to a nice juicy steak. I'm a dangerous carnivore too, after all!" Fahran answered Prescott, smiling: "In your dreams! With Chua as head of the department, you'll get tuna every day! Mackerel if you're lucky." Sebastian was a bit disappointed and moody. "I guess we can cook it with a vegetable like a tajine," he said, his lack of enthusiasm obvious. "I'll add some preserved lemon for a Caribbean touch... I could crumble the fish. Sun dried tomatoes, carrots and bell peppers..."

Prescott simply smiled.

Katherine Harrison walked into a barrack situated north of the secure compound. A few moments later, Tia Porter joined her and asked her to sit inside. In fact, it looked more like a small office than an actual barrack. Raymond Chua was sitting at the back of the concrete room; large black cables hung from the wall. He was typing on a computer keyboard and printing documents, sitting at a folding table. He was mechanically tapping his feet on the grass. There was no floor covering. This scene seemed quite surreal to Katherine. The man waved at her, tapping papers against the table. His sweaty hands left stains on the paper. "Please Ms. Harrison, Mrs. Porter, sit down. First of all, I thank you both for your time. I beg your pardon for this improvised office, it's not finished yet...but paperwork can't wait, even in the middle of the jungle! Katherine, I've been told you're never at loss for words. You like to tell stories, don't you?

- What do you mean? Are you saying I'm a liar?
- Of course not, you live to tell the truth. Or shall I say *your* truth? What I mean is that you're hungry for exclusive news and I find it hard to believe you'll be able to keep our work here a secret.

- You're right, there's a good chance I'll write an article that'll blow everyone's mind when I leave tomorrow.
- What if I ask you to sign a non-disclosure agreement today and offer you fifty thousand dollars in exchange for your silence?
- Fifty thousand dollars? Tempting, but my article will be worth much more. You said it yourself: I'm hungry for the truth.
- That's what I thought. My first idea was to take libel action against you before you publish anything. You'd be ruined and out of the picture before the trial. We'd also intimidate you in a variety of ways to make you lose your mind. But it'd be a terrible mess and a real pity to lose your skills as an archivist. So I've been talking with Dr. Porter here and we came up with another solution." He threw a small pile of papers on the desk and handed Katherine a pen. "If we can't buy your silence, inGen will offer you a job. Do you believe in astrology Ms. Harrison? I think you came here for a reason. It was your destiny.
- Why are you doing that? I don't get it. A few seconds ago, you were threatening to kill me and now you're offering me a job?
- Seventy thousand dollars a year...and it's a permanent position...
- Permanent? InGen is planning on creating dinosaurs forever? Why? Do you want to use

them as war machines, sell them like weapons? This is disgusting.

- Don't be ridiculous Ms. Harrison. It's out of the question, we have other wonderful things planned for our specimens...

- Can you tell me more about this job then?

- You've already met some of our animals, you'll be paid to take pictures and videos of these mighty creatures for our internal archive department. Eventually, your work will be released to the public. In this contract here, we're also offering you a job as head of PR.

- Head of PR for inGen, a nebulous and senseless company... no, thank you.

- You won't be working as head of PR for inGen... but for one of its brands. Read the contract.

- You locked me up in a room for days and when I managed to get out I was almost eaten alive by your carnivores. I've felt threatened by inGen many times. What makes you believe I'm going to sign your contract?

- Mrs. Porter will tell you more about the position. She's leaving for site A in a few days. Maybe you could go with her if you choose to stay.

- But the helicopter's leaving for the continent tomorrow." Tia immediately said to Katherine: "That's right. But you've been here for a while now. A few more days won't hurt. Come with me - it'll be a rare opportunity to visit site A. You're a journalist, so I'm sure you have the writing and photography skills we need for this new adventure. You could be the new voice of the company and work your wonders. Remember that talk we had together? This experience will change lives and amaze the world. Don't you want to be part of that bright future?"

Katherine didn't know what to say, her heart was pounding in her chest as if she was riding a roller coaster. The young woman was both stupefied and embarrassed. Her eyes wandered across the contract; driven by professional conscience and curiosity, the journalist could see between the lines the outline of a breath-taking dream. Why resist it? Why negate it? There was something magical about this archipelago, something gigantic and miraculous, something terrifying. Katherine Harrison was already under the spell of the island, she already wanted to stride along its paths and learn more about it. Maybe it was the opportunity she'd been waiting for her whole life, her ultimate journalist fantasy, unconfessed and unhoped for. Her heart slowly stopped racing. The young woman knew what she wanted and where she wanted to go. She grabbed the pen, reading another page of the contract. The rest of the world could wait. Katherine wouldn't leave with the other crash survivors tomorrow. She had better things to do here. "I almost forgot." Chua put a Polaroid camera on the desk. "Latest model. It's yours. I'll leave you to it."

The man stood up and left the barrack, a pile of papers in his hand. Under Porter's caring gaze, Katherine started reading the third page of the contract. She was captivated. A brand new world was opening in front of her.

"As you can see, it's a perfectly random deck of cards." Sitting on his bed, Segundo flicked through the playing card deck. Aileen was at his bedside, watching the magic trick. Segundo was resting his foot on a folding bed in one of the wings of the embryonic department. Julia had taken the girl to visit him - her company was welcome during his convalescence. The young man rubbed his left hand on his vest and put the deck on the blanket. He looked Aileen in the eye. "Please, cut the deck in half." The young girl did as she was asked and put the other half on the sheet. "Pick the first card and take a good look at it. Don't show it to me. I will try and guess which card it is using mentalism." Aileen identified the nine of clubs on the card. She loved magic. She smiled and put the card back on the deck. Segundo covered it with the remaining half and held the cards between his hands. "I'll try and guess your card." He looked deep into the Turner girl's eyes. "Your mind is easy to read, young lady! Is it the nine of clubs?" Aileen giggled: "Yes it is! That's impossible!

- Now that I guessed your card, I'll make it disappear from the deck! It's on my head...literally!" He patted his cap and lifted the

visor. On his head lay Aileen's card! The young man took the nine of clubs out of his hair to the little girl's delight and slid it under the deck. He flipped through the cards to show her they were all different. "Magic doesn't stop now - get ready to be dazzled!" He lifted the deck to Aileen's mouth. "Now, imagine you're a dragon: blow on the card and set the deck on fire. Come on!" The child blew on the deck, roaring. "Very good! Now look: all the cards have become your card!" Segundo the magician flipped through the deck once more and Aileen discovered to her amazement that all cards were now the nine of clubs! It was just unbelievable. The little girl clapped, laughing out loud. The young man laughed with her and put the deck back in its case. Julia was coming down the stairs, she walked toward the bed, smiling. "Don't let him fool you Aileen, it's a trick deck called a 'Svengali'. Magicians also call it a 'Radio deck'. Each alternate card is a nine of clubs but they're shorter than the regular cards. So when you riffle the deck, you only see the regular cards."

Segundo interrupted her: "Why are you telling her the trick?

- My grand-father had the same deck with the king of diamonds, sorry. That's why you always end up with the smaller card when you cut the deck Aileen, your fingers always pick the longer card revealing the smaller

one underneath. Segundo's deck is a Svengali deck with nine of clubs!
- You know a lot about magic, don't you? Segundo said.
- My grand-father used to practice a little. I loved watching him. It was fascinating. Sorry I ruined the surprise for your young audience but Aileen needs to know that illusion always relies on tricks!" She winked at her. The little girl looked thoughtful: "So it's not real magic?"
- There's always an explanation, answered Julia. You've learned a great lesson. Magic's a great fun way to remember that the supernatural does not exist. Come with me Aileen, Segundo needs some rest and I have something for you."

The young woman took the little girl by the hand and they both stepped out of the room. The place was quiet. Aileen was walking slowly. She noticed that the big hoses hanging from the ceiling ran all along the corridor. Julia opened an electronic door with her pass. The shutter opened from the left with an engine noise. They came into a lab. The room was huge. Workers were attaching devices to the walls. One of them was planning a wall with a circular saw, standing on a stepladder. Sparks fell down on the floor and went out on the shiny bright white tiles. Neon tubes glinted off stainless steel tables and lab counters. Julia walked toward a huge inbuilt terrarium. The glass case was about six and a half feet long and ten feet high. What could be hiding inside? Aileen let go of Julia's hand and stepped closer, intrigued. She pressed her nose to the glass. Julia put her hand on her shoulder and gently pulled her away from the tempered glass. In the terrarium, tall pale vines tangled around the top. Small green and red shoots grew on the wood. Aileen gaped like a child being given a bicycle or a doll on Christmas morning. Near the top of the terrarium, strange reptiles were looking at the wooden chips on the heated floor. They tilted their heads, looking at the blond little girl. These specimens had wings. Their body was covered with thin red down. They had a long, stiff tail ended by a sort of diamond-shaped "rudder". They looked like imps, small red gargoyles spying on their surroundings. The flying creatures were no more than 8 inches long and had smooth yellow beaks. A few small yellow feathers highlighted the bright colors underneath their eyes and at the back of their skulls. Sharp teeth protruded from their large horned beaks. One of the specimens flapped its wings for a second, chirping, and then stood still on its branch. Julia affectionately sleeked Aileen's hair. "See, you were right, dragons exist. Look, they're just babies, one month old.

- They're not really dragons, they're dinosaurs. They're Rhamphorhynchus." said Aileen. Julia stuttered, surprised. "How did you know that?" The little girl pointed at a sign bearing the name of the species at the bottom of the window. Julia congratulated the girl for her insight: "Amazing! You even said it right straight away! Even I struggle!
- It's magic!

- Yes Aileen, they are indeed Rhamphorhynchus. They are a genus of Pterosaurs.
- Flying dinosaurs.
- Exactly girl! When they're fully grown they'll have a wingspan of almost 6 feet. That's what the paleontologists say.
- Do they have names?
- No, they don't." Aileen pointed at little brown heaps on the floor of the terrarium. "Is that poo?" Julia grinned. "Yes, that's feces.
- Why is there a white part?
- Well, their systems get rid of anything the lizards don't need and this part is dedicated to calcium, hence the white color.
- It looks like chalk... What do they eat?
- We feed them mice but this particular species is supposed to eat fish.
- They eat meat, they're bad. Dragons that eat meat are bad.
- Dragons are just like other animals: they need food to survive. It's the circle of life.
- But dragons are bad, they breathe fire on their prey.
- To cook and digest them more easily. That's how nature works; they have to eat. The life chain is cruel sometimes. But dragons and men can live together. That's what we're trying to do here. Sometimes, the knight mustn't kill the dragon, he must let it live, give it a chance. Every creature in this world should try and understand the others.

- I'm a princess among dragons! And I'm going to live with them.
- You're so pretty, you definitely are a princess. With your beautiful golden hair, every frog prince on this island will fall in love with you!" The two girls exchanged giggles. Julia opened a drawer and repeated: "You're a princess, that's for sure. But with all that you've been through lately, you deserve to be knighted!" The young woman took a plastic knight toy out of the drawer. It carried a shield and a sword. The face of the hero was hidden by a silver helmet. She gave Aileen the toy. "Life is full of hardship and adventure and a knight always overcomes obstacles. You'll cut your way through the bramble bushes with your sword. You'll have the strength and the elegance of a knight, and you'll fight with your head held up high.
- I'll be a princess knight!" The girl took the figurine and pressed it against her heart. "Thank you Julia, I'll fight for justice and defeat adversity like a real knight!
- You already talk like a champion. Use it wisely. I bought it in San José for my nephew. But you deserve it more than he does. This toy makes sense with you, it's your symbol, your coat of arms.
- Do you think my mommy would have been proud to know I was destined to become a princess knight?

- I'm sure your mother is really, really proud of you. You met dragons and survived, any mother would be proud of that! Wherever she is, your mother loves you very much and so does your father.
- Daddy says she watches us from the stars every night.
- Your father's right Aileen. He is. You know...I lost my dad when I was about your age and I still miss him terribly. We have to learn to live without them day after day. It's our burden but love gives us wings. Life goes on." Julia walked toward another window a few feet to the left. "Do you want to be a mom too?" She invited

Aileen to come closer to the other terrarium. It had been sterilized. It was empty except for some branches 40 inches above the ground. The terrain behind the window rose above the rest, and Aileen hadn't noticed yet that, at the center of the terrarium, something was moving on the moss. It was an egg! A dinosaur egg. It was six inches in diameter; it was cracking from the inside. The Turner girl wasn't impressed by the size of the egg - she came from Australia and she'd seen emu eggs before. But *this* egg was about to hatch! Aileen knew it wasn't an ostrich. "Is it a meat-eating dinosaur-dragon again?

- No Aileen, not this one. It's an herbivore, it eats only plants.
- Where are its parents?
- She doesn't have any.
- It's a girl?

- Yes, it's a girl and you can be her mom and welcome her into this world if you wish.
- If she doesn't eat meat, then I can be her mom for the day.
- Who knows? You might be back in a few years. You'll see if she remembers you. You'll both have grown so much.
- Daddy will never want to come back here.
- Never say never!" The shell cracked and fell over to the left; the membrane was shivering. A piece fell down on the moss and Aileen saw the baby's head. "You can help her with the shell, but be very gentle." Julia put the little girl's hand into the clear gloves. The pair was going through the double-paned window. An air filter hummed in the vivarium. On the other side of the window, Aileen delicately put the piece of eggshell on the substrate, her hands weren't in direct contact with the animal. The small creature was only five inches long and her skin was khaki green. Aileen had never seen such a reptile. Her head looked too big for her body, her skull had a bony frill. Her crest had six notches. The baby looked like a shellfish. Darker green stripes underlined the bony protrusions. They gathered on the top of her head and went down, lining her eyes. The pattern repeated itself around her horned nose and the bumps on each side of her head. Thin bony stripes the same color as the eggshell embellished the little dinosaur's frill. Her three blunt little horns and pointy beak were white. The creature was covered in blood inside the egg. Her hind leg was pressed against her glistening body, she was hiding behind her front right leg.

276

Aileen pinched the lower part of the shell to crack it open. The newborn dived forward, freeing her hind legs for the first time. The little girl caught her with her gloves as she fell. She was fascinated; she had stars in her eyes. The baby dinosaur's gaze was kind and warm. The herbivore opened large yellow eyes with round black pupils. The wrinkled skin around her eyes made her look like a puppy dog. Her lower jaw was curved toward the back of her head. It seemed to Aileen that the baby was smiling to her, that she was filled with hope and joy. The animal crawled on her stomach and tried to get up on her legs. She dragged herself into the moss and the wooden chips like a little turtle. She struggled for a few seconds, then rested against a piece of bark. Blades of grass were stuck to her still-sticky skin. Julia was watching Aileen, who was all wide eyes and proud grin. "It's a little Triceratops," she said.

- It's easier to say than 'Rhamphorhynchus'.
- I agree Aileen! The other animals don't have names, only nicknames or code names. But since you're her mom, you can pick a name for her. Go ahead!
- For real? Can I? I get to choose all by myself?
- A privilege for princesses only! And knights. So you can definitely do it. You can call her Aileen if you wish.
- Like me? That would be a pity.
- Well, it won't be hard to tell you two apart!
- We could call her 'Muffin'. Her crest looks like a muffin, it's all puffy.
- You choose. It's a great responsibility.

- She's a girl so we can call her 'Miss Muffin'!" Julia wasn't sure. "It's better that TRI08 I guess...
- It's much better!
- Ok Aileen. Miss Muffin it is then!"

Aileen jumped into Julia's arms, giggling with happiness. Her cries of joy covered the noise of the fan. The little Triceratops sniffed the moss and put its beak on the twigs. It lay down on its side and closed its eyes for a nap .

The sun was shining bright in the cloudless sky. The branches of the jelly palm trees were softly rustling in the breeze. Leaning against a cage, George was watching the workers getting busy. He felt weariness weighing on him; he was staring at the foliage. Bradley Conway came his way. His boots and pants were caked in mud. He carried an M40 on his back, the butt and magazine banged against his shoulder with an annoying clink. Conway was smoking an El Unico cigar, the famous D8 of the Caribbean. Ash fell onto the ground and he blew a thick cloud of gray smoke. George squinted to keep the sunshine out of his eyes. "I thought smoking was forbidden here." Conway frowned and answered as calmly as he could: "those creatures were born in such a different environment from their original one, I don't see what difference it makes. A little smoke in the jungle won't kill anyone. They have to stop being so paranoid. Do you smoke?" He handed a cigarette and a lighter to George. The young man lit it and took a drag. He blew out the smoke. "I thought you were very strict about law enforcement. Do you cut yourself some slack from time to time?

- You don't need a special occasion to smoke a fine cigar. Even on this island." Conway noticed George's cut lip. "I heard what you did last night. Fighting those smugglers with your bare hands to defend people you hardly knew. It was noble, kid.
- I didn't want things to get out of hand.
- Yet they did. But you did your best. You were brave. You weren't afraid to get your hands dirty and I like a man with a firm hand.
- I just did what I had to do. But it didn't make much difference.
- There are always problems, kid. War's raging on this archipelago, it's not your fault. On this territory you have to be uncompromising, you have to know how to neutralize opponents, kill them if you have to. My employers are like that. They act. I do what I have to do too, even if it means I have to break a few fingers or take out a crook or two. It's war.
- You were in Vietnam, weren't you?
- USMC. I was in the 3rd MAF in May '65.
- Marine Amphibious Force...
- That's right. Conway was shooting puffs of smoke. I was responsible for all fighting

operations in the CTZ area. The Marines were first deployed in Vietnam to secure the airfield in Da Nang. But it was obvious that the military situation in the Northern provinces required more involvement of the ground forces.

- Is that where you were wounded?" Conway looked back over his shoulder. "War burn. It's my painful trophy. I don't really mind people calling me 'Lizard Neck.' I even enjoy the Marines pun. This fight wound defines me. You know a man from his scars. Do you have any?
- None.
- Yet you look like a fighter. You have the face of a boxer. Have you served in the forces?" George paused for a bit. "No.
- Policeman? Fireman?
- No.
- You know, when Chua looked into the past of every single crash survivor, he found information about everyone. Communication with the continent is bad. Anyway, he managed to get information about everyone to make sure it wasn't industrial espionage. Everyone but you.
- I'm just a regular guy.
- 'George Alistair'. No criminal record. No known address. No emergency contact. Maybe you're not as regular as you say you are.
- I'm trying to be a good citizen and stay out of trouble.

- Citizen of what? Where are you from? What about your birthday or the names of your parents? Are you going to lie to me?
- My family life isn't that exciting.
- I'm sure it is. Don't worry, I'm not interested in where you're coming from; rather, I want to know where you're going. You look like a nice guy. I don't know if you're running away from something, but if you're looking for a place to hide, this island is the best.
- What do you mean?
- I saw a lot of awful stuff in Vietnam. Some even say I did some terrible things. The country was a bloody battlefield, so yes, I killed. For duty. Not because I enjoyed it or because I took some sick pleasure in it, but because I had to. I followed orders, I obeyed barbarism without giving in to it and I fought for what I thought was right. That's what we're looking for here: men who can use their hands, maintain order and work for the greater good. I don't know who you are and I don't care. You can be whoever you want, start all over again or just live your life away from prying eyes. Men have died these past few hours, and with someone like you on our team, we may have avoided this.
- When are you sending the bodies to the families?
- They won't leave this archipelago. They'll be buried here. The families mustn't know - it was in their contracts.

- Are you saying they won't get a proper service? What are you going to tell the relatives?
- That they died at sea on a platform. The government of Costa Rica will announce their deaths. They're ghosts, just like everyone else working here. They knew it when they took the job; no one can know where they work and what they really do. It's all about non-disclosure. Families will get money, that's how it works, always...
- Are you asking me if I want to become a ghost too? George said.
- I think you're a ghost already. I'm offering you an opportunity. You work here with us, in the shadows on site B, you remain on the archipelago for a few years, you put money on the side for better days and you leave when you want. You're a free man. Think about it when you leave tomorrow. Stop in San José and find out what is best for you. This island could be your haven of peace, your secret lair; everyone wants one.
- It could also be my grave.
- You know that's impossible. You're already dead." Conway blew out smoke and raised his chin, looking cynical. "Do you have a job waiting for you on the continent? You said you had no family. What's holding you back? It could be a great opportunity.
- And what would be my job title here? Dinosaur supervisor?

-   You could join the tracker team, supervise transfers and all transportations on site. You met Barret and Jackson. Our teams are quite flexible here, I'm sure we can find you a job that'll meet your expectations. I can sense you have a good heart and the strength and courage of youth. InGen rewards hard-working people."

Conway and George heard a voice behind them. "And what about me? Will I be rewarded?" In front of the ferns stood Rodrigo Quintado. He had deep dark circles and had lost a lot of weight; his finger was trembling on the trigger of his gun. He approached George and Conway, signaling them to keep quiet; no one had noticed him in the busy camp. Conway stared at Quintado, his face was uplifted. Conway's head suddenly hurt, he ran his gloved hand through his straight gray hair and spun around to grab his gun. Quintado was coming out of the bushes, pointing his gun at them. "Don't even think about it. Just one move and I'll clean your ears with powder! You have something that belongs to me. Give it back and give me a boat, too! I won't hurt you if you cooperate." Conway lifted his hands in the air, looking around. "I don't know what you're talking about.

-   Don't play that game with me Boss. I saw your men loading my chest on that stupid train of yours.
-   So you came all the way from Matanceros to get some useless junk back? " Conway was

nervous but he tried to control the situation. George, for its part, didn't know if he should attack

Quintado or not. The crook was edgy and if George tried to act all heroic, they would probably end up dead. Quintado brandished his gun. "You're all going to die if you don't give me what I want once and for all! I'm done with these damn islands!" Conway rushed at him, pushing the barrel of his gun down to the ground.

Quintado kicked him hard in the back of his elbow so he would let go, then he gave him a straight right and an uppercut. Conway stepped back to grab his weapon. The crook broke his nose with the butt of his gun and opened fire. George charged him, pummeling him to the ground. Bullets whizzed and rebounded off a metal container. The workers stopped what they were doing to look at the far end of the perimeter. Quintado gathered his strength to punch George in the jaw. He pushed him back, kicking him in the shins. The hateful pirate didn't stop there: punches, knee kicks...He took it all out on the young man who rolled to the floor. Quintado ran to the center of the village; he shot a burst of gunfire at Conway. The Marine took cover; George did the same. The head of the camp was furious. Conway started yelling: "Kill him! Kill that man!" Two soldiers came running and tried to shoot him. Above, on top of the electric fence, a guard whistled. Quintado was shooting on sight, bullets struck trees and buildings. Men from inGen opened fire; projectiles were flying all over the place. Gunpowder rose in the air, bullets ringed on iron and banged on the bars of the cages. Workers were running around like crazy. Conway chased the smuggler, drawing his gun. Quintado emptied his magazine in Conway's direction and turned to a group of people. Without hesitation, he pulled the trigger, aiming at Fahran Nurdinah. Turner jumped to his left to get the architect on the ground. Bullets brushed past their hair. Sebastian stood in front of Prescott to protect him. The gun jammed.

Quintado escaped bullets coming from the left, he rolled behind a trunk and reloaded. The pointy palm leaves were pierced by bullets. The crook ran to a hiding place, avoiding the gunshots. As he was getting close to an iron facade, Quintado felt a projectile graze his leg. The bullet hit a rusty fuel jerrycan and a farming engine. A gas bottle blew up. Flames knocked him to the ground. The blast set several more fuel tanks on fire, and flames rose from the ground and swept through the buildings. A steel dumpster crashed onto the ground; steel squealed on the steep concrete. Orange flames reddened the iron, a huge cloud of black smoke filled up the place, ash and sparks surrounded Quintado. A nagging thump echoed in his ears. Everyone was lying on the ground, the explosion had knocked out a few people. The smuggler got back on his feet and walked to another building. He was casually shooting through the dark smoke, trying to make his way through the camp. He was shooting blindly, hoping he would hit someone, completely disoriented; the man had no limit, no mercy. He was obsessed with revenge and violence, he wanted to kill, bring his opponents down and leave this island for good with his loot. Suddenly, he saw Turner standing in his way. The man was looking most serious.

The air was dirty and Turner was thinking fast. He had a revelation: he had to step in and take Quintado out of the picture. Turner took advantage of the smoke to hit him on the ear. Quintado was taken by surprise but he immediately fought back, returning Turner's blows as fast as he could. Turner covered his face with his forearms and suddenly slammed his elbow into Quintado's mouth. Then he gave him a straight right to the cheek. The man retaliated with a kick to Turner's stomach. Quintado was about to shoot Aileen's father when Prescott interrupted him. The Irishman leapt at Quintado, striking him in the face. Quintado absorbed the punches, then violently slapped the middle-aged man with the back of his hand. Prescott's head whipped back and he grabbed his face with both hands, moaning. The enraged Quintado frantically kneed Prescott in the thigh, and Prescott promptly crumpled to the ground. The Irish looked up at his assailant, his face twisted with futile anger. Then his eyes flickered past Quintado's head, and his expression changed to utter shock and dismay. Prescott began to scream. It was not a scream of pain, or shame. Turner could tell the difference. Prescott was screaming with fear. Quintado whipped his head around to see what could possibly disturb Prescott so deeply. He suddenly became aware of the silhouette Prescott had seen through the smoke. Behind the embers and clouds of smoke, the rabid black Velociraptor, freed from its pit by the explosion, growled and snapped its jaws. The terrifying reptile leaned down, its massive body hovering above the ground, a good 6 feet long. Its dark skin blended in perfectly with the dust. The reptile leapt at them. Quintado hollered with surprise and stumbled backward, scrambling to get out of the creature's way. The beast gave Quintado a powerful blow with its tail, the thick scales whipping the man's knees and toppling him to the ground with a moan. The Velociraptor then sank its claws into the thick meat of Prescott's legs. The man howled in pain when he saw the sharp claws and the huge retractable sickle-shaped talon tearing through his calf muscles. Quintado howled at the creature in rage and shock, and opened fire on it as he struggled to his feet. Sand sprayed into the air as bullets hit the ground near Prescott, who was shrieking at the top of his lungs. One of the bullets grazed the dinosaur's tail. It hopped back, snapping its long jaw shut. Sharp teeth disappeared under sooty scales and the monster crawled back into the darkness of the smoke cloud. Its silhouette vanished into the dust; the animal ran away. Sebastian ran to help the immobilized Prescott to his feet. Fahran assisted him, dragging Prescott for a few yards. Turner took the opportunity to jump at Quintado, who was facing the other way. The angry smuggler grabbed his forearm and tried to topple him over. Turner knew that if he couldn't bring Quintado down, he would get shot; and that would be the end of his selfless gesture. He thought about his daughter, who was safe with Julia, somewhere among all this mess. Quintado was furious, fighting for his life and his shipment. He elbowed Turner in the gut. The physician let go but managed to grab the barrel of the gun before head-butting the smuggler. Quintado stumbled back, holding his forehead and cursing. He pulled the trigger, but Turner managed to take cover behind a small wall to avoid the bullets. He lay down on the steps of a little staircase and crawled up toward the entrance of the adjacent building. Pieces of concrete were falling on his hair as the rage-blind Quintado sprayed the path leading to the monorail with bullets. He followed Turner into the building, shooting at wood and glass. Windows shattered.

Turner had become the smuggler's target and he knew he wouldn't let go. He could hear Bradley Conway yelling a few feet below: "Kill him!" Turner ran across the little hallway and slid into the first streetcar wagon. The glass gate was open. Quintado shot the computers, projectiles piercing the wooden counters. Sparks came bursting out of the monitors and bullets blasted the walls. The man was destroying everything on his path! He jumped on board the monorail and aimed at the steel and glass structure. Turner hit the gun with his forearm and slammed his fist into Quintado's jaw. The gun clattered to the metallic floor and slid toward the crook's chest, which was stored in this particular compartment. A loud, metallic clink echoed across the capsule. Quintado fought back, punching Turner in the chest and then the chin. He threw the medical examiner against the control panel of the monorail. Turner felt the sharp corner of the dashboard make contact with his hip. He got punched once, twice, in the face. He slid down the window. Quintado pushed him against the wall and banged his head against it. Turner, breathless, spun around, locked his arms behind Quintado's neck, and thrust his knee into the side of Quintado's face. He kneed him again, harder this time. The smuggler somehow wriggled backward, set himself free, and kicked Turner in the side of his knee. Then he grabbed Turner by the collar and threw him into the back wall of the compartment. He spun around hopped over shards of splintered glass to grab his gun from the ground. That's when Quintado heard a grim hiss coming from behind. He turned around and realized with terror that they weren't alone in the monorail anymore. The terrible black monster was back, and it had just boarded the train. The Velociraptor growled, raising his head. Its reddish tongue licked its sharp teeth in anticipation. Turner looked at Quintado. He was shaking, his body was stiffening in terror.

Quintado aimed at the animal with his gun but Turner charged him. The smuggler opened fire, deflected bullets lodged themselves into the control panel, which shot sparks and began malfunctioning. Both men heard a woman's voice through the built-in ceiling speakers: "Automated departure initiated." The train doors closed. A few seconds later, the glass wall shut them in. The little train started moving. Turner heard the rail and concrete scraping the bottom of the compartment. The Velociraptor growled and sniffed the walls of the monorail. He pressed its snout against the glass and snuffed loudly, looking out the window. Mist spread over the glass. The streetcar was going faster and higher. It left the electrified perimeter of the village and went into the jungle canopy, about 30 feet in the air. While Quintado was distracted, Turner closed the distance between them and punched him in the face once again. Despite the fact that he was bleeding and exhausted, he managed to pack some power into the blow. Quintado dropped his rifle once again; it slid toward the door of the next wagon. The dinosaur approached the two men, its claws tapping the metal floor. There were only two wagons; a single doorway separated the men from safety in the other wagon. Turner ran to the door and frantically slammed his palm into a big red button. The door slid open with a hiss of compressed air. He ran into the other wagon and looked for the button to shut the door. Quintado sprinted after him, leaving his gun behind. The evil animal chased him, cackling. Its breath was irritated and short, and Quintado felt the hot exhalation tickle his neck; he mumbled what might have been a prayer in Spanish. The man barely made it through the door as it hissed shut thanks to Turner's timely reaction; Turner left his open palm on the button and caught his breath.

Quintado fell on top of him and the beast crashed into the glass wall behind them. The glass cracked as the result of the impact. The neighboring wagon was shattered and the capsule squealed on the concrete rail. The monster unleashed its rage on the window. It wanted to get through and devour them. How long would the door hold against its attack? Architect Fahran Nurdinah had mentioned that the railway wasn't finished. How high would the train stop? Would it even stop? Quintado had destroyed the control panel, so there was no way to slow the convoy down. Turner looked around the wagon. There were only a few metal chairs and jerrycans but no dashboard to pilot the monorail. Turner didn't get the chance to explore the wagon any further - the smuggler was already jumping on him from behind.

Their fight wasn't over. Quintado charged the Australian doctor and pushed him to the end of the capsule. Turner fought back, hitting Quintado in the ribs with his free elbow. Turner freed himself and threw his fists at the smuggler, then pushed him away with a blow from his knee. Unfortunately, Rodrigo Quintado was unstoppable. He grabbed a chair and threw it at the poor medical examiner. Turner's body was covered in bruises, his ribs ached terribly. Suddenly, a boot hit him in the jaw. The smuggler grabbed him by the hair and frantically banged his head against the glass. The glass cracked under the smuggler's brutal blows. Turner had blood all over his face. The man was going to kill him. Just like the monster standing in the other wagon, he was driven by rage. He was ruthless, he had a thirst for revenge and violence. He was now at the mercy of the monster who'd held his daughter hostage. Turner felt blood running down his forehead and blinding his eyes. The smuggler kicked him hard between the shoulder blades. The medical examiner collapsed on the floor. He saw the forest under the concrete columns, he looked down at the palm trees below, through the glass. Green hills spread as far as the eye could see.

The smuggler had burnt the camp to the ground and Fahran's monorail was badly damaged. What kind of a rat race had he gotten himself into? Turner looked for strength deep inside of himself and stood up. Quintado smiled, wiping the blood off his mouth with the back of his hand. "You won't give up, will you? You're tough huh big guy! For the love of God, what the hell are you doing on these islands? And what on earth is this monster?" Compressed air hissed and the door separating them from the other wagon and from the Velociraptor partially opened. In his rage, the beast must have pushed the red button on his side. But the door seemed stuck. The creature had probably assaulted it too much; the glass was cracked all over. Shards had already fallen to the floor. The monster charged again and the walls shook. The monorail was still moving. Turner took advantage of Quintado's exasperation and distraction to grab a folding chair. He dove on him and pummeled him with the chair. He could taste the blood in his mouth and red drops were falling from his nose. He wanted to live. He wanted to make it for Aileen. He wanted to see his daughter grow up. She looked so much like her mother already... life should go on, and Kenneth Turner had to survive to see it. He brought the chair down on Quintado's head and arms again and again, gasping, his sore limbs weighing a ton. He dropped the chair, grabbed Quintado's sweat-drenched hair and slammed the man's his head against the fractured glass window. Turner peered through the glass and saw the rail extending into the green mountains. The concrete viaduct ended a few hundred yards away. The construction stopped above a lake and the train wasn't slowing down. The engine wouldn't stop, making this a fatal one-way trip. Turner gulped, afraid. The glass streetcar was about to crash 65 feet below. While Turner was momentarily distracted, Quintado swung his fist at his face again. But Turner was faster. He picked up the metal folding chair and brandished it in front of him. The smuggler's knuckles hit the iron. He howled in pain. Turner smashed Quintado's left temple with the chair. The smuggler's legs gave way under his own weight and he fell into the window, which cracked and shattered. It was about to fall apart. At the back of the wagon, Turner noticed the door was also about to give in. The fierce dinosaur had slipped its head through the partial opening and had begun clawing at the air inside the capsule, cackling. Its eager shrieks turned Turner's blood cold; the monster was about to get in. The door bent and the Velociraptor pushed the glass with the top of its skull. It leaned on the door and it burst off its hinges with a deafening noise. Glass shattered on the iron floor and the fierce beast jumped inside, roaring. It was now or never: the monorail was above the lake. Unfortunately, Quintado gave Turner a rough and sudden uppercut. His teeth ground together and Turner felt his gums tearing. He crawled away backwards from his attacker and kicked at his face. The furious dinosaur suddenly pounced on Quintado, who screamed with fear and panic. He tried to grab a folding chair to protect himself, but it did nothing to protect him from the flurry of claws and teeth. Turner gathered his courage and ran to the end of the cabin.

He crouched and jumped against the cracked window. He held his breath as his body went through the glass. He felt the wind on his face; his own weight taking him down, falling. Turner thought about his wife. He was always thinking about his wife. He could still smell her, feel her warmth. He loved to kiss her neck. He thought about Aileen, about Julia. He wished upon his lucky star for his life, his clothes flapping in the wind. He stiffened his body, made it hard as wood, and took a last deep breath. His legs crashed onto the surface of the water and Turner entered the lake vertically. The impact was so brutal he immediately felt his ankle sprain, if not break. His aching body was suddenly immersed in icy water. It was a steep fall, Turner thought he was dead. He sunk to the bottom of the lake and blew the air out of his lungs to get back to the surface. The clear, blueish water was slightly salty. Turner caught his breath when he resurfaced. He coughed and struggled to float and stabilize in the water. He swam back to the monorail just in time to see both wagons fly off the incomplete concrete bridge, taking Rodrigo Quintado and the terrible Velociraptor with them. They crashed into the side of the mountain. The iron crumpled like a tin can, and the train exploded a hundred yards below. A fiery mushroom rose into the air, flames dancing and pointing at the sky. It was a crash nothing could have survived. The trees swallowed the hot sheet metal, which was now hidden by the lush vegetation. Turner swam on his back to the bank. He watched the black smoke from the train fill the sky. The sun was hiding behind the clouds, foreshadowing the night ahead. The Australian finally reached the sand, then crawled for a few more feet to reach the undergrowth. His strength was failing him. He lay down on his back, facing the clouds; birds were singing in the tree ferns.

Quintado was gone; his corpse was burning in the wreckage next to the first Velociraptor. The monsters were now resting in peace at the heart of the island. The fire rising from the monorail drew patterns in the sky. Turner thought about his daughter again and dozed off for a few minutes.

He knew Aileen was fine, he could feel it in his heart, paternal instinct maybe...the air got damper, minutes turned to hours. Turner was exhausted. He came to his senses and sat in the dirt, his socks still wet. He took off his shoes. The banks of the lake were quiet, the black smoke still drifting in the dusky sky. It was getting darker, the sun setting on site B. Turner had survived. For the first time in a long time, he felt calm and at peace. He'd been through life and had outsmarted death; he was ready to start over. He could take Aileen away from this archipelago and end all this. The ground shook next to him. Turner felt safe; nothing could hurt him now. The vibration was getting stronger. Was it another species of dinosaur? Another reptile ready to eat him alive? Turner stood up with difficulty and noticed a path behind the tall grass. A Jeep was parked behind a sequoia tree. Julia Barret came running to him. The young woman wrapped her arms around him; Turner winced in pain when he felt the bruises all over his body, but he ignored the feeling and buried his face in her long red hair. She smiled feebly, tears of joy were running down her cheeks. "You're OK! My wish has come true!" She looked him in the eye, pressed her shoulders against his and brought her lips close to his face. The young woman closed her eyes. Suddenly, the engine stopped and Turner heard Joe Jackson's voice interrupting them. "Night is falling, lovebirds. It's better to go back to camp now. The road is bad. Julia tucked her hair behind her ear, clearly embarrassed. She held Turner close and helped him walk to the vehicle. "Aileen's fine. She might be asleep at the camp by now.

- I had no doubt about it. Thank you for finding me.
- Teams have been searching the area for hours - you're lucky I found you Kenneth!
- I'm going to need a few plaster casts.
- I'm sure Aileen will enjoy drawing on them very much!" She made Turner comfortable in

the back seat of the Jeep and kept him warm with a blanket. Joe had the engine humming and drove onto a red dirt road. Bugs buzzed around the reddish trunks. The smell of pines tickled the nostrils of the travelers. The mountains of Isla Sorna disappeared in the semi-darkness as the forest watched over the vehicle in silence. Turner's heart was beating to the sound of nature. The grass swayed with each one of his breaths.

The weather was getting cooler. A few days had gone by but the forest was unchanged. Always the same trees, bunches of ferns looking exactly like other bunches of ferns. Katherine had a feeling she'd seen them all before. The gray Jeep Wrangler was speeding down a trail. The orange dirt road flew by beneath the young woman's eyes. Tia Porter was driving; for once, neither woman was chatting. Katherine was thinking back on what had happened these last few days. Her companions in misery had finally left the archipelago. They should be home by now. Chua and inGen managers had stayed true to their word. The air crash survivors had gotten the star treatment. The government of Costa Rica had chartered a helicopter to fly them back to San José. Or was it inGen? Tracker Julia Barret had been waiting hand and foot on Kenneth Turner and his daughter. Turner had promised inGen he wouldn't say a word about what happened. He had signed a non-disclosure agreement but had refused the compensation. Katherine had heard him talking to Chua before they left. The father and daughter had been through quite an ordeal. Katherine Harrison was glad to know they were finally safe. Cole Prescott, the funny guy, had pocketed the money; but his other leg had been torn to shreds by the black Velociraptor. By chance, the explosion had only freed the black raptor, and the other specimens had remained locked in their pen. The monster was dead somewhere on site B, in the jungle. A Mako shark had mauled one of Prescott's legs - the Irishman could never have guessed his good leg would be slashed by a dinosaur's claws just days later! George Alistair didn't leave with Prescott - he'd chosen to remain on site B. Katherine had no idea why - it just made the handsome young man all the more mysterious. She knew she would meet him again on Isla Sorna, which she looked forward to - she had developed a bit of a crush on the taciturn, courageous man. George had remained with Sebastian, Fahran and Segundo. The latter had been evacuated by boat; Katherine had left for site A on the same ship, first layover in Central America. She had seen Segundo throwing something into the sea, something that looked like a tube or a vial. Sitting on a chair, the young man hadn't dared to look at his foot for the whole journey. He had kept both his hands on his cap, nervously stroking the visor on his neck for an hour. The poor boy had been through hell and back; he'd soon be taken care of in San José, away from carnivorous monsters, away from construction vehicles. Raymond Chua and the foul Lizard Neck had stayed on site B. They had important business to attend to. Soon, Katherine would be in charge of something amazing, something crazy. The journalist couldn't believe she was on her way to her new job. The road would be long and full of surprise. Going undercover, pretending she was lost at sea almost amused her; she felt quite happy being dead to the rest of the world. Tia had quickly brought her up to speed on her new responsibilities as site archivist. Both women had barely spoken since they arrived on site A.

The endless canopy was hiding the sun as the Wrangler was driving through the trees. The mysterious site A was cautiously revealing itself. Birds were flying past the bumper. The air was dry. Katherine and Tia were alone in the Jeep. The Sabaneros were grazing their cows in a clearing. Cowboys from Costa Rica herded cattle with their horses. The vehicle drove onto a long dirt road that ran alongside a well-groomed plantation. Men were working amid stalks of sugar cane. Katherine could smell the scent of fresh cut grass filling her lungs as the Jeep approached two tree trunks. They were driven vertically into the ground on each side of the road. Katherine broke the silence: "What's it for?" Tia answered with a smile. "It marks a location. They're going to build a gate and an electric fence here.

- A new village in sight?
- Not this time. They're building one on this island, but this won't be the gate. This one will be much bigger. These two trunks mark the entrance to a reserve. It'll be spectacular, you'll see." Katherine glanced dubiously at the tree trunks as the car went by. "I've been thinking about inGen's slogan...'We make the future'. Wouldn't the public find it punchier if it were 'We make YOUR future?' What do you think? It works for me just as it is...

-   Interesting. I'll have a quick word with the board about it." Tia kept on driving for a few minutes before they reached a small camp on the left side of the road. She parked on the grass, stepped out of the Wrangler and headed for a gray metal shed. The construction bungalow was rectangular and about 65 square feet. "Follow me, Katherine." Both women went through the wire mesh gate. A small desk and furniture were arranged inside the workshop. Piles of paper were lying on shelves and on the table. The place really looked like a construction trailer, but Katherine quickly understood it would be her headquarters. Looking at the piles of files and the computer on the table, she was disappointed. But what did she expect in the middle of this new island? Was it really the place where the brand new archivist and head of PR was going to work? Cooped up in garden shed with one window? Tia comforted her: "It's quite basic I know, but there's everything you need here to start working. Your new life starts here.

-   I kind of hoped for something better to start my new life. Does this dump have a phone at least?

-   There will be - the workers are installing telephone lines. Just walkie-talkies for now! You'll find a list of channels and frequencies in one of the drawers. There aren't that many people on site A for now. Arnold's just got here, he'll take care of this. It's just roads and barracks and a new lab. Everything remains to be done.

-   Am I safe here, at least?

- You are. At the moment, there's no specimen living on this island. The only hazard here is genetics!
- Genetics and jaguars, Katherine said.
- Genetics and jaguars...don't be afraid. The fauna of Costa Rica is rich but shy. Nothing will trouble you here. No drug trafficker, no smuggler will land on this island, I promise. No one knows site A - it's not on any map...yet. You're safe.
- But what am I supposed to do here? Sit down and come up with communications strategies? Write about your specimens? Should I go out and take pictures?
- All in good time! For now, you need to learn and make up for lost time.
- Learn?
- You see all those files? You have to read them and understand what they're about. I want you to study, to feed on all this information. It'll save us time and make you far more efficient!" An engine roared behind the sheet metal walls, men were talking. Katherine was puzzled. "So I'm going to sit here and... read? I guess I can do that...
- You'll soon find out they're very good reads - inGen records are full of very interesting information. Today, we let you into the secret. Today, you'll understand the whys and the wherefores of our company. Our secrets are yours, yours to keep and to glorify." She spoke solemnly: "Katherine Harrison, welcome to..."

The door of the trailer slammed open. "Mrs. Porter, Mrs. Porter!" A young black man burst into the office, calling out to the geneticist in a French accent. "Mrs. Porter, you must come right away! You're requested at the lab!" The man was tall and athletic, his face smooth, a small mustache shadowing his upper lip. He was wearing shorts and a beige shirt that hugged his muscular body. He was handsome - Katherine couldn't help but notice. She felt the newcomer's gaze on her legs. He looked embarrassed and smiled cheerfully. Katherine thought it was funny and told Tia: "Well, you're not going to leave me here on my own, are you? We've barely arrived." Tia patted the young man on the shoulder. "Catch your breath Bernard. What is it about? Don't we have time to settle in first?

- Impossible. The embryonic department's asking for you. I have to escort you to the lab. Hammond's on the island. He rescheduled the meeting with the scientists; he wants to introduce the new head of the department now.
- Hammond's here!?
- Yes, he wants to meet you and introduce you to the new scientists on site. He wants to do it now, you know him, his impatience precedes him!
- But the lab isn't even finished, is it?
- It is and I have to take you to the opening ceremony right now. The first egg is about to hatch. Hammond wants to attend the birth of the first specimen. Hurry up!
- What? The T-Rex is hatching?

- They've detected some movement inside the egg. It'll happen soon. And you'll have a front-row seat. So please, Madam, will you follow me?" Tia Porter apologized to Katherine and left the office. "I'll be back in a few hours! Enjoy your reading!" The journalist couldn't believe it. "Are you sure I can stay here? Why can't I come with you? I thought there were no dinosaurs on this island!" Bernard started the engine and Tia waved at the young woman. "There was no dinosaur until today! See you later." Katherine found herself alone with a few workers.

The small camp looked pathetic but she resigned herself to her situation and sank into the armchair. Birds were chirping outside. All her life, she'd wanted to escape from something, she'd been free to go everywhere she wanted. When she traveled, she tried to get away from something. From boredom, from fear; from pain. But now, she was so lost, she could never go back. She stood up and looked at the branches moving out the window. The trees grew tall and became one with the greenery, they merged into the mountain, blended into the canopy to become a single individual. One huge tree with infinite hues of green, a tree that gave life and took it back. The forest shone with glowing shades of yellow. Katherine had taken a step toward nature, toward the horizon. She was alone with the island. She sat back in the armchair and looked at the carton folder lying in the middle of the desk. It was a white folder. It was heavy and full of papers.

The cover bore a circular logo. Inside the red circle, Katherine identified the skeleton of a dinosaur drawn in black ink on the cardboard. Judging by its sharp teeth, it was a carnivore. A few silhouettes of palm trees were scattered at the bottom of the circle. Katherine gazed at the logo printed on the carton folder for a few minutes. The young woman glanced out the window and opened the file.

EPILOGUE

South Florida. A few months later.

Pink neon lights were blinking and flooding the bar. A few shabby lampshades rested on bedside tables. Their yellow light contrasted with the soft atmosphere of the establishment. Antonio Keller was keeping a low profile, wearing a hat and sunglasses. It was dark in the bar and the man was trying not to attract attention, hiding behind his glasses. Of course the barman had made jokes about it. Hopefully for Antonio, it was his first time in Florida, it was unlikely someone would recognize him. Sitting at the counter, he was sipping a beer, looking at the I. The rooms were covered in wood paneling, stuffed alligators hanging on the walls. Two bikers were playing pool and laughing. Another one was hitting the pinball machine. Speakers hanging from the ceiling played Born on the Bayou by Creedence Clearwater Revival. Antonio was very far away from home; he'd never set foot in the Everglades before. The air was heavy, dozens of mosquitoes ground into the wood counter where humans had swatted them without mercy. Moths were flying around the light bulbs hanging from the ceiling. It was getting late and Antonio was losing patience. Suddenly, the man he'd been waiting for came into the bar. He walked past the aquariums and the fairy lights and sat right next to Antonio. He was in his fifties, bald, with a ring on his left ear. He reminded Antonio of this Procter & Gamble cleaning product character, Mister Clean, except with a goatee. White hairs bristled from his mustache to his thick chin. He was a powerfully built man, like a wrestler with coarse features; he didn't seem like the easy-going kind. But he was the man Antonio had come to meet in this godforsaken place. He knew him; the man, on the other hand, had no idea who Antonio was.

He'd just come in like every other night to have a drink. He waved at the barman and ordered a pint of Python. The local beer wasn't that bad, which had pleasantly surprised Antonio. The man's arms were bare; he wore a crocodile vest and a thick belt on his tight jeans, hugging his big, muscular thighs. His left arm was covered in scars, probably alligators. A necklace made out of teeth hung around his neck, he really looked like a guy from the bayou. His presence was quite intimidating. The barman poured him his drink and he went to sit alone at a table next to the jukebox. Antonio ordered another pint and joined him at his table. The man looked at him suspiciously and grumbled. Antonio Keller put the lager on the table and slid it toward him to break the ice: "You look like someone who needs a drink, or maybe two, after a hard day's work. This one's on me!

- You're buying me a drink? No one's ever done that here before. This is Ird...
- Believe me, it's not!
- I've never seen you around. To what do I owe the honor?

- To be honest, I was hoping to find you here tonight, Mr. Skinner"

The man looked at him with angry eyes, grumbled again and took a sip.

"I'm not interested.

- Let me introduce myself.
- I know them, guys like you, no matter what you have to offer, I'm not interested. Take your beer and get the hell out of here, I'm not for sale.
- I think there might be a misunderstanding here, I didn't come to hire you for your henchman skills. I just want to have a little chat with you, a little chat that you might even find interesting.
- I told you: I'm not interested."

Antonio laid a fifty thousand dollars cashier check on

the table and slid it toward Skinner. Skinner's eyes widened, then he squinted and shot Antonio a dubious glare. Antonio went on: "I've come all this way to meet you. My company thinks you're the right man for the job we have to offer. We'd like to do business with you.

- If it has to do with poaching, I'm done with it. I did my time, I have a clean slate, I'm done.
- You might have a clean slate, but also an empty bank account. We're just offering you a little help. I know about your little kangaroo bush meat business back in Australia - really creative! - and I also know you're quite good when it comes to crocodile

hunting. I understand why you moved to Florida, but that's really none of my business; I read your file.

- You read my file? Who the hell are you?
- Antonio Keller. Nice to meet you. My employer needs your skills. We won't ask you to kill any crocodile to turn them into bags or shoes, but you'll be dealing with reptiles.
- I'm not interested. I'm not skinning lizards anymore, I'm done with the fashion industry.
- My company has nothing to do with the fashion industry.
- Where are you based?
- Cupertino, California. But that's not where we'd like to send you.
- Where would you like to 'send' me then?
- To Costa Rica.
- You want to send me to Central America to steal reptile skins? Why there?
- It's classified, but I know you're reliable. Biological Synthetics Technologies needs the skin of one particular specimen, a fierce one. Our firm needs the flesh and skin of this creature to conduct a series of experiments.
- What species is that?
- That's totally up your street.
- Still not interested.
- You get fifty thousand dollars now and fifty thousand more when you deliver the skin.
- Are you sending me on a hunting trip to kill a protected species? Any coward could do

that. Find someone else, I like risk and danger. No species on earth can give me the thrill again. That rush of adrenaline... it's over. Be on your way.

- Believe me, you've never seen such a creature before. It's said to be almost 12 feet tall and 40 feet long, a carnivorous biped. It's the ultimate challenge for a hunter, the opportunity of a lifetime."

Skinner began his second beer, now all ears. "Are you saying a prehistoric species is still alive and kicking in Costa Rica? And nobody has ever mentioned it?

- Ancient specimens live on a private island off the coast of Costa Rica. Our acquaintance in the government calls it site C. The code name given by our competitor to this monster is 'Demon'. Do you have what it takes to hunt the devil, Mr. Skinner?

- Your 'competitor'? Another engineering company breeds prehistoric lizards? Are you kidding me? Take back your check and get the hell out of my face before I show you what I can do with my knife." He threw the piece of

paper at Antonio who picked it up and ripped it in half in front of him. He laid the pieces on the wet table and smashed them with his glass of beer. He took another check out of his inner pocket and gave it to Skinner. The hunter noticed the sum had changed, it was twice the first amount: a hundred thousand dollars. The Australian frowned: "Are you serious? Let me tell you, if you're not, I'm going to kick your butt. Nobody plays me like that.

- My employer never plays. Your travel buddy, Asger Hansen, figured it out right away. He agreed to join the expedition.
- Asger? You convinced Snare to go hunting?
- We know everything about his criminal past. He might have broken the law and the hunting code of ethics a few times, that's true. That's why we want him.
- Snare is a wild bastard. A blood-thirsty, delusional mad dog. I can't tell if it's a plus or not to have him on your team.
- Yet, money helped him make up his mind. Money's been scarce since he got fired from the alligator farm. And I'm not telling you anything new when I say selling lizard skins don't make an ambitious man happy. Are you ambitious, Mr. Skinner? I hear that you're saving money for your daughter and her son. This job could add a little extra to the pot. It's only for a week. Hansen and you could team up, you'll have all the equipment you need to survive and hunt on the island. You'll get paid to do what you like the best: risking your life. And you could help your family. Isn't it the profitable adventure you've been waiting for?
- Having Asger as a partner is a danger in itself.
- We only work with the best and you, Mr. Skinner, will be a great asset for our company.

- Don't butter me up so I say yes. I know my worth.
- Just think of it as a sporting vacation. You'll face a brand new species. All you have to do is survive and bring us the skin. That shouldn't be a problem for you. You said it yourself, you know your worth."

Skinner ran his hand over his bald head and through his white beard. Pink and yellow neon lights glinted off his forehead. He took the check in his hand, grumbled and frowned. His tone was thoughtful. The jukebox automatically picked a new song. Skinner knew the tune, it was 'Children of the Revolution' by T-Rex, released in 1972. It was one of his daughter's favorites. It'd been a long time since they saw each other. His grand-son must be growing fast. With this money, Skinner could visit them more often in Australia, he could even leave the United States and go back home. He looked up at Antonio Keller. "When is the expedition planned?" Antonio smiled and put his sunglasses on the table. He took a sip of beer and rubbed his eyes. "The ship is leaving next month."

The man at the pinball machine burst out laughing - he'd just broken his own record. The machine was ringing and blinking. Scores appeared on the screen. On the scoreboard, Antonio saw illustrations of dinosaurs. The colorful drawings flashed to the sound of tribal music crackling on the pinball machine speakers. The bikers cheered and drank to their friend. The pinball machine was lighting up on a regular basis and Antonio noticed the prehistoric scene shining above the screen. In the heart of the jungle, a threatening Tyrannosaurus was facing a Triceratops. The bright green leaves of the drawing popped into the darkness of the bar: drums echoed and an electronic dinosaur shriek made the pinball machine shake. The twisted shadows of the stuffed alligators on the walls created a brand new bestiary; frightening, mighty creatures were crawling up the walls, coming out of their lairs in plain sight. The dreams of men had disturbed their sleep; soon, they would awaken for good.

FILES

LINE ART CHARACTER DESIGNS
BY YERLIK ZHARYLGAPOV

KENNETH TURNER

AILEEN TURNER

LINE ART CHARACTER DESIGNS
BY YERLIK ZHARYLGAPOV

GEORGE ALISTAIR

KATHERINE HARRISON

LINE ART CHARACTER DESIGNS
BY YERLIK ZHARYLGAPOV

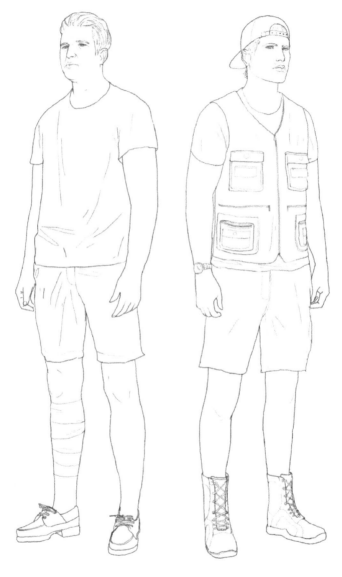

COLE PRESCOTT

SEGUNDO LETICIA

LINE ART CHARACTER DESIGNS
BY YERLIK ZHARYLGAPOV

JULIA BARRET   RAYMOND CHUA

LINE ART CHARACTER DESIGNS
BY YERLIK ZHARYLGAPOV

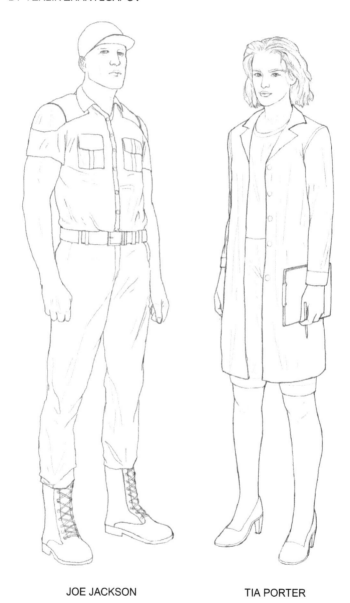

JOE JACKSON

TIA PORTER

LINE ART CHARACTER DESIGNS
BY YERLIK ZHARYLGAPOV

RODRIGO QUINTADO

LINE ART CHARACTER DESIGNS
BY YERLIK ZHARYLGAPOV

ERNESTO

SMOKEY

LINE ART CHARACTER DESIGNS
BY YERLIK ZHARYLGAPOV

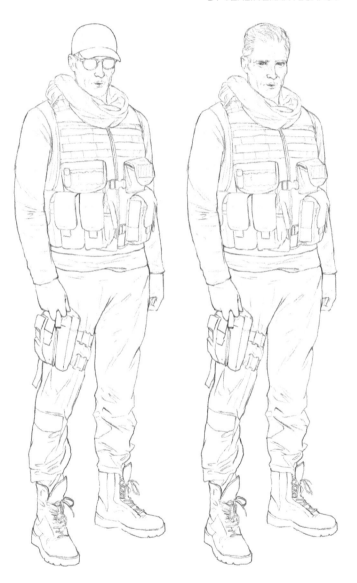

BRADLEY CONWAY « LIZARD NECK »

BARYONYX WALKERI
BY ROBERT JACK

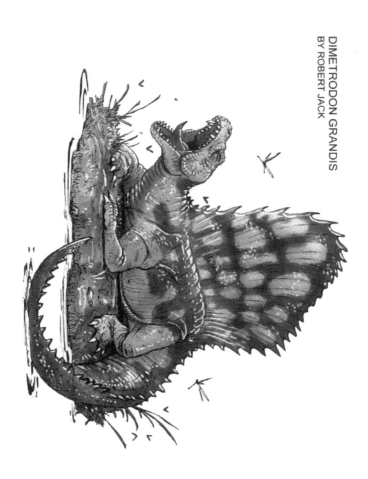

DILOPHOSAURUS WETHERILLI
BY ROBERT JACK

CARNOTAURUS SASTREI
BY ROBERT JACK

VELOCIRAPTOR MONGOLIENSIS
BY ROBERT JACK

VELOCIRAPTOR MONGOLIENSIS
FIRST SPECIMEN
BY ROBERT JACK

RAMPHORHYNCHUS MUENSTERI
BY ROBERT JACK

TRICERATOPS HORRIDUS
BY ROBERT JACK

ORIGINAL ARTWORK
BY ARAM PAPAZYAN

ORIGINAL ARTWORK
BY ARAM PAPAZYAN

ORIGINAL ARTWORK
BY ARAM PAPAZYAN

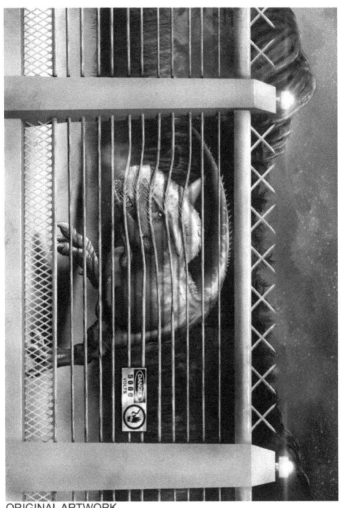

ORIGINAL ARTWORK
BY ARAM PAPAZYAN

TABLE OF CONTENTS

Life will find a way.

Printed in the United States Of America
Published in July 2020
ISBN: 9798630951526

CPSIA information can be obtained
at www.ICGtesting.com
Printed in the USA
LVHW051928191121
703844LV00019B/1941